BITTERSWEET DREAMS

Book One of the Alien Dream Series

K.S. Riggin

Table of Contents

Chapter One

"Rwawan become like Earth? No way!" Frall told the study group, laughing at my suggestion.

I shrank down into my seat, suddenly unsure. Was Frall right? Had I erred in my calculations? I used my hand computer to run the dynamics once more. Pollution factor increases times the number of years. Figure in the acceleration flow projection accommodations and . . .

"Knock it off, Clista," Frall interrupted, bumping my fingers so that the graph skewed off to the right. "You can't calculate this with those figures. *Donmire Industries* is working on the project, and they have already halted the acceleration. You can't continue to plot in the data's acceleration like it hasn't made any difference, and *Donmire* is on target for even more reduction next year."

"Yes, but our school project is based on today's figures," Gerga, my best friend, defended me.

That threw the group into total discord. There were six of us, and the dispute was divided pretty evenly. Three leaned toward keeping my projections, and the others were adamant about using Frall's more optimistic data. Yet, we weren't allowed to break off into two groups. We had to find a consensus and turn in our report.

"It's just stupidity to lash onto dead statistics," Frall continued arguing and trying to win over the group.

"These statistics are not dead. They're the most current available," I counter-attacked, angrily smoothing back a stray lock of my waist-length brown hair.

"They're from a year ago. Why don't you use *Donmire*'s figures?" Frall asked. "They're from last month."

I glared at him. "Any data from *Donmire* shouldn't even be considered. Not only did their studies *not* follow correct scientific procedures, but their data wasn't even collected by independent sources. That means it could all be false."

My words dissolved the group into even more chaos. Gerga called Theopolis a name. Theopolis retaliated with an even worse epithet. Semaph slammed his book down on the table and told everyone to shut up, which, of course, they didn't. And then, Frall raised up his hands and held them like he was trying to pull lightning down from the clouds.

"Look," he said when he'd finally gotten everyone to listen again. "We have to turn in something. If you guys want to be idiots about it . . ."

"Idiots!" I responded, gritting my teeth for his biased pushiness. "Isn't that like the kettle calling the pot. . ."

"And how is the project coming?" asked the proctor, sliding into an empty chair so he could check up on our status.

"It would be a lot better if Clista didn't keep arguing about the latest findings," Frall told him.

"What!" I yelled out, bolting out of my chair, ready to scream. Unfortunately, the round table we were sitting at somehow scooted toward the people on the other side of us, making me look like a fool.

"Ms. Pragan, sit down, please."

The way the proctor said it wasn't a request. I dropped down into my chair and tried not to look at anyone. Unshed tears were burning my eyes, and cinders blazed in my stomach. Angrily, I scooted my data, the diagrams, and the print-out of my calculations into a single pile and then fidgeted until I felt the proctor's eyes warning me to stop.

I sighed heavily. The white marble of our table's top carried veins of grayish black. The other four tables in the room were all the same, except different colors so the proctor could call out the groups by color names or send us to the correct table based on it. I wished very hard that I was sitting at the blue table. It had a really good team.

"How does everyone feel at this minute?" the proctor asked us.

Once more, the table erupted into a burst of angry words. The proctor looked us over, raised his hands, and asked *me* the same question.

I took in a shaky breath. "I can't reason with Frall. I can't make him see . . ." I wanted to say exactly how I felt, but tears took over, and I broke down.

Gerga moved her chair closer. Her arm went around my shoulder. I was glad for her support, but I was embarrassed. I couldn't look up. I felt everyone's eyes on me, yet my tears continued their downpour.

"I'm sorry," Frall said, but his apology was stamped out by the group's boos and hisses.

"Enough," ordered the proctor. "Remember this anger. Think about the cause of it. Recall how you felt when you were full with it, what your emotions were telling you to do."

The proctor paused a moment as if observing the effect of his words. Then he continued, "Good. Now, all of you, off to the exercise wing. Thirty minutes of cross country running for each of you,

3

followed by whatever programs you choose for the other half hour. Then report back at 15:00. Questions?"

No one said anything. Quietly, we all stood up and marched out. Apparently, we were the only group leaving. I looked back and saw several arguments occurring, but some tables were happily completing their task. I shot a glance, just as we walked out, at the poster on the rear wall. "Choose to work cooperatively." Had I really tried? I sighed as I shut the classroom door.

Frall chose the cross trainer next to mine. I hated to have him so close to me, but I said nothing. I was in the exercise wing to get rid of my anger, not to renew it. I turned on the chapter where I'd left off in my history book and continued working on my research project. Dictating as I ran, I slipped into a whole other mindset. I forgot about Frall and whether my calculations or his were the correct ones. I was swallowed up in mankind's exploration of the heavens.

"Earth's Solar System presented the greatest obstacle to space travel," I dictated. "The universe's great distances were an almost surmountable barrier. Time barred even the imaginings of further voyages. Breaching through time was the great step forward. . ."

"What?" I took off my headphones and glanced over at Frall. He was grinning at me with his devastating smile. The rest of him actually wasn't too bad to look at, either. His mane of hair was like black ink, curling about his ears as the perspiration dotted his neck.

"I couldn't hear you," I said suddenly, pulling my mind sharply away from its moment of absurdity in admiring the enemy.

"I said, do you really believe that time was all that stopped Terrans? How about doubt and disbelief. Money was an issue, too. The populace thought that it would benefit mankind to spend the money on other scientific aims, like the eradication of disease."

"This is not a shared project, Frall. Must you always argue with me?"

He raised his hands in the same gesture he'd used in the project room. I was bugged by his interference, but that didn't keep me from being impressed with his sense of balance on the exercise machine. I rarely let go of the handles while I was working out.

When I didn't say anything, Frall nodded and added, "I'm sorry, Clista. I shouldn't have said anything. I just happened to hear your words, and I thought . . . Never mind."

"Never mind? You're criticizing my *Advanced Thought Project*, and then you say, 'Never mind'?"

Frall pushed up the speed of his run and began to deepen the length of his stride. "Look, I just thought that you'd like the input, but I guess I was wrong."

I sighed and increased the grade on my own machine. "The thesis I'm writing about is how we broke down time into strings that we learned to ride."

"Yes, I understand that, but I think the depth of your project will broaden if you add the other components."

My legs were starting to ache, but I had no intention of lessening the grade of the machine. I sincerely needed a good, hard sweat.

Frall and I continued to discuss my project for the next twenty minutes. He did have some decent ideas. I didn't want to be impressed, but I was.

Dripping with moisture, I finally slowed down so I could cool off. Then I returned to my dictation, but I noted into my headset that I wanted to include elements of some of the things Frall had suggested. For some reason, I glanced over at him after saying that and found his eyes on me, smiling. Frall really wasn't as awful as I'd thought, at least when he wasn't in attack mode.

After I cooled off, I showered, grabbed a cold drink, and got dressed. Our group went back into the Projects Room together. We were all considerably happier than when we'd left. In fact, we were laughing and joking together as if nothing had occurred earlier. It was kind of strange when you thought about the difference between then and now.

The proctor was waiting for us. "Frall, you sit here. Clista, you sit next to him. You others, just sit close so we can all chat about what happened."

I would have bristled about the proctor's directive earlier. In fact, I might even have refused. But Frall was smiling at me and shrugging his shoulders as he made gestures like he was saving the chair next to him just for me. I smiled back and plopped myself down with an equally nonchalant smile. Actually, after our exchanges during exercise time, sitting beside him really was no biggie.

"All right, now what did you learn?" the proctor asked.

"Learn?" I said, sitting up straighter. "I learned that I don't want to be on the same project team with HIM!" I pointed at Frall like everyone wasn't capable of understanding whom I was talking about. I thought he'd laugh with the rest of us, but Frall just looked at me with such a funny expression on his face that I instantly felt guilty.

The proctor shook his head. "Anyone else?"

"I agree," said Gerga. "We never got anything accomplished trying to work with Frall. He kept sabotaging everything."

"Did he?" the proctor asked.

Where was the proctor going with this? I rolled my eyes and took a quick inspection to see what the others were thinking.

"Maybe we should have used BOTH sets of calculations and combined them into one report," offered Haleen.

"Right on," Theopolis agreed.

I didn't want to concur with anything that validated Frall's arguments, but I found myself nodding at the wisdom of Haleen's suggestion.

"Very good," the proctor continued. "And what interfered most with pursuing that line of reasoning?"

Semaph, who usually didn't add much to discussions, volunteered his opinion. "I think we had problems because we all took sides. I don't know why, but the girls clustered together, and then we guys all took the opposite side. Was that just a coincidence?"

The proctor chuckled. "No, that's quite normal. It's something built into the human framework, clustering together because of shared genders or cultural similarities. However, understanding that tendency means you can resist it."

"I didn't like seeing Clista attacked. That's why I sided with her." Gerga told everyone.

"I thought you agreed with me," I protested.

"I did. I mean, I do."

"Good," the proctor said, cutting off the discussion at that point. "You have all learned a great deal here today. However, Frall hasn't told you everything."

"What?" we each said, turning to him with puzzled expressions.

"I was told to be disruptive, you see. The proctor made me present data opposite to Clista's. Neither set of calculations is true, by the way."

I bolted up. "What are you saying — that we did all this for nothing? What about our project?"

The proctor asked me to sit down again. His eyes were sternly commanding. I sat, but I was definitely on the edge of my seat.

"Relax, Clista. I still feel sparks flying from you. You'll be free in a minute to go back to your exercise session if you wish, or you can try some deep breathing relaxations."

I let out an exasperated teakettle whistle of complaint, but the proctor ignored me and continued as if I hadn't voiced my irritation. "All right, students. You'll be doing many more of these projects together, and you won't know ahead of time if it's the project that is important or the lesson in teamwork."

I raised my hand, but the proctor shook his head. "Just think about it, Ms. Pragan. If you have questions tomorrow, we can discuss it further. But for now, you're all dismissed."

I didn't go back to the exercise room, do deep breathing exercises, or meditate. Since this was my last class for the day, I went home. Then, I dove into my room and started writing in my journal. Believe me, I had plenty to say.

In the days that followed, our debriefing over the project continued, and so did the pages of my journal. At school, we talked about how anger felt. Theopolis told everyone that it was "a wave of the ocean that swallowed you." Semaph thought it was like a "slap in the face." When the proctor called on me, I was embarrassed because I really couldn't define it. Anger just filled me with so much energy I felt like I could blast into space from the force of it. Of course, I didn't say that. I think I mumbled something about how it made me want to sweep up Frall's calculations and rip them into smithereens.

Frall laughed and said he'd be careful not to leave his homework anywhere near me. It was good that he said that because the proctor was eyeing me, and I could just see him writing a little nasty note about my aggressive tendencies in his little grade book. I wonder if it's true teachers do that.

Today, I found out that when Frall took that exerciser next to mine, he did it for a reason. He'd been told to engage me in a private discussion. Apparently, that's a technique for dealing with group division. I didn't say anything, of course, but I was really disappointed. I'd thought when he chose the machine next to me that he kind of liked me. You know what I mean. That was silly, I guess.

When I got home, I discovered that Mom and Dad were all whizzed about a discovery they'd made. Dad said they were looking for some gamite crystals deep in the Stormian Caverns, which they needed for an experiment they were doing, but then Mom slipped on some loose shale and slid down an embankment into a secret section — a place where nobody had ever been.

Of course, Dad followed her down. He strung up some scaling ropes, tying them securely so he'd have a way to get back up, and then, like some macho superhero, he climbed down to her and helped her back up.

Really, that's so romantic. I wish it had happened to me. I wish Frall had... What was I saying? I wouldn't be in a cave with him. He'd probably argue me to death.

Anyway, Mom was fine after the accident. I asked about that right away. At least she said she was okay, but I noticed that she was limping a bit when she thought no one was looking. (I even offered to serve dinner that evening. She gave me a big smile and said how thoughtful I was. I hope she remembers that the next time one of the proctors calls her and tells her my project reflects inferior analysis (like the time that actually happened.)

Anyway, Mom said that down in the new part of the cave, there were stalactites hanging everywhere, so big that she couldn't even stand up. Poor Dad. That must have been even worse on him because he's a lot taller than she is.

But Mom said she heard Dad making his way down the sides of the cavern, and so, having reassured him that she was fine, she shone her light around the recessed area she'd landed in. She said almost immediately, her eyes picked up on an aerie kind of phosphorous light. She turned off the flashlight, and that's when she saw it — a graveyard of the *Old Ones*.

We'd read about the *Old Ones* in school. They were aliens who lived a thousand or more years on this planet — long before we ever arrived. All of us Rwawans are immigrants from the planet Earth, but the *Old Ones* were probably the original inhabitants of the planet. At least, we think so.

Two years ago, I went on a field trip to the museum, and the docent talked on and on about the *Old Ones*. He said they were really advanced and that some of the artifacts had locks on them that we still hadn't figured out. That means that we don't have any idea about the purpose of at least half of the neat stuff the *Old Ones* left behind.

We don't know how to read their language, either. So all the places where there's scribbled directions, warnings, or information, it's all still a mystery. The *Old Ones* could have been a friendly race or a warrior race. Gerome, one of the guys in my Interplanetary History class, says the *Old Ones* could even be mustering up enough firepower to drop bombs on us. Or maybe they could be constructing something that would make our lives super miserable. He thinks they're still alive and in hiding.

The proctor of the class didn't like Gerome's suggestions, but there isn't any proof that Gerome's wrong. All the artifacts we've found date back about a thousand years. That means that the *Old Ones* could have gone somewhere else for a while. And I suppose they could be still around in hiding — and they could be vicious like Gerome thinks. I bet they're friendly. Wouldn't an older species have learned to get along with people?

Still, I don't know what Rwawans could do about it even if the *Old Ones* did turn up and act war-like. Earth blew up pretty close to four hundred years ago, so we can't retrace our steps, and we don't have any fuel to take us off the planet even if we had another planet to go to. I think the best bet is just to hope Gerome's wrong. Besides, why would the *Old Ones* want to destroy us? Maybe we could all be friends, supposing they're not all dead, which is what the proctor says is the probable answer to the mystery of their whereabouts.

But anyway, I was talking about my parents and their find, and I think that it's so silver-gold cool that they've discovered *Old One* artifacts! I can't wait to tell everybody about it, except that my parents won't let me yet. Dad says it has to remain a secret for a while, at least until he and Mom have time to catalog all the artifacts and to do a complete examination of what they think they've discovered.

I bet if I could tell Frall, he'd be impressed. He's always talking about how he wants to go out on the digs, and here, my own parents have apparently stumbled on the find of the century!

Mom let me see some of the artifacts today. The piece I liked best was a silver necklace. It wasn't really all that pretty, yet there was something about it that drew me. It was only a simple chain with a round, dangling, circular piece of metal, yet I couldn't take my eyes off its center. At first, I thought the disk was plain with no markings whatsoever, but the more I stared at it, the more I wanted to look at it, touch it, and put it on.

"I don't suppose I could have this, could I, Mom?" I asked, barely able to wrench my eyes away from it.

Mom, bending over a far more (to her) interesting torch-like object, didn't say "no." Actually, she didn't say anything. She was busy taking etchings off the strange writings on the torch's side.

Dad didn't say a word either. He was scribbling away in his journal, recording exactly what they'd seen and done during that day while they were inside the Stormian Caverns. I started to ask again, even though I knew they'd say "no" — if they ever tuned in, but then I stopped and stared at the medallion. It was calling to me. I don't mean it talked to me or anything, but yet, I knew. It wanted me to touch it. It wanted me to . . .

"Clista, how about some dinner?" Mom asked. "You want to do the honors tonight?"

I had taken a step closer to it. My hand was raised, frozen at half-mast, reaching to touch the necklace. I pulled my gaze and my hand away and looked up at my mom. "What?" I asked.

"Where have *you* been?" she questioned. "I've called your name three times. Are you all right?"

Mom's face was crinkled up in worry. I knew in a minute she'd be striding forward to put her hand on my forehead, checking for a stray virus.

"I'm fine, Mom," I told her before she could advance into the mother-worry zone. "I was just thinking about that necklace. What do you suppose the spirals on it mean?"

"Felix, I think Clista's coming down with something. Could you check her over?" Mom asked.

My father looked up. His eyes shot a diagnostic survey over my body and then returned to my mother. "She looks fine to me," he said.

Mother was frowning even worse by then. She put down the torch-thing, cited a last minute observation, and then walked toward me.

"Felix, come over here, please," she said.

Sighing, Dad shut his book, stood up, and with strides exactly like Rwawan's Long-Legged Bird — which really wasn't a bird since it had no feathers, but we called it that for some reason, he joined us and tilted his head as if that helped him to see me better.

"Clista wants to know about the spirals on that necklace," Mother said.

I was wishing by then I hadn't asked about it. I was pretty sure I was about to receive some kind of long, academic lecture.

But my father was strangely silent. He looked down at the medallion, looked up at my mother, and then stared at me. "What spirals?" he asked finally.

Dad wasn't much of a practical joker, and my mother was even less of one. I gazed at their faces, thinking that maybe this was something new they were trying out, like an experiment or something, but they didn't have the look that came into their eyes when they were trying to become scientifically distanced from the results.

Then they always looked kind of hopeful, like something fascinating might come out of it. There was no such detachment on either of their faces at the moment. Dad's forehead was puzzle-crinkled, and Mom had a lifted eyebrow, which she usually reserved as her worried expression.

"Are you saying you don't see the spirals?" I asked them to halt whatever strange mystery was occurring.

"There's nothing there," my father blurted out. "You see circles?"

"I think she's coming down with something. Maybe her eyes have been affected," Mother suggested, reaching out to give me the forehead touch I'd sensed was coming.

"I'm not sick," I told her, but I held still. It was always better to get it over with.

"She doesn't feel warm. Better go lie down, Clista. I'll see to dinner."

"No, you won't," my father said. "It's my turn."

I rolled my eyes. All that fuss was about programming the Food Processor, which took less than five minutes. It didn't take much effort either: choosing which vegetable, which soy selection, the desired beverage, and dessert. Big deal!

I marched off, shaking my head in confusion over the spirals. I figured Mom and Dad could argue it out between them.

But once I got up to my room, I started trying to figure out what had happened. It was so weird that neither of my parents could see the circles inside the disk. Those spirals were as clear as . . . well, Frall's big ears, for one thing. I laughed, thinking about his ears and his nose, and his smile and . . . never mind about that. I didn't want to spend time thinking about Frall.

He was just an irritant, except today when he'd smiled at me . . . He really does have nice teeth, too. Isn't that a peculiar thing to say? Like, I'm talking about the Big Bad Wolf, except I like the way Frall flashes them. It's not like his teeth are big or super white or anything. It's just that when he smiles with his teeth showing, you just have to smile back, and then it hits you right in the belly button, and you feel all warm and tingly.

Darn, I said I wouldn't think about him, and here I was going on and on. GRRR.

But, back to my parents and that strangeness down in the basement. You see, I knew Mom and Dad were old. All parents are, but my parents weren't that old. Why couldn't they see the spirals? I'd never noticed either of them having vision problems before. Shouldn't at least one of them have seen the design, even if the other couldn't?

It was so odd. I decided that I'd better keep a watch on them. Maybe I needed to needle them into having vision tests. Maybe *they* should see a doctor. Maybe they were sick. Then, I suddenly laughed at myself because I sounded just like my mother.

Later that night, I dreamed about the medallion. Somehow, in the dream, I brought it into my room — an impossibility with my parents' alarms set on the basement and its collection of *Old One* artifacts. But in my dream, I put the silver chain around my neck, and the medallion hung down against my skin. I was looking at it as it lay there, getting warm against my skin.

As I watched, the spirals blazed into an intense cobalt blue, and the necklace burned me. Frantically, I tried to take it off, but it melded itself into my skin. My fingernails pried at it. I remember even taking a knife and actually cutting into my skin, trying to remove the glowing horror, but though I felt the pain of the knife's insertion, my skin healed instantly around each cut.

In my dream, I tried soap, ice, and heat, still attempting to remove the necklace. I don't remember how the nightmare ended, but when I woke, the first thing I did was touch my chest. I breathed the largest

15

sigh of relief when I didn't feel the medallion there. The dream had been that vivid.

I'd never had a dream so real or one that frightened me as much. I didn't want to go downstairs and see the artifacts again. I was suddenly afraid. What if the necklace called to me, and I obeyed? What if my dream was a warning?

I skipped breakfast that morning and popped a nutrition pill. Then I sonicked my teeth clean. My hand shook as I brushed my hair. My skin felt clammy. I decided that it must be because of the math test I was having later in the morning. That's what I hoped, anyway. Dreams can't make you sick, can they?

As I rushed out the door with the quickest of good-bye kisses to my folks, I yelled out, "Got to go study at school." Then I shut the door, listening almost automatically for the self-modulating click of the lock.

I disconnected my scooter from its recharger unit in the car storage unit and jumped on it. The ride to school was so quick I almost didn't have enough time to breeze away the cobwebs of dream-worry before I arrived. But as I parked my vehicle in the student scooter stands, I ran into several of my friends — and Frall.

"May I talk to you for a moment?" Frall asked, pulling me away from a discussion I'd just started with Gerga about our plans for the midweek half-day.

Gerga elbowed me in the ribs and said loudly enough for anyone in the vicinity to hear, "Look who's making sweet talk with the enemy now."

Of course, I laughed it off, but my face was feeling like someone had torched it. I hoped I wasn't blushing. "I'm sorry about that," I said to him as Gerga walked away. "She thinks I'm still angry about the other day."

"And you're not?" he asked, touching my arm with a book he was carrying. My face grew even hotter.

"Of course not," I answered, a bit hesitantly because I wasn't sure it was true. "You did what you were supposed to. I guess we'll all have roles like that to play in future sessions. You may be ready to throw something at me when it's my turn."

"Then let's be friends in between," Frall said with a warm smile. "That way, you and I can build a rapport that allows for opposing views."

Somehow, Frall and I had ended up over at the side of the quad. The other students had all gone in, and so we were alone. There was no one to wave to, nobody I needed to speak with before class. There was just Frall and his serious, dark green eyes studying me as if he were trying to figure out my thoughts.

I nodded in agreement. "Sure. No problem, but I've got to go now," I said. My voice trailed out so it finished in a harsh whisper.

That was the worst thing that could have happened. I meant to sound forceful and sure of myself. But obviously, I hadn't. Frall broke into a full, even more devastating smile, and before I could recover from it, he picked up my hand, placed a folded paper in it, and turned and walked away.

Because of our talk, I was almost late to class. I stumbled into my first room with my hand clutching the note, my face so pale, apparently, that several commented on it. The proctor called on me right away, even before I could pull myself back to normal, which also meant that I had no time to open and read what Frall had written. It was a nightmare trying to keep my thoughts on the proctor's words.

Then, I had to go up to the front and give a demo on the new spacesuits we students were testing for *Cronoks Lab*. The suits weren't connected to a breathing apparatus or anything, but the safety flaps and the various important details about the hook-up, *IF* we were ever to use one, had to be demonstrated.

Later, I led the class in a discussion about the elements we needed to check for in the suits. Together, we developed a checklist for keeping track of our difficulties: how hard was it to strap and unstrap the necessary sections for ease of waste deposits (Yes, that means going to the bathroom.), how comfortable was the suit for sleeping, which activities were made more difficult because we were suited up, which areas of the suit became uncomfortable with the passage of time, etc.

Next, I passed out the suits, making sure that every student received the one designated for him or her based on height, weight, and body type.

The testing and reporting back to a company was all normal stuff for students of our age. Giving input to the labs was part of our service to the community. It was one of the ways we brought in funding for school materials and how we gained true work experience. Of course, the real carrot, the reason most of us did it, is the hope that the contacts we made with a company could lead to a good job offer after the academy.

All of that was in my mind as I sorted and dealt with a few minor problems. I was in charge because I'd been elected the coordinator of the project. It would be my job to collect, compile, interview, and analyze all the findings.

The next step would be to take that information to Cronoks Lab and present it to their executive board. Presentations were something I was good at, and therefore, probably the area I'd be going into after graduation. (If a company thought I had enough potential and offered me a job, I'd be guaranteed further training at the university, something a company usually paid for if a student were willing to sign a five-year contract with them. Good deal, huh?)

Normally, I very much enjoyed developing a checklist and organizing the data production process, but on that day, I'd have preferred just to slip down in my desk seat and read a certain note that someone had given me.

Unfortunately, I couldn't, and the rest of the morning continued just like that. After class, my friends gathered around me, still discussing the experimental spacesuits, which we'd begin to wear the next day. However much I seriously wanted to break away and go off and be by myself, I couldn't. Already, everyone kept talking about how I wasn't acting like me. I told them it was because I hadn't slept well. Remembering the truth of that, I shuddered.

"Are you sure you're not sick?" Gerga asked for the third time that morning.

I was just about to answer her when the girls backed away from me.

"What's wrong?" I sighed. "I'm not sick, and I'm certainly not contagious."

"How do you know?" Frall asked.

I jumped. "Don't sneak up on me like that!" I said, backing away from him like he was the one with the contagious germs.

"Clista, what in the world is with you today? Calm down, girl," he said, grabbing hold of my elbow.

My eyes followed his hand. He saw my look and let go, backing off as if I'd bitten him. "Sorry, Clista. I don't know why I did that."

His face had turned as pale as mine must have looked a little earlier. Understandably so — touching someone without permission was a definite no-no.

"Don't worry about it, Frall. I know you didn't mean to," I said, staring at the buttons of his shirt, mainly because I didn't know where else to look.

Frall's eyes lifted up to scan my face. I met them and inhaled sharply. There ought to be a rule about eyes as green as his. I worked on my breathing. In, out, in, out. Calm, collected... and ready to scream with the tension. Frall's presence made me feel jumpier than a Rwawan hopper bug.

"Did you read my note?" he asked after a moment of watching me fidget.

"I couldn't," I said, shaking my head. "This morning, I had 'Leadership Training,' and it was my turn to instruct the others on the wearing of the experimental spacesuits. We start our trial week this afternoon after school."

Frall nodded. I could tell he was listening; his eyes were glued to mine. It was flattering, but it made me dreadfully nervous. I shifted the extra suits I was holding in my right arm and unintentionally dropped one of my heavy math books. Of course, Frall picked it up, blasting me with another sugar-charged smile. I felt like a klutz.

"Thank you," I began, but then I didn't know what else to say. I needed to leave to go on to my next class, but I didn't want to be the one to rush off again, and I was dying to rip open Frall's note. Should I do it in front of him?

"I'd better go," he said. "We don't want to be late. I'll talk to you later, ok?"

He turned so abruptly, I was left with a mouth full of words still all mixed up and unformed. I glanced down at Frall's note. It was poking out of my leadership manual. I looked up again, just in time to see Frall dart into his class. He must have broken a new record for speed walking. I stared as the door of his room closed.

"Hey, what are you doing, Clista? We're late. Let's go," said a friend rushing by me.

I turned and followed, grabbing at the spacesuits I was about to drop.

"When do you start wearing the suit?" Bisto asked as I was draping them across an empty table behind us. I didn't answer until I'd dropped down into the seat.

"This afternoon," I told him. "When I get home. Then, I turn into an asteroid miner. Will you still speak to me, then?" I chuckled as he rolled his eyes.

Bista was one of my best friends. He was also the top math student in the class and my tutor. Every time I got stuck in the morass of mathematical calculations, he came to the rescue.

I pulled out Frall's note, opened it up, and read the first line, "Do you think . . .

"Did you finish that problem I left you with?" Bisto demanded. That was the one he'd worked with me via computer the night before. It had a truly stinky transbilateral. I think I'd done it right. I pulled out my paper and handed it to him.

"Put away whatever it is that you're looking at," Bista ordered. "This is not right."

Never has a sigh been so warranted.

It wasn't until lunchtime that I finally got to read the note. Then I went into the bathroom, sat down in a stall, and opened the by then very crinkled paper. No one elbowed me. No one ordered me to study, asked what I was doing, or tried to jerk the paper out of my hand. It was sublime.

Dear Clista,

I suppose it's silly to write this in a note, but I wanted to tell you that I enjoyed talking to you on the cross trainer the other day. If it hadn't been for that project, the one that made your eyes flash with the most intriguing lights, I might never have had the courage. (It's strange what a person will do for a good grade and yet would never be brave enough to do on his own.)

You see, you always have a group of people around you. I could never get close before, even if I'd had the daring. I can understand why everyone forms a circle around you — you're vivacious and fun and wonderfully smart.

The truth is that I'd really like to continue our conversation about the early days of space travel — or any other topic you're interested in. What I mean is — I'd like to get to know you better. What do you think? Do I have a chance?

Please let me know, Clista. I'll be easy to push away if you're not interested, but if there's any possibility that you might be interested in getting to know me, I'd really like that.

Frall

"Oh, my stars," I cried out. (Thankfully, there was no one else in the bathroom, but just in case, I kept the rest of my thoughts silent — which wasn't easy since I felt like singing.)

The letter was so beautiful! I sighed and then read it again and again. My eyes had "intriguing lights"? Wow! He thought I was vivacious and smart?

At that moment, space lift off would have been a cinch. I could have donned my spacer's suit and risen up into the sky, floating high enough to peek in on all the moon colonies and the various space-docking stations. I felt that good!

A group of girls entered, chatting and gossiping about someone I'd never heard of. My helium evaporated. I finished my basic needs, clicked the recycle button, and came back to reality.

A few minutes later, I rejoined my friends. I guess I was a little quiet. They chided me about it and then teased me over whether I'd be starting up a new fashion with the spacesuits. I played along, munching on my sandwich and drinking my strawberry yogurt drink, but I was really thinking about Frall and the wonderful things he'd said.

As if he picked up on the thought, he came walking out of the senior's hall. His eyes scanned the benches and tables and stopped when they saw me. He paused for a moment, reading me. I should have hopped up and called out for him to come over. Even a wave would have given him a sign, but I just sat there, gazing into his eyes. It was enough. He came striding over, his smile — friendly and natural, his green eyes even greener in the sunshine.

I moved over, and my friends did, too. It was that easy. Frall sat down and ate lunch with us and laughed and talked as if he'd always been sitting at our table. I liked having him there beside me. It seemed like the sunshine, sparse on the North Continent — the upper region of Rwawan where I lived — was warmer that day, or maybe that was just Frall's smile and the way I was feeling.

That night, I thought I'd go home and pour my heart out into my diary. I had so much to say. The day had been so special. I would have, but there were other things happening that evening, and none of them had anything to do with Frall's smile.

Chapter Two

When I arrived home, Mom and Dad were upset about something. They wouldn't tell me what the problem was, but I knew there was something. They both barely ate anything at dinner, and when I tried to explain about the spacesuit test program and why I'd come down to eat suited up, Mom got up without a word and left the table. Dad's eyes followed her, looking worried, but he remained sitting with me and tried to keep me company.

"What's with Mom?" I questioned him like every good daughter should when a parent acts strange.

"She's just tired tonight," he said, avoiding my eyes like he does when he's hiding something.

"Dad, really. What's the problem?" I asked again. This time, I picked up his piece of carrot cake and held it away from him so he'd look me in the eye.

He sighed heavily, sipped his cold coffee, and shot a glance in the direction where Mom had gone. "Give me back my cake, and we'll talk about it," he said grudgingly.

I'd put my helmet on the table between Dad and me since Cronoks Lab didn't require us suit testers to eat through suit tubes. We kids were just supposed to wear the main part of the suit most of the time so we could get a good understanding of its weight and how it made us feel after keeping it on for long periods. Anyway, that's the reason why the helmet was lying there next to Dad, but that didn't explain why he kept stabbing at it with his fork, right on the company label:

rat-a-tat-tat, rat-a-tat-tat. I wandered if that was a clue for what was bothering them. Were they mad because I was doing work for Cronocks Lab?

I gave Dad back his cake, and he used his fork for another purpose, but that strange behavior was just one more thing I needed to write down in my personal diary. Dad was usually Mr. Calm. He never twitched or demonstrated nervous habits — not usually, anyway.

He caught me staring at him and set down his fork. He'd finished eating his cake by taking four monstrous bites of it. He folded his arms and started clearing his throat — a sign that a lecture was coming.

"You see, Clista," he said, assuming his teaching face. "The company that you're doing your report for is the one that's been harassing us at the cavern." He paused to pick up his mug of coffee and gulped down most of its contents.

"No, I take that back," he said, placing the mug down. His right hand reached up to grab at his chin. Then he rubbed at the evening's darkening beard shadow. After that, his hand continued upward, wiping at his forehead, although the room was far from warm.

"I shouldn't say *harassing*, I guess," he continued. "Let's just say, complicating our research. That's why your mother is a little bit unhappy about the project you're working on. She's starting to hate Cronoks Lab. Understand?"

I nodded. "Of course, Dad. Cronoks is causing you difficulty, so Mom is bugged that I'm working with them."

Dad smiled, pleased with my summary. "Exactly. I hope this is a one-shot deal, this lab work you're doing." His hand dropped down onto the top of my helmet, and once again, the rhythm of the beating tom-tom distracted my eyes and ears.

"I mean, you're not thinking of applying for their scholarships, are you?" Dad burst in with a raised voice, another behavior quite unlike his usual soft-spoken manner. He looked angry, too. I put my fork down and gave up on eating my piece of cake. I didn't need it anyway.

What happened to a spacer if he grew too fat for his spacesuit? I wondered about that for a second and decided to jot the question down in my Cronoks Lab notebook. Maybe Cronoks would want to insert some stretch into the stomach area of the suit, just in case. It was a great idea. Would it be enough to get me hired?

The discussion with Dad continued ominously. I hedged my answers. How could I tell Dad which company I'd go to work for? Was Dad trying to limit my options? Was he saying that I should avoid Cronoks Lab just because he and Mom didn't like them? What was going on out there in the Stormian Caverns, anyway? My parents usually got along with everybody. And besides, why should Cronoks Lab interfere with the work of two archaeologists? What business was it of theirs?

Of course, I asked Dad these questions, but he didn't want to talk about it. (Why don't parents ever want to discuss the things that bother them when *they're* always telling *us* to talk about everything?)

The situation really left me in a strange position. What should I do? Without more information, I couldn't decide anything. And the worst of it was that Cronoks Lab had actually been my number one choice. If the company offered me a scholarship, it would be very, very hard to turn it down, especially for something so nebulous, like the fact that they might be causing my parents a little difficulty out at the caverns. Should I mention that possibility to Dad?

I sat there a moment, watching him finish off my dessert. The carrot cake was his ultimate favorite. I was glad I'd passed it to him. I thought maybe it would cheer him up. But when he finished, he went back to pounding on my helmet. I decided that the timing was not quite right to discuss future career possibilities. Besides, I needed to think some more about the situation and to write it all out in my diary. Writing was the only thing that calmed me and let me sort things out.

It was Dad's turn for the dishes. I stood up, picked up my helmet, and placed it back on my head. Then I paused to give Dad a pat on the shoulder and a quick hug and kiss, which I discovered is next to impossible with a helmet on. (Another note I must make in my Cronoks Lab notebook.)

I also observed the slight stiffness of my knees as I headed up the stairs. That didn't really bother me, but it did make me very aware of possible restrictions. I bet I'd be a rotten soccer player while wearing the suit. Could I swim in the school pool? I climbed up the stairs slowly, heading for my room and my two different diaries.

"Clista," Dad called. I turned around. He was standing down at the bottom of the stairs. Seeing his expression, I walked back down.

I guess Dad was pretty good at reading faces — even when they were inside helmets. He took two steps up and kissed my forehead right on top of the helmet. "Don't worry about any of this, honey. It will all smooth over. In a few days, we probably won't even remember this conversation."

If only that were true. In the weeks that followed, it became more and more important to remember everything Dad had said. I wished I'd pried and asked him more questions until he finally broke down and told me everything. I should have. He never would have stood up to my persistence. I wished I'd told him that maybe I might want to go to work for Cronoks Lab. Hindsight. If only. . .

But I didn't know that night, so I just scribbled in my diaries and went to bed, still wearing the helmet and the spacesuit.

That night, I dreamed again about the necklace. It called to me, wanting me to put it on. Strangely, in my dream, somehow, I was at Cronoks Lab, and they were offering me a position. I don't remember what answer I gave. I just remember that I was torn with guilt because my parents' sad faces were watching me. Mom was crying, something she never did, and Dad was sitting in a chair, stabbing my helmet with his fork.

That was the nicer portion of the dream. Then, it turned into a series of nightmares.

In the morning, when I woke up, I had a painfully stiff neck. Dutifully I wrote my sleeping difficulties and the neck problem in my Cronoks notebook. I didn't mention the part about the dreams, but for some reason, my nightmare haunted me through the day, dropping stray parts into my studying and test taking, giving me flashbacks of scenes. It was very strange, and the necklace, the disk of the necklace I'd seen down in the basement, was the vision that haunted me the most.

Chapter Three

At school that day, there was a great deal of teasing. We space suited students were dubbed the "astronauts," and a variety of jokes sprang up about our getting stuck inside the suits and never getting out. Some nasty people — mainly younger students — said that we'd be stinky by the end of the week, which, of course, was utter nonsense since even without the hook-up for air tanks, the suits were self-cleaning.

My painfully stiff neck was probably helped by the rigidity of the helmet. By lunchtime, it no longer bothered me. During our break, Bista helped me with another of the unconquerable math problems, and Frall not only ate lunch with us again but managed to see me at least twice at odd times during the day. Despite the morning's unpleasant beginnings and lack of sleep, the day had turned wonderful.

At least until I got home. When I let myself in, Mom and Dad were already there. That was very unusual. They'd been staying at the caverns most days until around Three Moons, the time when three of Rwawan's five moons became visible.

I could hear them down in the basement with their finds — cataloguing, discussing, and examining each item, as they always did when they were home. I wasn't eager to join them. I wanted to write in my diary before I forgot all the things I wanted to say about Frall and my day, but Mom, hearing the door announcement of my arrival, called out for me to come join them.

"Clista, have you seen the necklace I showed you?" she asked before I'd even gotten to the bottom of the stairs.

I was pretty sure I knew which one she meant. I wasn't aware if there were others, but that particular necklace had certainly made an impression on my consciousness. I shook my head.

"It's gone," Mom said, eyeing me suspiciously.

"Wasn't the basement alarm on? No one could have broken in," I reminded her.

Mom didn't say anything, but her eyes were giving me that look of examination like she could see into my brain.

"I sure wouldn't come down here looking for it," I told her. "That thing's been giving me nightmares from the day you showed it to me."

I hadn't meant to blurt that out, but my father's head reared up, and he was suddenly attentive. "Nightmares about the necklace? Tell us about them."

Both my parents were staring at me like having nightmares was important. I didn't understand it, but I sighed, dropped down onto one of the examination stools and tried to collect the wisps of what seemed now only very blurry recollections. I told them everything I could remember.

"The necklace has summoned you," my father said almost immediately, making it sound like that was a good thing.

I rolled my eyes. "I wish it hadn't. Its summoning, or else the helmet I had to wear, gave me a stiff neck this morning. I feel like I didn't sleep all night."

"Perhaps you didn't," Mom said with the strangest note in her voice. I turned and stared at her.

31

It was lucky that Mom didn't tune into the part about the helmet. I sure didn't want her to go huffing off again just because I was testing the spacesuit for Cronoks Lab, but she hadn't seemed to notice that part. She was still pondering Dad's comment about the necklace having summoned me.

"So you think there's still power in the possessions of the *Old Ones*, Felix?" Mom asked my father, her eyebrows perched like they were question marks, hanging high on her forehead.

Dad's eyes didn't move from my face. I knew I was being studied as closely as one of the artifacts. He didn't answer Mom.

"What happened in the last dream, Clista?" he asked softly.

The helmet was really starting to bug me. I felt distanced from my parents like I couldn't see them eye-to-eye. I took it off and set it down on my lap.

"I told you, Dad. I don't remember. I just know that I was dreaming about the necklace again, and it wanted me to . . ." I stopped because I really didn't know exactly what the necklace wanted — to touch it, to put it on, to wear it? It was all silliness anyway. Why were my parents so interested in my dreams? And what "power" was Mom talking about? I'd never heard anything about the *Old Ones* having power.

"Come here, Clista," my mother ordered sharply.

Obediently, I slipped off the stool, plunked the helmet down, and went over to stand beside her.

"Look at this," she told me with a sharpness in her voice that said I'd better do what she said or else. I attempted, as I often did, to read her face, but Mom didn't give much away. Dad always said Mom was the ultimate poker player. I wasn't really clear about what that meant except that it was a game people used to play, a game in which they tried to hide their reactions from each other. I'd have been lousy at it. Mom would have won.

Mom held up a light orb of the *Old Ones*. She and Dad had shown me several of them when I'd been invited to see the artifacts that day. I identified it so Mom would know I really did pay attention to the things she told me. Then I waited for her to speak, shooting a glance at my father to see what his eyes would tell me.

"I want you to touch it," Mom said.

Dad was nodding. My eyes flew back and forth between them. What was going on? They never let me touch anything. This was really weird.

"But you always say . . ." I stalled, trying to understand why they were acting so strange and why I felt frightened by it.

"Just do it," Mom repeated, her lips stretched taut with tension and a slightly waxen look as if she'd been biting them repeatedly and had robbed them of any blood.

I took off my space gloves and placed my hand on the orb. Without warning, it lit up and spread light across the basement in a soft, slightly rosy glow.

I retracted my hand immediately. "I didn't do anything," I whispered before either of my parents could speak.

Dad walked toward me. When he stood close, he positioned his hands on my shoulders. "We're not angry, Clista. We're jealous. The *Old Ones* have chosen you. They've summoned you, and both of us would have given anything for that link. But we're not angry with you. Do you understand?"

I took in the air with great gulps. I felt tears in my eyes, but there was no reason for them.

My mother formed the first beginnings of a smile. It was weak, but it let me see that Dad was right. She wasn't mad at me, either.

"But what does it mean?" I asked.

For one thing," Mom said, walking closer and touching my cheek with a loving gesture, "it means that we need you down here for as much time as you can give us. Will you do that, Clista? Will you help us understand these artifacts by touching them and telling us what you feel?"

"You want me to help you?" I whispered, not really grasping her words. "Here, in the basement?"

"We need you," Dad nodded. "We need you very much."

I don't know if you've ever stood outside a door and wanted in so desperately that you sometimes felt like just kicking that door down. Of course, I'd never do that, but it was the feeling I'd had for years. There was always Mom and Dad, together, secretive, and then on the outskirts, me.

Maybe I was the comic relief, the one who entertained them with my childish ways, but I'd always felt like a tag-a-long who kept interrupting them with my silly, kid-like needs. Their sense of duty had been the link between us. Oh, I know they loved me. I don't mean to say they didn't, but they loved their work more, and their love for me sometimes only got the crumbs of what was left.

I never realized how much I'd resented that until I found out what being inside that basement, inside the locked door, meant. For the first time, my parents made room for me between them. They actually saw me as someone who could work *with* them. It was as if I were no longer the add-on appendage, the child who amused them when they had a spare moment. I'd suddenly become a person.

However, I was describing the scene in the basement, wasn't I? And here I am, hopping forward in time.

After the light orb turned on, Dad asked me to check if I was wearing the necklace. I almost stormed out then. Was he accusing me of stealing and lying? It took some reassurance from both of them before I actually looked. Despite all the dreams, I never believed what Dad was theorizing, but he was right. It was true. The necklace lay around my neck.

Chapter Four

Of course, any sane person would say that was an impossibility. Either the necklace had journeyed upstairs and fastened itself on me while I slept, or I had somehow walked downstairs, into the basement, through the alarm, and slipped on the *Old One's* artifact over my head and inside my spacesuit.

To be honest, neither hypothesis was logical. It just couldn't have happened. It was absolutely ridiculous for me to have the necklace around my neck, yet I did. And just as in the nightmare I'd had, it was, unfortunately, a permanent fixture — melded to my skin.

Yes, that brought tears and a raging temper tantrum. I reached for a knife my dad had been using to cut apart a box. I stabbed myself, attempting to cut my skin at the place where the necklace joined it. I was that determined to remove the thing.

"Stop it," my father ordered, and he grabbed the knife away. Tossing it into the sink, he took my shoulders and shook me gently.

"Think about what happened in your dreams, Clista. Remember that. The *Old Ones* were warning you. They prepared you for this. That necklace cannot be cut off. I doubt there's any way it can be removed."

Tears flooded my eyes in doubled force. I covered my face, fell limply to the ground, and sobbed. It was my mother who sat down on the cold, hard flooring. Taking me into her arms, she talked me calm.

"We can try some chemicals on it, Clista. Maybe electricity will disconnect it, or electro-magnets . . ."

"Do you think so?" I asked, gulping back the sobs and wiping my eyes. "Can you get it off? Please, Mom, please."

"Hush, Clista. We can try, but the necklace is really pretty. It isn't so awful. I wouldn't mind if it had attached itself to me. I'd be honored."

I cried more then. I didn't agree with her concept of what was an honor, but my tears were petering out. The idea that maybe Dad could do something gave me hope. I stood up and assisted my mother, who rose a bit stiffly, grimacing and moaning about getting old.

I laughed. "You? You'll never be old, Mom. You and Dad are too busy, too full of life."

She laughed and hugged me again. Then Dad came over and joined us, giving my shoulder a squeeze of reassurance.

"I'm sorry, Clista," he said. "We never would have brought the necklace home if we'd had any idea it would do this. We just didn't know. There was no reason to think . . ."

I threw myself at him, needing the feel of his arms around me. As he held me, I leaned against his chest and listened to the steady beat of his heart. That reassured me somewhat. I swallowed the last fragments of my tears, and then I pulled away. "Will you try what Mom suggested? Please, Dad?"

He nodded. "I doubt either of those things will work, but I'll try, Clista. As you know, the *Old Ones* were far beyond our technology. We can't even begin to understand what makes their tools function. It's like a peek into the future, a future you're connected with. Is that so bad?"

"Yes," I sniffled. "Because I don't want it. I never asked them to do this to me."

Dad didn't say any more. He reached out to touch the pendant. "Ow," he yelled. "That thing's hot. Is it burning you, Clista?"

I shook my head, puzzled by his reaction. I reached down and touched it. It glowed slightly, tingling my body, but it didn't burn.

"It does light up, Dad, but it's not hot. It doesn't hurt me to touch it."

"What light?" Mom asked as she reached out, far more gingerly than Dad. She, too, attempted to place her hand on it, but almost as quickly, she withdrew her fingers, shaking her hand and blowing on it as if it were aflame.

"We can't touch it," Mom cried out. "It forbids us."

"I don't understand any of this," I said, feeling sick to my stomach. "Nothing happens when I touch it, except . . ."

"Except what?" my father prodded, his eyes lit up with curiosity and the same scientific zeal I'd seen at the beginning of each of his projects.

I was familiar with the protocol. I calmed and lowered my voice. I was science-trained. I knew what was expected. "It glows when my hand approaches. Can't you see that?"

As I demonstrated, my hand approaching the pendant slowly, I watched as it lit up again and turned radiant with the same blaze of red and gold a person saw inside a candle flame. I looked up to glance at my parents. Both of them were shaking their heads. They saw nothing. Why? Why couldn't they see the medallion's glow? And what did it mean that I could? What was its purpose?

Just as the light was mine alone, I thought about how it tingled my body, the way it made me feel itchy and desperate to move or to do something. Suddenly, I recognized the feeling. It was exactly like when an afternoon grew hot, and the sky rumbled. That same feeling of restlessness came over me then — like the air was charged.

I tried to explain all that to my parents, but I could tell they didn't understand. I couldn't imagine my mother ever feeling like this. She was too poised, too contained. Dad, maybe he could have, but he fought against such moods and emotions. He believed that feelings were something a scientist suppressed.

I sighed loudly and heavily. If my parents couldn't touch the necklace, what could they do? "Can we still try those things, Dad, even if you can't touch it?"

My parents assured me that there'd be no problem with that. It was just that I would have to be the one to apply them. Dad turned toward the locked cabinet where he kept all the chemicals. He brought out several and began to mix them. One by one, I tried every mixture, compound, and smelly substance he handed me. Not one of them had the least effect on my pendant.

Nor did heat or cold, the electromagnet, the electric current, or anything else we tried. The necklace reacted to nothing.

"I hate it!" I yelled when we'd come to the end of all their suggestions.

"No, Clista. Don't feel that way. Don't you see," Mom said, "This means you're the favored one of the *Old Ones*. I'm pretty sure that means that their protection is on you. That's a good thing."

Mom picked up the knife that Dad had thrown into the sink. She walked toward me. "Give me your hand, Clista," she ordered.

Eyeing Mom with a great deal of doubt, I put my hand in hers and watched as she attempted to pierce it with the sharpened edge. The knife refused to cut.

"Interesting," declared my father. "So, wearing the necklace throws some kind of shield over her. I wonder what other things she's protected from."

"I would guess every weapon we Rwawans know about," Mom said, attempting next to throw a book at me. I almost ducked instinctively, but I stood still, figuring it wouldn't hurt too much if it hit me. The book fell short. Mom repeated the experiment over and over with different things. Nothing ever touched me.

Being safe was a good thing. That part I liked, but the glow and the tingling bit was going to take some getting used to.

I jerked my hand away from my mother before she could try the hot stick on me. It was used for heating chemicals and would make a bad burn if it touched the skin. Dad, seeing my reservations about more experiments, called a halt.

"Okay," I said, backing up a little from my mother's zeal. "What else is this thing good for?"

Mom looked at Dad and shook her head. Dad raised his eyebrows almost up to his hairline. Then they stared at each other as if they couldn't believe I'd ask such a stupid question.

"With the necklace you are free to go inside places we're not allowed," my mother said, taking up the initiative.

"It looks like you can use the artifacts, too," Dad said. "They've ignored our attempts at turning them on, but the light orb sure responded to you."

"You're so lucky," Mom told me again. "Who knows what wonders you'll be allowed to discover. You might be able to read their writing. Look here. Can you read this?"

Mom shoved a book in my face. I studied the scribbles. They looked a little like the stems and petals of flowers or miniature clouds, but I couldn't read them.

"Too bad," said my father. "If you could have read them, that would really have been a miracle."

Mom sighed again. "Clista, maybe you don't appreciate it right now, but in time, you'll feel grateful for the honor. I know I would be."

Mom's eyes were red from holding back tears. I looked down, feeling guilty. To desire something so much and to see it given to another person who didn't even want it was a horrible punishment. I was sorry I'd complained so much. Maybe my parents were right. I tried to believe it.

"It's really quite attractive on you," my father said to cheer me up. I turned and smiled at him, and then Mother smiled at both of us, and it was like after a storm. The air was miraculously all clear again, and the itchy mugginess was gone.

I stopped fighting the will of the *Old Ones* then, and I began to explore exactly what I could do. We already knew about the light orb. I touched it and turned it on again. Then I went around touching the other items, but none of them reacted to my initial contact.

"Concentrate," my mother scolded. I realized then that I'd been thinking more of bed than of forcing something to come alive. But I was really tired. I told her that.

Both of them looked down at their clock pendants and gasped. It was long past when I usually went to sleep.

"Go to bed," my father said, kissing me goodnight.

Mom looked slightly worried. "I hope you don't have any tests tomorrow. Maybe you should stay home?"

"Clara," my father cautioned her, with half-hearted sternness, then chuckled at her expression.

I shot a glance back at her and saw her look of chagrin. She wasn't concerned about my getting as much rest as she was hoping to have my help all day. I laughed, too.

"Sorry, Mom," I said. "I have a leadership report to work on. Can't stay home."

I kissed them both goodnight and slowly climbed up the basement steps. I shut the door at the top and walked up to my bedroom, dragging my feet, half in tiredness and half because I was reviewing everything that had happened. My stomach growled. I'd missed dinner, but it was too late at night to eat. I promised myself I'd have a good breakfast in the morning.

It was only when I got to the top of the big staircase and was about to enter my room that I realized I'd left my helmet down in the basement. I longed to forget about it and sleep minus its distraction, but I really did want that scholarship from Cronoks Lab. I turned about and went back down the stairs to get it.

The door to the basement was still closed. I put my hand on the button to identify me, but I stopped before I made contact. Through the door, I could hear the voices of my parents. They were talking about me and about Cronoks Lab.

"Maybe we should tell her what they're doing," my mother said.

"She needs to concentrate on school, not on our problems."

"Her being attached to the necklace means she's entered our realm," my mother told him. "If they find out about it, they'll never let her go."

"You have to remember, Clara, our daughter didn't volunteer for this. This has all been against her will. I don't think that before this came up, she had the slightest interest in the *Old Ones*. We can't influence her to follow in our steps. We have to let her decide her chosen field."

"Even if it's at Cronoks Lab?"

"Even there, Clara, because just as I said, in the end, it's her decision."

I don't know how much longer I would have stood there listening. It wasn't the right thing to do, but it's difficult not to listen when your parents are discussing you. But I was suddenly seized by a huge yawn, and I was so tired I felt like I could curl up at the basement door and go to sleep. I couldn't stay there any longer. I needed to get my helmet and go to bed.

I knocked and entered. Neither one of my parents looked the slightest bit guilty about discussing me. I'm sure they didn't realize I'd heard their words, but I know if someone had walked in on me when I was talking about them, I'd have been embarrassed.

I explained the reason for my return, walked across the room, picked up the helmet, and left with a yawning "Good night."

Dad mumbled something, but he didn't look up. He was pretending to be engrossed in a huge manual he'd previously shown me, which was full of writings about the *Old Ones'* artifacts. Mom was sketching in her science journal. As I walked by, I glanced over her shoulder. The illustration she was working on was a perfect likeness for the light orb I'd managed to turn on.

Mom had listed the measurements in the margins of the page. As I watched, she was carefully inscribing and diagramming tiny, but neat comments that noted details not visible in the sketch. I stood by her side a moment, intrigued by the quality of her work, and then I issued another "Good night," which wasn't answered by either of them. Tiredly, I trod up the steps of the basement and returned to my room.

Chapter Five

That night, I had many dreams. My parents were in danger. There was an explosion. Someone from Cronoks Lab was inside the cavern. I saw his white coat and his goggles. He had on an explorer's helmet. In his hand was a shovel. I think he was digging. Was he trying to help my parents? Maybe, but everything was confusing. Time wasn't sequenced right. It kept looping and sputtering out.

In the morning, when I woke up, I felt groggy again. My eyes were red-streaked and puffy. Gray pillows lay beneath each eye, the telltale markers of the ugly visions I'd had during the sleepless night.

I stuck my head into a vitalizer and allowed the mist to refresh my eyes and face. When I finished, I caught a stray pimple bulging from beneath my skin. I zapped it with Pimple Gone. The ugly thing retreated nicely. Then I stepped into the shower, turned on my music, and let the water massage my body to the tune of Brez Nev's *Powder City*.

Needless to say, I felt much better when I exited. I had worried slightly about the necklace being damaged by the water, but when I got out, it was as shiny as always and just as dry. I eyed it in the mirror and tried to decide if it looked good on me. Parents lied about things like that sometimes. However, the necklace wasn't ugly. I decided I halfway liked it.

I dressed, pulling on a pair of jeans and a Brez Nev souvenir T-shirt. After all, I figured it didn't really matter what I wore. Nobody would be seeing my clothes. That was kind of a dis. (That's Brez Nev's talk for "disappointment.") Clothes were something we kids picked to show our mood and our attitude for the day. Mine would have to be "astronaut-look." I laughed at myself for caring. "Vanity," I said with a chuckle.

I turned on the spacesuit's clean cycle. I could have done so while I was wearing it, but that morning, I just wasn't up to being a model suit tester. In fact, I resisted putting the thing back on. I was feeling slightly claustrophobic about it. Of course, I wrote all of that down, but I wasn't really sure how much of it was because of what I was going through personally or my reaction to wearing the suit.

Irritated with the sudden cumbersomeness of it, I tugged and pulled carelessly, almost hoping it would rip so I wouldn't have to wear it. It didn't. I secured it shut, put on my helmet, and allowed maintenance to perform its medical examination of my body. I negated the hair, face, and body washes since I'd already taken care of those, but I clicked on the teeth cleaning and nail trims. That part was kind of cool.

Mom and Dad were already in the kitchen when I went down to breakfast. I could hear them talking as I walked down the stairs.

"I need a cup of coffee badly," I said by way of greeting.

Mom laughed. She was a morning person, and Dad was always happy no matter what time of day. Their smiles were almost more than I could take that morning. I wished there was a smile screen on the helmet face that I could darken. The helmet adapted itself to light and dark, but smiles didn't seem to affect it.

"Poor Clista," Mom said, "We kept you up way too late. Tonight, it's early to bed."

"Mom, I'll probably have a paper to write. Whenever I'm thoroughly exhausted, that's when one of the proctors decides to assign one."

Dad laughed. "I remember that," he said. "You've heard of Murphy's Law? Well, that's Proctor's Law."

Even I let out a snicker at that one, and then, strangely, I started feeling better.

"So what do you think of the Cronoks Lab suit?" Mom asked.

I choked on a swallow of coffee and had to recover from my coughing spell before I could even start to think about an answer to Mom's question. Why was she bringing up Cronoks Lab? I thought she hated talking about them.

I examined her. Her face, unlined and smooth as a twenty-year-old's, was looking even younger that day. Not realizing that I was staring at her, she glanced at my father, and her mouth sweetened into a perfect smile. Mom looked beautiful at that moment. I sighed, wishing I had her looks, but I took after my dad. My cheekbones weren't as high, my eyes not as almond-shaped, and my hair was dark and curly which was totally different from her reddish blonde.

"I think it's a good spacesuit, Mom. I don't know anything about the company."

That seemed to appease her. She took a sip of her coffee, smiled again at Dad, and then broke off a piece of her breakfast nutritional bar, which she nibbled on as she went back to reading her archeologist's journal.

I didn't wait around until she got to another pause in the book. I was too tired to fence even gentle probing. I finished my coffee, grabbed a stoshberry bar, and high-tailed it out the door with my usual quick goodbye.

When I got to school, Frall was waiting for me.

"Hey, what took you?" he asked, laughing because I was actually earlier than I'd promised to be.

"Parents," I told him, rolling my eyes. Of course, he couldn't see my gesture. Hiding behind helmets looked like it was going to be hard on relationships. I wondered if Frall still remembered what I looked like.

"What color are my eyes?" I asked him when we'd seated ourselves over in the student quad.

Frall started to laugh. "That's easy — spacesuit brown."

"That's what I thought. I hate wearing this thing," I complained.

Frall placed his hand over my gloved one and squeezed. "Your eyes are hazel, Clista. They change color with whatever you wear. I've seen them blue as sky or gray as fog. I've watched as they darkened to green or hinted at brown. And they're full of sparkling highlights that madden a guy because he can't grab hold and figure out exactly who you are."

I was glad then that Frall couldn't see my face. It felt hot as volcanic ash. I laughed nervously and withdrew my hand. It was a good thing I did so because Bista, Gerga, Semaph, and Theopolis all came rushing into the quad, pounced into our conversation, and slid comfortably into the table benches on each side and across from us.

"Did you hear?" they asked.

"Hear what?" Frall and I both questioned at the same instant while we tried to read their excited faces.

"Cronoks Lab is giving us another project. This one is about the *Old Ones*. It seems that the lab has found a rare instrument, and every student in the school is going to touch it and see if the thing reacts."

"Reacts? What kind of instrument?" I asked, puzzled.

"You know from the *Old Ones*."

"An artifact?" Frall and I said at the same time.

He looked at me and laughed, but I was too caught up in the news to return his smile. "What do you mean about its reacting? Reacting to what?" I asked, sensing that something bad was about to destroy my day.

"Artifacts are ancient. Nobody knows anything about them." Frall lectured. "I've never heard of one of them reacting to someone's touch," he added.

Semaph jumped up. "What am I doing sitting here? I'm going to see if I can wake the thing up. Must be magical."

Bista thought about that for a minute. "Yeah, me, too." He swung his leg around the bench and stood up. "Hey, Semaph, wait for me. I'm feeling lucky today. Maybe I'll be the one to fire it up."

"You're leaving us?" Gerga said with a pout on her lips.

Bista sat down instantly. His eyes brightened along with his smile. "I wouldn't dream of leaving you, Gerga. I think I'd rather stay here, actually. After all, if this instrument has been dead for centuries, I doubt it could be all that exciting. And what are the odds it would see me and come alive? Frall said none of them responds to someone's touch. Maybe Cronoks Lab is just trying to make us study or something."

Frall shook his head. "Zero to nothing. Artifacts don't turn on and off, and they're not magical. Anybody rushing over there is wasting their time."

"Cronoks Lab doesn't think so, " Gerga said. "They wouldn't have brought the thing here otherwise. And someone said that there were five scientists with it."

"We really don't know what artifacts do and don't do, Frall," I said, thinking of the light orb that had flared up when I touched it.

"Yeah, I know. Artifacts are what I want to pursue after graduation. I want to be an archaeologist."

"Hey, that's what Clista's folks are — archaeologists. Didn't you tell me that they catalog artifacts for the museum, Clista?" Gerga asked.

Frall stared at me. "You've got to be kidding. Do your parents really work for the museum? You've got to introduce me to them. I'd love to watch them work. I'd even volunteer my time. Do you think they'd be interested?"

I shrugged. "I'll ask."

I was thinking about how hard they were working in the caverns. Frall looked strong. They might be willing to use him. However, I needed to think about that some more: the ramifications, the questions, the probings of my mother if I introduced Frall to her. But my brain just couldn't focus on it at the moment. It was doing somersaults about the news my friends had brought — an *Old Ones'* artifact at school.

Where had it come from? I remembered my parents' anger with the company, but wouldn't my parents have told me if they suspected Cronoks Lab of stealing? Could that be the problem? But just maybe the artifact didn't come from there. Maybe this was just a coincidence.

Of course, I knew that any archaeological finds my parents dug up were not really theirs to keep. They belonged to the Rwawan Museum — except for one necklace that would never end up there . . .

I reached up and tried to touch it. The spacesuit prevented that, but the necklace grew warmer than it had a moment before. I wondered if it was glowing again. Did it sense that I was thinking about it?

"Clista, I thought you'd be excited. Isn't Cronoks Lab the company you wanted to work for?" Gerga elbowed me.

"You want to work for *them*? Theopolis asked. "That would be a good choice for you, I suppose. Me, I want to go someplace off Rwawan, to explore other worlds, to live on maybe one of our moons."

"You would," said Gerga. "You'll probably end up on Shlam, where there's nothing but volcanoes."

Theopolis cracked an uneven smile. He'd probably been practicing it for hours in front of a mirror because the smile was perfect for him. It was the crookedness of it that teased and the way you could just see the tiniest bit of his teeth. The smile came out looking mischievous, good-natured, and adorable. All the girls had once voted Theopolis as the cutest smiler on campus.

"Shlam wouldn't be my first choice," he said, still smiling that heart-throbbing smile at Gerga. "Not unless you'd be there."

Gerga took it in stride, not even blinking. She gave him a swift grin and laughed — just as if he hadn't just thrown his heart at her feet. She turned to look at me. "So, shall we all get in line? I'd love to have something exciting happen when I touch the artifact. I wonder what it is they expect to happen? What would the thing do to show it was turned on?"

"I bet Cronoks Lab has no idea either. Otherwise, they wouldn't be taking it to various schools to have everyone touch it," Theopolis said.

"Yeah, maybe if the right person lays a hand on it, it pulverizes them. For all we know, anything's possible with the *Old Ones*." Bista was only joking, but he was so intent on glowering at Theopolis for making a move on Gerga that he didn't see Gerga pale at his words.

Then, when he turned and saw, he added, "Tell you what. I'll hold your hand while you touch it. That way, I guarantee you'll be safe from anything bad."

Gerga shook her head and laughed. "No thanks. I don't think that holding someone's hand will stop the thing from pulverizing me, but I'll let the others touch it first. I think I'll plan to be too busy to take my turn."

"Clista, how about you?" Bista asked. "Need a hand to hold?"

Frall had taken hold of mine. I blushed and withdrew it. Then I shook my head. "Thanks, Bista, but I think I'll be fine. I've got too much work to do to go around touching silly artifacts. Speaking of work, could you check over my equations, pretty please, Bista?"

That morning as I went to class, everyone was talking about the exciting opportunity of touching an *Old Ones'* artifact. I thought it was more interesting to speculate about where the company had gotten the notion that an artifact might react to someone's touch. I'd never read anything about humans being able to activate such devices. So why did Cronocks Lab believe it was possible, and why were they bringing it to schools?

Oh, I suppose the latter made sense. The young were more pliable. They weren't resistant to trying new things, and research showed the pathways for the brain connectors were still open and loose. For that reason, a young child would be the ideal, but a young child would have an interfering parent. One of us, on the other hand, so close to employment age, could easily be entrapped . . .

Now, why had I said that? Entrapped? Was it just because of what my mother and father kept hinting? I wanted to be hired by Cronoks

Lab. Didn't I? Yet, why was I so leery of them all of a sudden? I really needed time to think about this situation and to figure out where it was all headed. I wished that math class would allow me to sit and process life drama, but it wouldn't. I sighed and turned my attention to "quantitative expressions of deviant planes."

After class, I had just taken my seat in Language Development when I heard the newest gossip. Cronoks Lab was taking their artifact from room to room, making sure that *everyone* tried it. How had they gotten permission from the school?

That didn't take me long to figure out. Cronocks Lab was the sponsor of several programs. Money.

Would a student have the right to refuse? Could we be forced? That brought me back to my original question. What made Cronoks Lab think that someone could turn on the device? Sure, *I* knew it was possible. But how did they know?

Thinking about how my parents and I had discovered that down in the basement and the how and why of it, brought me the most horrible thought. I *couldn't* touch the artifact! It probably would turn on for me. I was wearing the necklace.

I was in danger. If Cronoks Lab discovered that I was wearing an artifact, Mom and Dad would get in trouble, and I'd become the Lab's newest Rwawan science project, the nonpaid, non-volunteer kind.

My body broke out into a cold sweat. My mouth dried. I could hardly swallow. My head began to pound. Each moment, as the class continued, I pictured the scientists coming through the classroom door. The artifact probably wouldn't even wait for me to be hauled up to the front of the classroom, kicking and screaming. It would start flashing and turn itself around and point at me. Then a siren would go off and …

"Are you coming, Clista?" a friend asked, pulling at my spacesuit. I gasped and looked around. Everyone was leaving. I'd made it through the class. But what about the next class and the one after that?

I sighed, picked up my books, and followed Storba out the door. "I'm not feeling well," I told her. "I think I'd better go home."

"I'm sorry. What does your suit say?" she asked curiously.

I glanced down at the body readout. High levels of stress: body temperature elevated, pulse rate fast, blood pressure in safe quadrants but above normal for occupant. Adrenaline flowing throughout the system.

"It says that I'm not feeling well," I told Storba, smiling wanly.

My friend waved goodbye and called out, "Feel better," as she walked off to her next class.

I felt like telling her that I wouldn't be feeling better until Cronoks Lab left the school, but, of course, I didn't. I only waved with a weak flutter of my hand. Then I turned toward the Academy Office.

Bad luck seemed to be following me that day. As I entered the nurse's headquarters, a man with the words Cronoks Lab emblazoned across the pocket said, "Well, what do we have here? One of our testers! How's the suit doing?"

I was glad my face was covered by the tinted faceplate of the helmet. It meant that the man, a senior department scientist, which it said on the label of his gray lab coat, couldn't peer into my eyes and read my horror at finding him there.

"I haven't been sleeping really well. Is that a side-effect of the suit?" I asked. "That may be all that's wrong with me, but I'm just not feeling well."

"Interesting," he said. "Better let me take a look. We wouldn't want one of our spacesuit testers getting sick on us."

I would have backed up and thought up another excuse if I'd had the opportunity, but the man grabbed one of the suit's outer links and propelled me toward him before I could speak.

"Ah," he said. "I see."

Why do people do that? Don't they know that if they're experts who are supposed to know everything, an "ah" and an "I see" means that they're holding back information? When they do that, it sends our already high blood pressure even higher. What did the "ah" and the "I see" mean?

"Let's take that helmet off for a few minutes, shall we?"

Again, I was ready to reverse my steps and run back to my classroom, but there was no way I could. I was trapped between the counselor's desk and the Cronoks Lab scientist. The man unsnapped and lifted. Then, he placed the helmet down on the chair. "There," he said. "Doesn't that feel better?"

I nodded. "You're right. I guess I just needed some more air."

He frowned at that, picked up the helmet, and examined it. "No, the air outlets are fine. They weren't blocked. Maybe you just panicked?"

My head reared up. "I'm not claustrophobic," I said. "May I have my helmet back, please? I think I better get back to class."

"Not until we check you over, young lady. What's your name? What class are you missing?"

I darted a look of "help me" at the school counselor, but for some reason, she wasn't interfering. In fact, she was staring at the scientist with so much admiration I doubt she even noticed I was there.

"Clista," I answered him. Then I paused to check my watch because it seemed like I'd been in the office for hours, even though I'd been standing there for only five minutes. I sighed heavily. "The class I'm missing right now is — Leadership."

"How interesting," the man said, "the exact class where the artifact is. We don't want you to miss that, do we? I'll walk you there."

"Oh, I don't need you to do that," I stuttered. "Besides, I'm still feeling kind of dizzy. Maybe I should lie down for a while. Could I do that, Ms. Jayfor?"

She hummed and hawed about it, not wanting to contradict the scientist, but I could see she didn't see any reason why I shouldn't.

The man's face darkened. His left eye was twitching. He smoothed it still, and then he smiled, nodded, and said, "Well, Clista, if you're still not feeling well, that's certainly a reasonable thing for you to do. Don't worry about it, though. We'll bring the artifact *to you*. I wouldn't want one of our potential employees to miss out on seeing it."

Chapter Six

As he left the office, Ms. Jayfor led me into the small room where a cot was kept for any ailing students. I lay down and closed my eyes. I was really in a fix. What was that expression — out of the sunshine and into the solar flares? That was me!

There was a transceiver next to the bed. I picked it up and buzzed my folks. Dad answered. I filled him in on what was happening. He sounded as worried as I was and said, "I'll be right there. Give me fifteen minutes." Then he disconnected.

I lay back and shut my eyes, trying not to worry. I guess I fell asleep. I don't know how that could be possible, with my thoughts racing around like charged electrons, but I woke to the sound of loud voices. One of them was my father's.

I bolted up. That was the wrong thing to do. My head was whirling. I almost collapsed. Instead, I clung to the cot, closed my eyes, and waited for the chaotic madness inside my head to dissipate.

I could feel the heat of the necklace burning my skin. The pain of it was tolerable, but there was a warning in it. Something was wrong, very wrong.

"Dad," I called out.

Apparently, my voice contained my fear. He came barging through, ignoring Ms. Jayfor's mew of distress.

"What's wrong?" he said.

My whole world was crashing down, so that seemed an odd thing to ask me, but he meant what new calamity had occurred. I opened my eyes and saw that the scientist had followed my father into the room. Ms. Jayfor was standing there wringing her hands and uttering sentences that all began with "Really, I don't think this is quite. . ." With the scientist, my father, and another strange man wearing the gray lab coat of Cronoks Lab all inside the room, it felt extremely crowded.

"Please, I need to talk to my father ALONE."

"Oh, dear," said Ms. Jayfor. "I'm afraid I must insist. He is her father, and she wants to . . . Please . . ."

Although her ability to issue orders was a bit weak, her gestures more than made up for it. The two men and Ms. Jayfor backed out of the room and closed the door.

"Dad," I whispered. "There's something wrong. I don't know what it is, but the necklace is burning me. It doesn't feel at all like it did in the basement . . . and I feel sick. I can't walk, and I'm really scared."

Dad was there at my side in an instant. His arms surrounded me, and he hugged me close. "Don't worry, sweetie. I'll take care of it. It must be the thing they're bringing in here. You don't have to touch it. I'll see to that."

I shook my head. That was the wrong thing to do. Dizziness overtook me. I sagged into my father's strong chest and lay there for a moment, absorbing his warmth and love. Then I breathed in a very shaky breath and tried to figure out what the necklace was telling me.

Dad's heartbeat was calming, but it couldn't hide the flood of information that hit me at that instant. I gasped and swallowed hard. If someone had slapped me in the face with a dead animal, told me I'd flunked all the week's tests, and distributed my personal diary to every student in the academy, it couldn't have been any worse than the waves of horror I was feeling.

"Dad, you don't understand," I said. "What Cronoks Lab has brought to the Academy doesn't feel like the *Old Ones'* possessions. I haven't seen it, of course. I just feel it. I know this doesn't make any sense. None of it does, but you see, it's wrong. It's . . ." I gulped and tried to control my words, but the super-charged repulsion I was feeling for the Cronoks Lab artifact was robbing me of the calm my father's presence had brought me.

"Where is it?" I asked my father. "Is the thing outside that door? Did you see it?"

Dad shook his head. "They were bringing it here, Clista, but I told them they couldn't make you do anything against your will. You don't have to touch it. I won't let them force you. In fact, they have no right to demand anything of you kids."

"Dad, you're not listening," I blurted out.

He pulled back. "I understand you're upset, Clista, but you . . ."

I think I was in for one of those big lectures, the ones about treating my parents with respect and consideration. I probably deserved it, but NOT at that moment!

"Dad, PLEASE."

He stared into my eyes, picked up my wrist, and tried to take a reading. Of course, he couldn't feel my pulse through the spacesuit's heavy fabric. He sighed loudly and with considerable displeasure, then turned the suit's Vital Signs Monitor in his direction so he could examine the data. Then, as if not trusting anything the Cronoks Lab would tell him, he once more stared into my eyes.

"What exactly are you talking about, Clista? Are you saying that the artifact Cronoks Lab has is NOT something that once belonged to the Old Ones? You mean it's malevolent to them?"

There was a knock on the door, and without waiting for an answer, the gray-suited scientist who'd blocked my going home came barging in carrying the thing.

I screamed. The necklace was searing my flesh. "Take it away," I yelled. "Take it out of here."

The scientist stopped, confused. My bloodless face must have frozen him temporarily, but that didn't stop my father. Dad strode toward the scientist with such anger I could feel the red lava of its rage.

"Get that thing away from my daughter," my father yelled. Then he pushed the man backward and slammed the door in his face.

The relief I felt was like a cool shower on a hot day. I knew the artifact was still outside the door. I could feel it pressing in on me, its evilness a preying monster, yet I had been given a reprieve for a moment. I breathed in deeply with gratitude.

The air cleared. The stark evil that had burned my lungs, weighted down each indrawn breath, and buzzed inside my head like a thousand attacking mosquitoes, retreated. The sound of its silence helped me marshal my defenses. But I knew that it would return. The battle was inevitable.

My father was staring at me, his face an aged cask of lines of worry. He felt my attention as it centered on him. He swallowed and said, "I'm afraid I may have ended your chances for employment with Cronoks Lab."

How strange that I could go from screams of panic to a loving smile in such a short period of time, but it was as if the seconds we had between us were crystallized into moments of awareness. "You saved my life, Dad," I told him. "Thank you."

Dad started to speak, but I held up my hand. I had to explain to him what was happening. I needed him to understand before the next encounter came.

Again, I whispered, unsure how thick the walls between the outer rooms and this room were. "I think you should know, Dad, that the connection between the *Old Ones* and myself is growing stronger the longer I wear the necklace. There is Power in their gift, a Power that is so much stronger than anything I've ever felt.

"It's like living in darkness and suddenly being given light. It's not a bad thing like I thought at first. It doesn't frighten me anymore — especially after feeling the wickedness of that other force. I accept the bequest of the *Old Ones*. They have given it to me for a reason. I honor it, and I pledge my life to their need."

Dad was listening all right, but at my first words, he deflated and sank into a chair, a man bombarded with more than he could accept. His hands rose up to cover his face. Because of that, I couldn't tell what he was thinking. I wanted him to look up, but I couldn't push him faster than he was able to handle the knowledge I was giving him. I knew he needed time to adjust, but I had so little of that. A minute rushed by, a minute of precious time, but still, I waited.

As the silence continued, I calmed my breathing and slowed the beating of my heart. I gathered in the quiet, like one who harvests wheat seeds in the cup of her hands. Thus, I corralled the Power, sipping Force from the air as most people breathe in a fragrance.

When my father finally looked up, his eyes were haggard with great puffs of shadow, but he was resigned and once more willing to listen. The scientist had pushed the father aside. Curiosity once more ruled.

"What does it feel like?" he asked.

I shook my head. "We can't talk here now, Dad. Besides, the enemy comes. You must stay where you are. Do not come between the instrument the man carries and me. Okay?"

Dad shook his head. "This is difficult, Clista. As your father, I want to protect you, but I believe you when you say that the Power of the *Old Ones* is inside you now. I will stay in the chair as long as you're not hurt."

I nodded. I would have spoken, but the door flew open. The same scientist walked in, carrying the *Tworst of Twent*. Once more, the evil lashed out at me, but I was ready this time. I channeled the lines of Power and invoked the *Old Ones*. My hands stretched open, small finger against the small finger, my palms each a cup for Goodness.

The man stopped and froze in the doorway. Once more, his eyes sped to mine. "What are you doing to me?" he asked in a panicked voice. "I can't move."

"What you have in your hands is the *Tworst of Twent*," I told him. "It is the personification of evil. Like goodness, it cannot be destroyed. It must always exist. But in the hands of mankind or a like being, it carries great malevolence.

"Long ago, the *Old Ones* buried it deep inside the caverns. They placed protections all around it, safeguards, so it would not ignite this world with its malice. My parents unfortunately removed the safeguards, and somehow, the *Tworst of Twent* came into your possession. It must be returned to its resting place. It cannot be allowed to reign."

"What silliness is this? The Power of the *Old Ones* — that's all a myth. Have your parents put you up to this?

"It's coming from you, this strange force. What are you doing to cause it? Where did you find a weapon to stop my movement?

"Or is it Felix I should be speaking to? I called Cronoks Lab. It didn't recognize your name at first. But further digging found you. The company told me that you and your wife are the archeologists in charge of our dig. Clista is your daughter. Is that what this is all about? I know there have been some problems, but . . ."

"My father has no control over the Force you feel. The *Old Ones* guide me and protect me. They will not allow you to come closer."

"This is ridiculous. I won't be ordered about by a child. Felix, tell her to turn it off, or there'll be serious consequences. You know what I mean. Tell her to stop it NOW."

"You're threatening me without understanding," I told him. "Put down the *Tworst of Twent*. It won't help you. It doesn't bring wealth or power, and you're not going to find anyone who can control it. It never works that way. Although it will grow stronger the longer you hold it, the person possessing it doesn't. The *Tworst of Twent* is not a channel; it's an expeller. It sends out negativity."

I had given the man all the information the *Old Ones* had told me, but I could see that his eyes held nothing but disbelief. I thought it likely that under the influence of the *Tworst of Twent*, anything I said might be impossible for him to grasp. Yet the *Old Ones* believed that he could still free himself if he were originally a good person. With the full explanation, they were giving him that chance.

Once more, I tried to get him to release the artifact. I really didn't want to see him die. "Please, place the *Tworst of Twent* on the floor, and then I'll let you back away. The *Old Ones* will allow that. They'll give you your life if you do it now. But if you don't separate yourself from the evil you're holding, the *Old Ones* are going to preserve your body and wrap it inside their protections forever as another of their safeguards."

"You're mad," the scientist said. "I won't put this down. Never. It's mine."

My hands were filled with Power. I closed my eyes and summoned the action. Threads of blue, twine-like web began flowing down between my fingers. That did not alarm me. I was prepared. But my father stood up, ready to come save me.

"No, Dad," I called out. "I'm fine."

He sat back down on the edge of his chair, the lines of worry forming deep veins across his forehead.

The Cronoks Lab man was struggling. I could see his face fighting against his confinement, but I knew he couldn't break through the Movement Chains of the *Old Ones*, and the *Tworst of Twent* could not aid him at all.

So almost leisurely, I let the webs strengthen and grow full as a giant's beard. Then I rose and walked closer, fighting against the repulsion I still felt.

"Will you put it down?" I beseeched him one more time. "This is your last warning."

"Never," he barked out again with such ugliness in his face, I saw that the *Tworst of Twent* had already sent its thorns deep inside his mind.

When I'd advanced the necessary steps, I raised my hands in front of my lips, and I blew. Like the lightest bubble, the threads rose and floated across the air. They hovered a moment above the wide-eyed scientist and then slowly drifted downward. As they landed, they spread, cocooning him as if he were the nucleus of a shimmering, blue atom.

I watched his face, still vile with rage. As the fibers slowed, knitted, and sealed him inside, only the man's eyes stared out, glowering and glaring with wrathful determination. And even as they, too, were covered up, hatred was the last thing he projected.

When it was over, I dropped my hands and retraced my steps. Then I fell face down onto the cot and sobbed.

My father was at my side at once. He said nothing about what had happened, no recriminations, no orders to undo what I had done. Instead, he gathered me into his arms and rocked me like the child I had once been.

When someone knocked on the door, I dried my tears and stood up. The blue cocoon, which included the scientist and the *Tworst of Twent*, hovered above the ground. It still shimmered somewhat, looking like a dew-moistened spider's egg sack.

I stood beside it and cupped my hands open, as I had done once before, small fingers against small fingers to gather in the Power. When I felt saturated with it, I placed my hands on opposite sides of the cocoon and allowed the Power to circulate about the sack-like shape.

Once more, a knock sounded on the board. "Grenan," the man called out. "Is everything okay?"

I ignored the interruption and continued with what the *Old Ones* were instructing me to do. There was no sound in the swirling winds that swept around the cocoon, but I felt them, and I planted my feet more firmly. It didn't matter. Almost before I had done so, the gray winds of movement died down, and the webbed man's sack began to diminish in size.

"What in the stars . . ." my father cried out in a harsh whisper. Then he stopped and was silent. I didn't turn to look at him, nor did I answer. The Power took all my concentration. It filled my mind and drove me forward.

When the cocoon had shrunk to the size of my pocket, I clapped my hands to halt its shrinkage and to empty the Power from my possession. Then I reached out and plucked the slightly spinning sack of *Tworst of Twent* and the scientist, Grenan, and I slipped them into the pocket of my spacesuit. Finished with that, I turned and looked at my father. "Now, what should we do?" I asked.

Perhaps that seems ridiculous since I had taken charge of so many other things, but the *Old Ones* couldn't help me deal with the reactions of my own people. They were, after all, aliens and perhaps as ignorant of our society as I was of theirs.

But my question served two purposes because I think my father liked it that I had turned to him for help. He put his arm around me and cooed, "Don't worry, baby. This may be unpleasant for a while, but we'll get through it."

I kissed him on the cheek and said, "Thank you, Dad."

That was all the time I had before the door burst open, and the remaining scientist, the academy principal, and a tall, bulbous-nosed stranger I'd never seen came rushing into the room.

"What is going on here?" Mr. Caroom, the principal, demanded.

Chapter Seven

My father was calm. He picked up his jacket and led me forward. "I don't understand what you mean, Mr. Caroom. My daughter is ill, and I'm taking her home. Why are these two men here? Is there some problem?"

Mr. Caroom sputtered for a moment. His eyes shot around the small area where so much had happened. Of course, he saw only the single chair in the corner where my father had sat and, on the other side, the cot and the small table beside it. Nothing was in the least disarranged.

I placed the helmet, which Grenan had thankfully returned to me, back on my head and latched it properly. My days as a product tester for Cronoks Lab were probably over, but at least the helmet could serve me as a cover. I was just too tired to mask my face from any on-lookers. Using the Power had drained me.

"I thought . . . I was told . . ." Mr. Caroom began. Then he coughed and turned to glare at the scientist next to him. "You said he was in here, Mr. Choffee. Where?"

"But I don't understand it? Grenan came in here with the artifact. He was going to show it to the girl. She was supposed to touch it," the scientist replied.

Mr. Carroom had been glancing over at us. With the man's words, the principal's head swiveled back to glare at Mr. Choffee. The principal's eyes bulged as if he couldn't believe what he was hearing. "Let me see if I understand this," he said. "You're saying that you knew this girl was sick, and you were going to force her to touch some silly, old artifact?" His face reddened even as he spoke. All of us students knew that was a warning sign, like a storm brewing, black clouds in the East.

"Grenan's not here. It's obvious that *he* has better sense than to bother a sick child. But I think you and I need to talk. Come with me, Mr. Choffee," the principal demanded.

The scientist was still looking wildly around the room. He darted over to the bed and got down on his hands and knees to search under it. "But you don't understand," he told Mr. Caroom as he stood back up. "Grenan came in here. He had the artifact, and he never came out. What have they done with him? Where is the artifact?"

"Well, he's not here now, is he?" Mr. Caroom said, laughing unpleasantly. His face, as he shot a glance at my father and me, darkened even further until it resembled the cooked inside of a burned sugar beet.

"I'm sorry for all this," the principal said, nodding to my father. "I hope Grenan didn't bother you or your daughter. None of this will ever happen again, I promise.

"And you, young lady, ah, Clista, isn't it? I'm very sorry you're feeling under the weather. You go home with your father and get some rest. You do look drained. Have you been studying too hard?"

The principal shot a glance at my father. "Today's students are so driven. It's quite different from when you and I were in school. We knew how to moderate ourselves, didn't we?" He winked at my father and nodded at him again.

Then, darting another look at me, he said, "Feel better, Clista, and stay home and rest tomorrow. That's an official order, you hear me? I mean, as long as your dad concurs."

I smiled rather shakily and said, "Thank you, Sir."

Then my dad took over for me, shook hands with Mr. Caroom, thanked him, and pushed me forward toward the door.

"But, Grenan . . ." I heard Mr. Choffee say once again just before we walked out through the door. We didn't pause. We slipped out of the office without any word of explanation.

I was very glad that Ms. Jayfor had not yet returned from her errand. It was probable that as taken as she'd been with Grenan, she would have had her own questions, ones we didn't have answers for. Luck was with us.

Dad and I walked through the school hall, straight through a mob of kids, none of whom were seniors like me. I was relieved that my friends weren't around. I didn't want to answer their questions, either. I kept my head down and walked as fast as possible. We had just reached the door to the outside exit when our good fortune winked out, and someone yelled out, "Clista!"

I turned around to see who it was, but I already knew. I really wanted Dad to meet Frall, but the timing was off. For one thing, I hadn't prepared Dad for this situation. I knew he'd have a ton of questions about any guy I liked, and the relationship I had with Frall — if you could call it that, wasn't nearly firm enough to bear the kind of deep probing Dad would want to carry out.

"Clista, what's wrong?" Frall questioned, his long-legged stride bringing him over to my side almost instantly. Worry shadowed his face.

"Nothing. I'm just going home," I told him, feeling his eyes probing. "I'm not feeling well."

Dad shifted his stance. I knew what that meant. Hurriedly, I made the introductions. "This is my friend Frall, Dad. Frall, this is my father."

Of course, Frall flashed his gorgeous smile and stuck out his hand for Dad to shake. But then the two of them stood eyeing each other like I was a bone they were about to fight over.

I tried to connect them better. "Frall is interested in archaeology, Dad. He was hoping he could come over and talk with you about it sometime."

Frall was too busy to pick up the cue. He was still measuring my father with his eyes.

Dad, however, remembering his manners, came out of the caveman stance first. "Nice to meet you, Frall. Clista's friends are always welcome at our house. Stop by sometime. My wife and I would be happy to talk about Stormian Caverns and our work there."

I suddenly became aware of the change in the atmosphere that comes when it's time to be hustling to the next class. "Aren't you going to be late?" I asked Frall, glancing around, expecting to see the other kids rushing by.

Strangely, Frall didn't seem worried. He ignored my question, continuing to make eye contact with my father. "When would that be, Sir?" he asked. "I'd love to come by after school today."

Dad coughed, the kind that means, help me out of this, but I wasn't about to. I was once more staring into Frall's eyes, wishing that he could come with us right that moment. Luckily, Dad couldn't see my expression. The space helmet was very good for covering up such things. If I hadn't had that on, I'm sure Dad would have seen the silliness of my grin as I stared up at Frall.

"Maybe tomorrow would be better, " Dad said. "Clista's not feeling well today," he added to remind me as much as Frall.

With my father's words, I felt a wave of fatigue once more, slapping at my tired body. It was suddenly all I could do just to remain standing. "I'm sorry, Frall," I mumbled in exhaustion. "Dad's right. I'm really not feeling well, not at all."

I managed to get that full sentence out before I fainted. I guess, from hearing about it later, that my collapse surprised my dad. It was Frall who caught me, and he then insisted on carrying me out to Dad's Fly-By. I wish I'd been awake. Imagine being in Frall's arms! But on the other hand, I guess it was just as well that I wasn't. How embarrassing if any of the kids had seen that. They'd be snickering for months.

Dad told me later that Frall even kissed me on the cheek, right on top of my helmet, just before he shut the door of the vehicle.

Darn, it just wasn't fair. That was the very first time Frall ever kissed me, and I didn't even know it. I didn't even feel it! Even worse, there was Frall giving me that princely, "I hope you're feeling better kiss," taking the risk that I could have been contagious, and doing it right in front of my father — talk about courageous! Frall is just so incredibly wonderful!

Chapter Eight

Dad took off in the Fly-By and flew us home. Of course, I don't remember that either since I was still unconscious.

Mom had left the dig early, too, and was waiting for us at the house. When she saw Dad carrying me in, since he refused to allow me to walk, she got very upset and started ranting about the Academy, Cronoks Lab, and the spacesuit I was wearing. I think she would have gone on to blame more things if Dad hadn't hurriedly told her I was just very tired.

I honestly am not sure I could have walked, even though I argued with him about it — feebly. I felt like someone had stolen all my bones. My body was limp.

Mom demanded that I go right to bed, and I didn't protest. Dad carried me upstairs, Mom at his side, scolding me the whole way. Then she shooed Dad out of the room, helped me into my nightgown, and tucked me in.

"I'm going to go downstairs and fix you something nice to eat," she told me after kissing me on the cheek. My eyes were already shut, and I was floating in the softness of my bed, so my mother's voice sounded distant. I didn't answer her. I hardly heard her footsteps as she walked away.

She told me later that she heated up some soup and brought it up to me, but she said I refused to open my mouth for the spoon and just kept mumbling something about a cavern and rock piles. She gave up, patted my head, kissed me, and left. I don't remember any of that.

The next day, my parents stayed home with me. That's probably when Cronoks Lab rigged their cave, or at least I suspect they did. I blame myself for what happened, although Frall says I shouldn't, but if I hadn't been ill, my parents wouldn't have stayed with me, and then . . .

But I didn't know that then. That night, I slept soundly in the freedom of innocence.

When I finally woke, my mother brought me food again. I was hungry then. I ate all the soup and wanted more. I dressed and followed her downstairs, where I ate two sandwiches, a couple pieces of fruit, and emptied a bag of yogurt chips. Then, and only then, was my belly satisfied.

Later, after I'd dressed in my spacesuit once again, I joined my parents downstairs in the basement. I spent my time there touching various artifacts that they indicated. Several of the items came alive. One was a weapon that didn't look in the least bit dangerous, except that I instinctively knew that it was. I placed it back down most carefully.

A crystal triangle lit up, too. I thought it was the most interesting, but the *Old Ones* asked me not to tamper with it — not with words, but by making the object so hot it burned me when I touched it. There was also a round, flat-shaped item that glowed. The *Old Ones* gave me no instruction concerning that.

I turned it upside down and searched for levers, but I couldn't find anything, nor could my parents, and none of us could discern its function. The rest of the items remained dull to the touch, but Dad and Mom were pleased with the triangle and the weapon. They bent over their separate journals and scribbled away happily.

I didn't care one way or the other if any of the artifacts reacted to my touch. After the previous day, I just accepted. I guess you could say I had become acclimated to being in link with the *Old Ones*. It had changed my life, but since there was apparently no way to undo what had been done, there was also no use fighting it. Anyway, I savored the fact that it brought me into my parents' research lab. That part was fun. I loved having them ask me questions and having them listen. I felt older, wiser, and more valued.

I was pretty sure that Dad had told Mom about the day before. She asked me nothing about it, but I caught her eyeing me strangely several times. I knew somehow that it was related. I wondered when her flow of questions would begin.

Whatever Dad had spoken about, it became very obvious that he had completely forgotten to discuss our scheduled afternoon visitor because when the house computer announced his arrival, Dad moaned out, "Darn, I forgot to tell you about Clista's friend. I told him he could stop by after school."

I went running up the stairs to get the door, but I heard the edge in Mom's voice as she demanded, "And who, exactly, is this friend? Would you please explain why he is coming over?"

I chuckled. Let Dad deal with that. I wouldn't have to, not at least while Frall was there, or so I hoped.

I felt like stopping to check my hair and see if I looked okay, but I still had my suit on, so there wasn't anything I needed to do to primp. I laughed at that, recalling how Frall had still known the color of my eyes.

Yet, I'll admit, I paused and smoothed down my suit. It was, actually, only an avoidance, for, you see, I was suddenly afraid that it might be awkward seeing Frall outside of school. I took a deep breath, stilled my shaking hands, finger-touched the door, and gave permission for Frall to enter.

He shot inside the moment the door slid open. Then he seized me in his bear-like grip and said, "Are you okay? I was really worried yesterday."

I nodded, but I didn't have time to get an answer out before he demanded, "Where are your parents?"

"Downstairs," I told him, thinking that Frall meant he was more interested in meeting them than in talking to me, but I'd completely misjudged his intent. He seized the moment. Gripping my helmet with two hands, he unclasped it and lifted it up. What followed next maybe wasn't a kiss like I'd seen in the vids, but when Frall's lips pressed against mine, they were warm and interesting. There was no question that I liked it very much.

The thumping coming up the basement stairs alerted us. Frall and I drew apart abruptly. I was just fastening my helmet back on when Dad reached the top, opened the door, and looked out.

"Ah, there you are. Clista's mother will be up in a minute. Let's go sit down at the kitchen table. That's more or less our conference room, and amazingly, there's often food there.

Frall laughed exactly as he was supposed to. I was amazed at his poise and adaptability. He didn't let on in any way that he and I had just shared a rather interesting moment of closeness. Thankfully, I don't think my father realized either.

In the kitchen, I plopped down in my usual chair, feeling like the world was spinning again. It wasn't the *Old Ones* confusing me this time. It was my own emotions. Dad ordered some pizza, dialed in drinks, and passed our plates and napkins. Frall, sitting on the opposite side of the table, gave me a wink.

There are definite advantages to wearing helmets. I wondered if I was being unfaithful in not listing them all in my Cronoks Lab journal.

I sighed and smiled back at Frall, and asked him about his day. Embarrassingly, I sounded just like my mother.

That thought must have brought her out of hiding, for she sped into the room like a whirlwind, spinning the atmosphere into the danger zone.

"So — Frall, isn't it?" she asked, knowing full well the name of the boy sitting at the table.

Frall stood up, using old world mannerisms. My mother's eyebrows rose a bit, but she said nothing. Such things did not impress her.

"Nice to meet you," she told him, taking his hand with a grip that was, I'm sure, every bit as strong as my father's. Mom believed that she could measure a person's character by his or her response to such a handshake. I watched both Mom's and Frall's faces, but neither displayed any reaction. Was that a good sign?

The pizza came out of the Food Vendor, it's protein and vegetable toppings sizzlingly enticingly. I breathed in the smell and eagerly held up my plate for a serving.

When everyone's slices were doled out, we dug in, no talking for a good five minutes. Then, as the edge of hunger diminished, the questions began.

After the first couple of minutes, I realized that Frall wasn't nervous at all but was, in fact, responding with questions of his own. He was using Mom's attack to gain information. Inside my helmet, I began to smile, unbelievably enjoying something that I'd dreaded.

A while later, Mom broke into one of her rare smiles. Then she laughed and raised her hands, palms up in defeat. "You win," she told Frall, laughing.

"Does that mean a trip to see those artifacts at Stormian Caverns?" Frall pushed.

Mom and Dad shot a glance at me. I shrugged and then shook my head. I hadn't said anything to Frall about the find, only that they were working there.

Frall caught my look and explained. "Cronoks Lab told the classes all about the artifacts when they toured the school. I was looking forward to touching that relic of theirs, but for some reason, Principal Caroom pulled it. About the time that Clista left school, the scientists departed. I'll never get to see it now, I guess."

I wished I could give Frall the horrid thing. It was still in my spacesuit pocket and had given me the worst nightmares, which was probably the *Old Ones'* way of ordering me to take the thing back to the Stormian Caverns.

"Tell him."

The voice was so loud I stared at my father, thinking he'd yelled at me.

"Tell him!" came the command once again.

My hands went up to my ears, and I covered them. "No!" I said. "I won't."

Both my mother and father ran to my side. Frall stood up and stared. I felt the movement of my parents, and it registered, but I was too busy listening to the voice in my mind. "Tell him," they ordered again, and that time, I heard more than one person giving the command.

I felt faint and sick. *The Old Ones* sounded like they were there, beside me, inside me, speaking in my mind!

"I don't understand this," I told my father, looking into his eyes. "The *Old Ones* are talking to me now. It's not like before. That was like a residue of knowledge. These are actual voices. But I thought the *Old Ones* were dead. Aren't they?"

"Clista, we'll discuss this later. We have company now. Remember?" Mother said, trying to nudge me into silence.

"Take him to the basement," the voices ordered.

I shook my head, trying to fight the new burden the *Old Ones* were placing on me. But they wouldn't leave me alone. Their voices were escalating. "They want Frall to see the artifacts," I told my parents. "They've ordered me to show them to Frall."

"Clista!" my mother cried out.

"Wait," Dad said, catching her arm and her attention. "Are you sure, Clista? It's what *they* want, or is that just what you want?"

"What are you talking about?" Frall asked. "Is there something wrong with Clista?"

I wanted to laugh. He thought I needed mental therapy, and maybe I did. Maybe the voices were only in my mind. Maybe I was going crazy.

"Am I imagining this, Dad? Maybe Frall's right. Maybe I'm flipping out."

"Stop that, Clista," my father said sharply. "You didn't imagine what happened yesterday or what happened with the necklace. If the *Old Ones* say that Frall must see the artifacts, then we must show him.

"Come with us, Frall," Dad said, rising. "You wanted to see Stormian Caverns? We'll show you just what they held."

Frall, for the first time since I'd met him, looked uncertain. He sat there, staring up at us. He glanced first at me and then at my parents. "Are you saying you have artifacts here? From the *Old Ones*? Like the one that Cronoks Labs had yesterday?"

"What they had wasn't from the *Old Ones*," I told him. "I know this is weird, Frall. I don't understand it, either. I'm not even interested in archaeology, but they chose me, and now I think they're communicating."

"Clista. The *Old Ones* lived thousands and thousands of years ago. They're dead, really dead. We know that . . ." Frall said.

"We don't know anything about them," my father said. "They're as much a mystery as they were when we first discovered this planet. But Clista has brought us new information. If you follow us downstairs, you'll see why we believe her."

Reluctantly, Frall stood up. Leaving the pizza, the drinks, and the mess from our eating, he and I followed my parents.

"Do me a favor," Frall said, drawing me aside before we went down the stairs. "Take off that suit, at least the helmet. I need to see your eyes, Clista. Otherwise, I'm not going to believe anything. This is just too strange."

I nodded. Then I unlatched the helmet, placed it on the table in the living room, and took Frall's hand. Thus, I led him down into the basement.

"Wow!" he cried out when his eyes took in the rows of tables with their hundreds of relics. "Stars! I'll believe anything you tell me now. This is unbelievable."

I was still holding Frall's hand. I drew him over to the table where the *Old Ones'* light orb leaned up against the wall. "Touch it," I said.

"Are you sure?" he asked, his eyes traveling to my parents for permission. When they both nodded, Frall reached out and lifted up the ancient lamp. It glowed, just as it had for me.

"You have the power," I whispered.

My father stepped closer. "That's not possible. How could both of you .. ?" He stopped and stared, the pupils of his eyes darkening and widening, for Frall had not only turned on the light but had made the orb change colors as his hand moved about its base.

In wonder, I reached out and touched Frall, wanting him to look up, wanting to know what his eyes were saying. As my fingers made an impact with his, the orb's light wavered and then brightened further into a beacon so strong I blinked from its sudden brightness.

"I don't believe it. They're complementary," my mother said in a hushed tone of astonishment.

I dropped my hand abruptly and turned toward her. "What do you mean?"

"Wait a minute," Dad said, and then he rushed over to the ceiling-high bookcase that lined one wall of the room. His fingers scanned the volumes of tomes, walking the spines as if his touch could read the contents. Then, with a jubilant cry, Dad yanked a bulky, olive-hued text off the shelf and brought it over to us.

"Clara's right. I think I read it in here," he said. "Yes. Here it is. There's something we came across where two people can form a link, a special link … But what I can't remember is whether it was a theory or something the archeologists actually encountered."

Frall and I stared at each other. Sure, maybe there'd been some magic in the kiss we'd shared, but alien matchmaking was a bit too much for either of us to swallow. Already Frall was shaking his head, his face full of doubt and . . . distaste.

"Maybe anyone who came down here with me would have set off that flare of light. How do we know that it's only Frall and I who are complementary?"

"Thanks a lot," he said, pretending to laugh, but I saw that his face held anything but amusement. My words had hurt him.

"I didn't mean it like. . ." I started to explain.

"Hush, you two," my father interrupted. "I've found it. 'It is written that Power is strengthened when multiplied by two.' That was found and translated — one of the few statements written in more than one language. It was found over thirty-five years ago in the Messler Caverns on the opposite side of Rwawan.

"Look, this is all interesting, but I've got to go," Frall said, interrupting my father when he was just about to read another ancient passage.

It was my fault. Frall was reacting to my rejection. "Please, don't go. I didn't mean . . ."

"Anyone could do what I just did, Clista. You said it yourself. I bet your parents could," he said, pointing to them.

I stopped his mouth with my finger. "Frall, please. Nothing happens when my parents touch the artifacts. Absolutely nothing, just like nothing happens when most people touch them. Hundreds have tried.

Why do you think Cronoks Lab brought that piece around for everyone to touch? Somehow they found out that it's possible for a human to waken an artifact, but they didn't find anyone who could. Except you can, Frall, and I can. That's why the *Old Ones* wanted you to come down here. They knew."

Frall was staring into my eyes, but he said nothing, remaining silent as he listened and measured my words. When I finished, he glanced over at the *Old Ones'* light and said, "What else are you keeping from me?"

For a second, I debated. What if he told someone? What if he … but Frall was just like me — trapped in this strange drama. Besides, I really didn't have a choice. The *Old Ones* had already told me that. For some reason, they wanted Frall involved.

I unsnapped my spacesuit, tore the Velcro strip apart, and exposed the necklace that the *Old Ones* had fastened to my neck.

"Stars and comets, Clista," Frall said. "Why are you wearing that?"

"Because they chose her," my mother interrupted. "Just as they've chosen you. Clista didn't ask for it. She doesn't even want it, which is quite droll considering that Felix and I would give everything we owned to have that connection — but the *Old Ones* are the ones who choose, and they have found us, for some reason, unacceptable." My mother stopped for a moment to wipe a tear. I'd never seen her cry before. I stepped closer, but Dad was beside her almost immediately, his arm around her, his lips whispering in her ear.

Mother couldn't speak then, so Dad took over. "As Clara said, apparently, the *Old Ones* have chosen you, Frall. That's an honor. And, it seems that your wish to learn more about them has just been granted."

"No. I don't believe any of this," Frall said. "And even if it were true, this isn't what I want. I intend to be an archaeologist, not some alien's pawn."

I nodded. I'd felt the same way at first, yet they hadn't given me a choice. How could someone fight a Power that spoke into your mind or wrapped necklaces around your neck while you slept? Would Frall really get to choose? Maybe he was wise to back away.

"Thank you for dinner," Frall told my parents stiffly. "I'm glad I had the opportunity to meet you, even if I can't help you with this project of yours."

My parents nodded, but they were already engrossed in study. My father had urged my mother to sit down, and then he'd brought over that heavy volume from which he'd read us the section on "complementary."

"I'll say goodbye to Frall, and then I'm going up to my room," I told my parents, but they didn't answer me. They were bent over the book, their heads together, talking in low tones in that unity that so often didn't include me. I blew them a kiss and walked up the stairs with Frall.

I could feel the coldness emanating from him. His body was stiff, and he made sure that we didn't touch as we climbed. When we reached the front door, I paused and placed my hand on his arm. "I'm sorry I got you into this," I said. "I understand exactly how you feel. Really."

Frall removed my hand and let it go. His eyes shot a glance at the door, and then he looked at me, but it was like there was no recognition. Even his eyes had grown frost.

However, he listened to my words, then he shook his head and said, "This is just too creepy for me, Clista. I don't believe in Magic or Power or whatever you call it. The *Old Ones* are gone. Sure, they're interesting, but they're dead.

"I don't know what your parents are telling you, Clista. I mean, they're nice and all, but somehow they've made you think all this stuff is true. It just isn't.

"I think you need help. Maybe you could talk to the counselors at school, or you could drop in at the clinic or. . ."

His hand reached out to touch the door. It slid open, and I saw he was ready to bolt outside.

"So you think I'm imagining all this," I said. "What about the light orb? What about the way it turned into a beacon when we were both touching it? And you think I dreamed up this necklace, Frall? I thought it was only my imagination, too. But then I woke up, and the necklace was on my neck, and I couldn't get it off. Did you notice that? Do you think that's false, too? Or is that part of my craziness?"

"I didn't say you were crazy, Clista. Let me see the necklace again," he half-ordered, half-requested.

Again, I unsnapped the collar of my suit and unfastened its sticky seams. Frall placed his hands on my shoulders and bent closer to study the necklace. "May I touch it?" he asked.

I nodded. "Yes, but it won't come off, and my parents had no part in that. In fact, they tried everything they could think of to remove it. And I assure you that this necklace is NOT a fantasy, Frall. It's very real."

Frall probed the necklace with his fingers. He felt all around my neck, searching for the catch, but, of course, there wasn't one. Then he turned me around and peered down at the back. He tried to jerk the thing off, but although his fingernails dug into my skin, there was no space between skin and necklace.

Finally, as if tired of it all, Frall sighed and dropped his hands. "Ok, I guess you somehow unlocked one of the artifacts of the *Old Ones*, and now you can't get it off because you don't know the secret of it. That's still not magic. That's advanced technology. But don't try to tell me that the thing came from a dream you had. Your parents had to have found it in one of their digs."

Frall's eyes were blazing, like he was angry with me. Was that because I was forcing him to confront what he didn't want to see? I thought he'd wanted to look at and touch artifacts. Yet, he didn't act like he was enjoying seeing them anymore.

Remembering his question, I tried to explain. "Of course, my parents found the necklace, and I saw it that first time on a table with the other artifacts. That's why I kept dreaming about it, but I didn't go down into the basement to get it. There's an alarm. It would have sounded if I'd opened the basement door during the night.

And don't say that my parents placed the thing on me. They'd never do that. Besides, you saw how jealous my mother is of the fact that I get to wear something of the *Old Ones*. You heard her. She wanted to be the one they chose. If it were as simple as just putting on a necklace and having it stick, believe me, my mother would be wearing this now."

Frall eyes traveled the necklace. Once more, his fingers stroked it, and then he took his hands off my shoulders and drew back. His eyes, as they stared into mine, were only slightly less suspicious. He still thought I'd taken a walk into crazy, and the warmth we'd shared between us was now gone.

"Okay," he said, "Like I told you, this is just too strange, and I gotta' go. My folks'll be worried. You going to school tomorrow?"

I nodded. Frall said nothing more as he slipped out the door. His feet crunched the gravel walkway. I heard the sound of his stride speeding up as he distanced himself. It sounded as if he couldn't wait to get away. He never even paused to look back, although I yelled out, "Goodbye. See you tomorrow."

I stood, leaning on the doorframe, and watched Frall mount his sky scooter. His body was lank and agile, and like everything he did, he sat the scooter ramrod straight with ease and skill. He lifted up swiftly and in a manner so individualistic I knew he wasn't riding on automatic. Without a wave of goodbye, although he knew I was still standing there watching, he shot straight up into the evening clouds.

It was the edge of dusk when Frall took off. The sky was just darkening into bruises against the pale gray of the horizon. Heavy cumulous clouds were blowing in, the kind full of thunder and lightning and the heavy windstorms we often received in the spring. As I watched, those clouds speedily filled in the place I'd last seen Frall's scooter. I shuddered from their cold moisture and from the gloom inside me.

Still, I didn't move. I wanted to think about all that had happened. I smiled for a second, recalling how Frall had kissed me when he'd first arrived and how, for a short time, I'd almost had a boyfriend.

"Oh, Frall," I sobbed. At that moment, I felt the first of the evening's raindrops.

I backed inside and closed the door. My eyes were stinging. Tears dripped down my cheek. I wiped them off and gulping back my despair, I turned away and set forth to clean up the kitchen.

Chapter Nine

The next morning, clouds were heaving great volumes of tears. It was a perfect match for my mood. I showered, changed my clothing, and sonicked my teeth.

Heading downstairs, I peeked in on Mom and Dad. They were sitting at the breakfast table, their heads together as usual, sipping coffee from bright-colored mugs as they discussed the artifacts. I waved and called out that I was heading off for school.

"Eat some breakfast first," Dad called out.

"Maybe the Power feeds her," Mom said, laughing, and once again, they launched into another discussion. Neither noticed as I grabbed a Complete Bar from the food machine and let myself out.

For once, I was glad for my spacesuit. I knew it would keep me dry and warm despite the increasingly rough winds and the turbulent downpour.

The day before, Dad had recovered my scooter. As I looked it over, I was relieved to see that it was undamaged from its overnighter in the school lot. I sat down on it, placed my hands over the 'on receptor,' and soared up into the sky. For a moment I battled the air currents, and then I stabilized by putting it into automatic. The winds were more than I could contend with.

Thus I flew safely, but I rode a ride so rough, it brought pink to my pale cheek. The weather was only the first of the warnings I had that told me dark times were blowing in.

My friends all gathered around me in the courtyard that morning. Bista demanded to see my equations and diagrams; Theopolis touched his fingers to his lips and made a kissy noise to tell me how much he'd missed me. Semaph relayed information about a new project opportunity, and Gerga snapped nastily because I hadn't returned her call after Frall left the night before — but how could I explain what had happened? (I hadn't even told her about the *Old Ones'* gift although she and I had been best friends for always.)

No one asked me where Frall was. Either they didn't miss him, or they didn't want to mention his absence. So I sat on the bench where two days ago he and I had held hands and made future plans. It was difficult not to let on how miserable I felt.

Although the courtyard was a covered area, we weren't indoors, and the winds soon switched directions. The blasts of cold, wet spray drove us inside the Academy walls. In the passages within, the first person I saw was HIM. "Hey, Frall," I called out. He looked me over with eyes as cold as the winds and turned and walked away.

I'm sure everyone witnessed it. It was like being slugged in the stomach. I froze, my face probably a complete wreck of agony.

Bista was the first to react. He pushed the others aside, threw his arm around me, and said, "He isn't worth a single tear, Clista. Remember, I'll always be here for you, no matter what." Gerga piled into the love fest next, and then the others surrounded me and did a group hug.

Before I could respond, Bista pulled away. I stared. His face was reddening. He didn't look at the others — or at me. "See you later. I have a test to study for," he called out and strode off towards the library.

"What's with you? You've tossed over Frall and now moved on to Bista?" Gerga snapped at me.

Her words were so uncalled for my mouth fell open, and I stood in shocked silence.

Theopolis tried to calm her, but Gerga was spitting like an angry cobra, a snake we'd seen in the videos of our history class. Theopolis and Gerga broke away and steered to the right. I glanced at Semaph, but she had nothing to say to me either. She shrugged and took off after Gerga and Theopolis.

So that left me more or less directionless for a good twenty minutes before class. With nothing to do, I drifted over toward my first class. That was the worst decision I could have made. Ms. Jayfor, who often prowled about looking for incidents in the hall to relieve her boredom, spotted me. "There you are, Ms. Pragan," she called out. "I'd like a word with you in the office if you please."

I didn't want to speak to her at all, but I was pretty sure such a talk was inevitable. With a sinking feeling in the pit of my stomach, I followed her into the den of catastrophe.

I had one portion of luck. Mr. Caroom was passing through on his way to circumnavigate the Academy. "Ah, Clista," he said when he saw me. "How lovely to see you looking so much better. You're still pale, but I think you're less tired looking. How do you feel?"

I felt like a person must feel when a wave knocks them down and they can't swim. The ocean brine was heading down my throat, my breath was almost used up, and those Terran sharks we saw in Terran horror movies were approaching. Of course, I didn't say that to him. I smiled and told him that I was feeling better.

"I was just about to ask Ms. Pragan about the whereabouts of Grenan, the missing man from Cronoks Lab," Ms. Jayfor mentioned to Mr. Caroom.

Of course, she didn't know about the blow-up the principal had had with the other scientist. Poor, Ms. Jayfor. Mr. Caroom immediately sent me off to class. Behind me, I heard him launch into an attack that caused Ms. Jayfor to sputter a swarm of apologies.

I had a pop quiz in Government that I was ill-prepared for, an oral presentation assigned while I was out in Leadership, and a whole new line of thought that was entirely over my head in math class. Bista, who wasn't sitting by me, either ignored or didn't see my pleading looks. He rushed out the door before I could grab him for help.

Then, I saw Frall talking with a beautiful red-haired girl who'd just started at the Academy. Once more, he ignored me, passing me in the hall as if he'd never seen me before. So I was crushed, mutilated, and walked over. How could the day get worse?

Just before lunch, Ms. Jayfor called me into the office.

I expected that I'd be alone with her and she'd ask me all the questions for which I had no answers. But that wasn't so. It was much, much worse. A man from Cronoks Lab was there, as was Mr. Caroom and the school psychologist.

"Sit down," the principal said, "We need to talk with you, Clista."

My eyes traveled the group. Their faces were like death masks, parched and drawn. My heart sped up. My palms grew clammy.

"There isn't any way that we can do this gently," Mr. Caroom said. "I'm afraid we have some very bad news."

The faces around me were suddenly like poured acid. I clung to the armrests of the chair I was sitting in, my heart stopping to listen.

"What's wrong?" I asked, still thinking that the bad news was about the missing scientist. Were they going to accuse me of murder?

Would they lock me up? Why wasn't my father here? Why hadn't they called him?

Mr. Caroom reached out and took my hand. His was rough and sweaty. I didn't like the feel of it, but my mouth had dried, and I couldn't speak. I didn't dare pull away.

"Clista, we must all be strong when bad things happen. We, here at the Academy, will be there for you. Do you understand?"

No, I didn't. I didn't understand any of it. I was underwater again, going down for the last time. My lungs were empty. I couldn't breathe.

"There's been an accident, my dear," Mr. Caroom continued.

I still thought he was talking about the other day, about the missing man. That hadn't been any accident, but I couldn't tell him that. Grenan shouldn't have attempted to force me to touch the artifact. He shouldn't have insisted on keeping it when I explained about its danger. But I wasn't going to talk about that. I kept my eyes lowered, trying to think of what I should say, waiting to hear the actual wording of their accusation.

"There's been a cave-in . . ."

That brought my eyes up. That wasn't what I'd expected to hear. A cave-in? What did a cave-in have to do with Grenan's disappearance?

Ms. Jayfor was wearing strong perfume. The flowery essence of it was making me sick. My hand flew up, covering my mouth. I inhaled sharply and couldn't remember how to let it out, how to breathe.

"I'm afraid, Clista dear, your parents are presumed dead," Mr. Caroom continued.

The faces around me were monsters' faces. I gagged and stood up. Then I bolted into the little room I'd occupied before. I stooped over the sink and emptied my stomach. There wasn't much inside me, but the spasms went on and on, mixed with my tears.

The woman followed me. I recognized her as the school psychologist. She stood behind me, her hand on my back. I resented her presence. I started to tell her so, but then her arms wrapped themselves around me, and I couldn't speak. Waves of tears weakened me. She let me go so I could wash my face and rinse out my mouth. But the tears kept up a steady stream. My nose was like the morning's rainclouds.

"I don't believe it," I told her. "It's a lie. Cronoks Lab just made it up."

Ms. Evans' arms tightened around me once more. She cooed to me as if I were a baby. I sobbed into her blouse. At one point, I repeated my words, again blaming Cronoks Lab. She didn't argue with me.

"We'll find out, Clista," she said. "But remember, you're not alone. Hold on to that thought. We'll be with you through this. We won't leave you."

Later when the first wave of tears had passed, Ms. Evans lay me down on the cot and left for a moment. I heard the water running in the sink. I was embarrassed that she was cleaning up after me, but I couldn't move or even speak to apologize. She returned seconds later with a warm, moist cloth and washed my face, the whole time telling me how she'd see me through my sadness.

"There's nothing wrong with my parents," I told her, regaining my voice. "They're just doing research deep inside the caverns. They'll come out. They're not…"

A second blast of weeping ended my words. Ms. Evans lay down on the cot and held me as I cried. She didn't mention my parents again.

She took me to her house a little later. I didn't want to go. I wanted to go back to class and have everything be normal. I wanted to go home and wait for my parents. I wanted to start the day all over again and never hear the word "cave-in."

Ms. Evans' house was very small. Her kitchen stretched into the living room, and the two small bedrooms were only square boxes with simple beds and chests of drawers. She had no basement.

I wandered about, touching things, looking at her books and the pictures of her husband, killed while exploring the volcanic moon, Shlam. There was little of Ms. Evans in the house, only wisps of flavor – a cyclamen plant, green but unblooming, a hanging wreath made of dried wildflowers, their browns and whites nicely accented by dried yellow sprigs of the uncommon and daisy-like stirpup. Pictures of her dead husband were the only other human-like addition. I wondered at the sparseness of her decorations, but I didn't ask. I just paced and asked her when I could go home.

The authorities had already called my uncle, my father's brother, so he could come to take care of me. Uncle Cristoff was my only blood relation. I'd never met him. He and my father were not on speaking terms. I wondered why, but I didn't care — just like I didn't really care about anything except going home and waiting for my parents.

Ms. Evans got out a puzzle and tried to get me to place the pieces together. I tried to make her happy. I'd find a piece, put it in, and then stand up and start to pace until she called me back to the table again.

I wanted to call Gerga, but then I remembered that she was angry with me. I desperately needed to call Frall, but, of course, I couldn't. I knew he wouldn't talk to me.

Outside, the rain poured down. Thunder tormented the sky with loud cracks and rumbles. Lightning feathered the darkening sky. It was a long afternoon, relieved only by the lovely flute melodies that

Ms. Evans played on her sound system and the cocoa she kept plying me with. I think the last cup must have had something medicinal in it, for I grew sleepy, and she talked me into going to bed.

I slept through the night and was up with the dawn. Bird song woke me. My eyes flew open. The sound and feel of the morning was wrong. I flung myself up, visited the john, and crept out through the front door to begin my long walk home. Halfway there, I realized that I was passing the school. I stopped by, picked up my scooter, and flew up into the sky.

I guess I knew I wouldn't find my parents at home. Yet, still, I looked. The first thing I noticed was the broken lock on the basement door. The alarm had been disconnected. My eyes scanned the empty tables in the basement. All the artifacts were gone.

Several vacant spaces in the bookshelves told me that someone had also made themselves at home with my parents' private collection of research texts. If I'd been angry before, it was nothing to the fury I felt then.

I had time to tour the house, searching my parents' room for other signs of theft. But when the police came, they ignored my words about the burglary, hardly glancing at the broken basement door. My being young should not have been a handicap. They should still have been willing to listen to me. I lashed out at them with scalding words. It was unlike me, and I felt guilty for it, but I think I was justified.

One of the policemen shot a restrictor on me. It slowed my speech and my movements. Thus, when they led me out of the house, I couldn't fight them. I could barely mumble an objection.

They took me back to Ms. Evans. She came out to the poliflyer and talked with them. Then she opened the backdoor, helped me out, and walked me inside her house. She lay me down on the couch.

As the restrictor shot wore off, Ms. Evans didn't bother to scold me. She even listened as I told her what I'd found at my house, although she admonished me when I kept saying that the burglars were Cronoks Lab.

"You don't know that is true," she insisted, but I think she believed me because she said. "It seems as if they could have waited. But weren't the artifacts really theirs?"

"Cronoks Lab wasn't the client," I explained to her. "My parents worked for the museum. Cronoks Lab was only funding the project, an agreement which permitted them to study the research, not steal everything."

"When your uncle comes, we must tell him this," Ms. Evans said. "The police are expecting him today."

The bit about my uncle was not welcome news. It chafed me to think about a stranger having governance over me.

"I'm only a year shy of legal age majority. Do you think the courts would force me to go with an uncle I didn't want to live with?"

It was the first time I'd even thought about a future without my parents. It was not that I'd accepted their death, but I had begun to reformat life just in case.

Chapter Ten

My uncle didn't come all that day. I spent most of the morning, afternoon, and evening pacing the floor back and forth. When Ms. Evans would call for me to come sit, I'd put a puzzle piece into the large frame we'd begun the day before. I'd pop them in with a kind of restless energy that kept me nervously fidgeting like the chair had thorns. But the puzzle couldn't hold me. I mostly walked the carpeted floors of Ms. Evans' house.

I begged her to allow me to go to the Stormian Caverns and see the site where it had supposedly happened, but Ms. Evans wouldn't let me. "Wait for your uncle," she kept saying, but it didn't seem like he was in any hurry to arrive.

I thought a great deal about the strange Uncle Cristoff, this man who had suddenly, legally become my guardian. I'd never seen his picture. I didn't know if he had a family or what he did for a living. In fact, I knew nothing about him but his name and the fact that he didn't like my father. That was enough. I hated him for it.

Just after nine that evening, there was a knock on the door. Ms. Evans told me to get it, knowing that it must be my uncle. I shook my head. I didn't want to see him. I was too busy building up hatred against him as if he were the one who had caused my parents' misfortune.

The knock came again, louder and more forceful. I sank down lower into the couch, wishing I could flee.

Ms. Evans finally rose and went to the door. She waved it open, and in walked my father. I sprang up and ran into his arms, crying and laughing at the same time. "You're okay," I sobbed. "I knew you were. I didn't believe them. Where's Mom?"

But there was something wrong. My father's arms weren't holding me close. He wasn't kissing and hugging me back. I looked up into his face, and a chill sank down inside me. This man wasn't my father. He looked like him — exactly like him, but he wasn't my father.

I pulled away and backed up. "Who...?" but I suddenly understood. The realization doused me with horror. My father and Uncle Cristoff were twins.

I bolted and ran into the small spare bedroom where I'd spent the night. Throwing myself on the bed, I burst into tears. I'd just lost my father a second time.

A while later, Ms. Evans came in and tried to talk me into coming out to meet my uncle. I wouldn't have anything to do with him. The betrayal was too great. I told her I never wanted to see him again, not ever again. How could I bear to look at him, knowing he wasn't my father, grieving each time I glanced into his deceptive face?

Ms. Evans sat down on the bed. "He seems very nice, Clista. Don't you think he deserves a fair chance? He did come all this way to see you."

I shook my head emphatically. I knew I was being irrational, but too much had happened. I was miserable and full of hate for my uncle, for Cronoks Lab, and for the way my parents had been stolen away. There was no room inside me for acceptance.

I heard my uncle's voice talking with Ms. Evans late into the night and then came the silence of sleep. I planned to get up and run away, but the quiet took me with it. I fell into its slumber.

Once more, I woke to the songs of birds. I lay there for several moments and listened, wondering how they could sing, how they could feel so much joy. Listlessly, I rose only when I was desperate to use the bathroom. *He* was in my room when I returned.

"Leave me alone," I cried out, wondering if I should just run out of the house and keep on running, but I knew the police would hunt me down again. They would bring me back to this forgery of my father. He owned me. Isn't that the way of it? Until I reached the majority, the police would always bring me back to him.

"I don't need you," I told him. Then the tears started up again, splotching my face and wavering my eyes until I could hardly see the man standing inside the room.

"Can we go into the other room and talk?" he asked. "I want to discuss the role of Cronoks Lab in this."

All thought of flight left me then. He had my attention. "They killed my parents," I said. "Then they stole the artifacts, breaking into the house to do it. Did Ms. Evans tell you that?"

"The other room," he said, gesturing. "And lose the helmet."

He came toward me. I backed away. He was nothing like my father in speech patterns or in his thinking processes. I eyed him coldly. "Why?" I asked.

"I suppose I could tell you it's because I'm your legal guardian, and I say so, but I would have hated anyone who said that to me, so I'll tell you the truth. You see, I want to read your face. Besides, you owe me that for making me sleep on the couch. It was way too short."

He laughed like my father. That stung me. But he'd been honest with me. Without any argument, I unsnapped my helmet, pulled it off, and set it down on the chest of drawers. Then, I followed Uncle Cristoff into the living room and sat stiffly on the couch.

Ms. Evans must have heard us talking. She came out of her room, dressed and ready for the day. "I'll go start coffee," she said. I watched her open up the cupboard and take down three mugs. The smell of coffee soon flavored the air.

While we waited for a mug of the brew, I started talking, and then I couldn't stop. I might not trust my uncle, but at least he was willing to listen to my suspicions.

His eyes, my father's eyes, stared into mine as I tried to relay all that had happened. I knew what he'd said earlier about "reading me." Apparently, that was precisely what he did. He scrutinized me like my father used to scrutinize texts written about the *Old Ones*. He read into me.

Ms. Evans brought us the coffee. I sipped mine and tried to dodge around the story of my necklace. I could hear the fragility of the tale without it, but how could I trust both Ms. Evans and a man I didn't know? Would either of them believe me? Would they think, like Frall, that I was unbalanced? Cautiously, I danced around it and filled in as best I could.

"And what really happened to Grenan?" my uncle asked. "Although, perhaps just as interesting is what made Cronoks Lab think that an artifact could be empowered by someone's touch?"

I shrugged, not having any answer that was suitable to tell him. I could see from his eyes that my uncle thought I was lying, but he didn't call me on it.

"All right," he said. "We'll let it go for now. I suppose you've got questions for me?"

Of course, I did. Like why had he never visited us, and why had he and my father fought, what did he intend to do with me and what was he going to do about my parents' murder? But it wasn't the time for such questions.

"Will you take me out to Stormian Caverns?" I asked. "I want to see it."

Leaving my question hanging, Uncle Cristoff picked up his untouched coffee and drank it down with one tip of the mug. Then, he placed it back down on the table and rose. "Thank you so much for your hospitality, Franca," he said to Ms. Evans.

I'd never heard the psychologist's first name before. I stared at her, curious, and then I saw the strangest thing. She blushed. Did that mean she liked my uncle? I was still pondering that when she rose and politely murmured what a pleasure it had been to have us there.

"You must keep in touch with me, Clista," she told me.

"Wait! I'm not coming back here?" I cried out. "I thought you promised to help me through this." So much for diplomacy. I'd just blurted that all out, glaring at her like she'd done something horrendous.

I know I sounded ungrateful. Ms. Evans had been really kind to take me in as it was, but I couldn't understand what had happened to all the promises she'd made about being by my side throughout the grief. Was I supposed to be finished with that now, or was the responsibility being dumped on my uncle's shoulders?

Angry with her rejection, I turned on my uncle. "Listen, if you think I'm going back with you to Steron, clear on the other side of Rwawan, you're wrong. I'm scheduled to graduate from the Academy in three months, and I'm not leaving here until then."

Both of the adults began to speak at the same time. Seeing the problem, my uncle stopped and nodded politely for Ms. Evans to go first.

She grabbed my upper arms and stared into my eyes. Speaking much louder than she did in her normal voice, she said "Shame on you for thinking that, Clista." Then, to soften the blow, she leaned forward and kissed my cheek. "I want you to see me as often as your uncle allows. Anytime you need to talk, I'll be here for you. I mean that, Clista. Anytime. But you're not my ward. I can't keep you here. I don't have that right."

I was crying again. I hated the tears, yet everything seemed to make me weepy. I wanted to argue with her and with my uncle, but the sobs interfered with my voice.

My uncle cleared his throat. Then, with an extremely gruff voice, he ordered, "Enough of this. I never make promises for futures I can't see. Clista, get your things. We're leaving."

Maybe if he hadn't looked so much like my father, I would have disputed his orders, but I was still crying and unable to speak. I returned to my room and picked up my backpack and the few things I'd collected when I ran away to my house. Then, I walked out of the door of Ms. Evans' house with a perfect stranger.

In silence, my uncle flew us back to my parents' house. No sooner had we entered than he sat me down at the kitchen table and demanded, "First, fix us some breakfast — I assume you can work the mechanisms of your kitchen faster than it would take me to figure them out, and while you're doing that, I suggest you change your mind set about me because whether you like it or not, you're stuck with the status quo. That's a fact. No argument."

I started to rise in order to follow his directive, but he grabbed my arm and halted me. "I'm not through talking," he said. I dropped back into the chair, staring at his hand on my wrist. His grip wasn't painful, but it was decisive. I knew I couldn't break free. It wasn't even worth the effort to try.

"Like you, I want justice, and I intend to get it," he continued. "But, I'm not a patient man, and I won't put up with your evasions. When you sit down to tell me the parts you left out before, you better plan on telling me *everything* you know, suspect, or even have dreamed about."

He wasn't asking, yet I nodded my head that I understood. He released me then, and I stood up and walked over to the food machine to prepare our breakfast.

I didn't know this man who'd suddenly come into my life. I had no reason to even trust him except that he wore my father's face. My brain was swimming with unanswered questions, but I agreed with what he'd said. The most important thing was my parents. I needed to know what had happened. I needed revenge for their deaths if it was true that they'd been murdered. For the moment, I would do everything Uncle Cristoff said.

Having decided that, I placed the prepared food down on the table and sat down to eat. Then I begin to tell him about the *Old Ones*. Of course, I had no proof of the light orb turning on or the reaction of the other artifacts to my touch. Since those were all gone, I couldn't prove it, but I did show him the necklace, and I brought out the Cronoks Lab's artifact in its shrunken cocoon.

As it dangled in my fingers, I knew it didn't look like the dangerous object I claimed it to be, but my uncle's eyes inspected me as much as he eyed the artifact. He examined my necklace, running a knife about its edge and searching, just like Frall had, for the catch. When he was done, he sat back and again examined my face.

I fastened and snapped up my spacesuit and waited for the verdict, but Uncle Cristoff seemed in no hurry to give one. He picked up his untouched coffee, and again, with one tilt of the cooled mug, he downed the contents. Leaning forward on his elbows, he said then, "Congratulations. Crazy as your story is, I believe you."

I was grateful he'd accepted it, but I'd wasted too much time in telling it. I cleaned up our mess and began to pace, telling him again how urgently I needed to go to Stormian Caverns.

"No," he said. "Not yet."

He stretched out his legs as if he had no intention of going anywhere quickly. His leg reach was long. His limbs dominated the small space of our kitchen. I tore my eyes away from them and pleaded again.

"I thought you wanted clues," I said. "And, what if my parents are still inside, blocked from getting out? What if they're running out of air? What if they need us?"

My uncle raised his hand to stop my words and said, "There's nothing to see."

"How can you say that? My parents might be . . ."

Once more, he stopped me with that dismissive wave of silence. "Look, Clista, I'm not good at this. I've never been married, and I don't have any kids, so dishing out emotional stuff isn't something I have any finesse with. The truth is that they're dead, Clista."

"How do you know that?" I burst in. "Just because Cronoks Lab says so? Maybe they are lying about all of this. Maybe ..."

"Clista, stop it. Calm down and sit."

He issued orders like a person used to commanding. I wondered again who he really was. What did he do for a living? But that was for another day. I wanted to understand about my parents and why we couldn't go check out the Stormian Caverns. I sat down, hoping he'd at least tell me why he was so sure.

He reached out and took my hand in his. His was rough and large and felt exactly like my father's. Tears swam in my eyes.

He squeezed. "I've been to the cavern, Clista. I saw their bodies."

I sprang up and covered my mouth. It was all I could do to stop from screaming like a mad woman. "Why didn't you tell me? Why did you let me go on hoping?"

He didn't speak. He just stared at me, his eyes so full of misery I couldn't say anymore. I dropped back on my chair, lay my head down on the table, and cried. I'd wept so much lately; it was a miracle I had any tears left, but this time, I was too drained to cry long, and the feel of his eyes on me made me uncomfortable.

When he saw me looking up at him once again, he stood up, walked over to the sink, and wet a towel. He tossed that to me and sat down.

"Why didn't you take me with you to Stormian Caverns? When can I see my parents'....bodies?" I asked, breaking down again.

He shook his head. "They'll be buried tomorrow. They're not pretty, Clista. It will be a closed casket. Remember them as they were the last time you saw them. It's better that way."

"I don't agree with you. I need to see them."

"There's no time to talk about that now. We'll discuss it later. Right now, I want you to help with the accounting."

I dried my eyes and concentrated on not crying. I had no idea what Uncle Cristoff was talking about with this "accounting" of his. I think he was waiting for me to ask so we could change the subject.

Once he'd explained that he wanted to tally what was missing so we could file a police report, I understood and approved. Together, we went down into the basement and began the survey. My parents had always kept excellent records with much more detail than I could ever hope to recall, but the thieves had stolen all the records, along with several important texts, the hard drive of the computer, and my mother's sketchbook.

I wrinkled up my nose, scratched my head and tried to remember exactly what artifact was placed in each space of each table. That took several hours, and I knew I was missing some. I did the best I could. I was grateful that I had worked with my parents down in the basement so recently.

Afterward, Uncle Cristoff searched through my parents' clothes pockets while I investigated under the mattresses, the carpeting, and inside all the bedroom and basement books. I even rummaged around my room, just in case something was hidden in there.

While we were discussing lunch, my uncle got the idea that my parents could have placed something behind the drawers in the kitchen or even in the refrigerator, but those searches came up empty-handed. However, my idea that there might be something in the unused spare bedroom unearthed my mother's diary. She'd hidden it underneath a chest of drawers in the corner. With shaky hands, I opened and found, taped to the inside, a letter for me and one to Cristoff.

I knew my mom had been suspicious of Cronoks Lab, but in her diary, she gave us the specifics of it — the names, places, and events that had fostered that belief.

"We've got them," I said through another bout of tears because, in the letter to me, my mother had written how much they loved me. "This is evidence. Let's call the police now."

Uncle Cristoff held up his hand for silence. "We'll investigate the Stormian Caverns first. Then we'll call in the cops."

"But you said…"

"I'm going to check the house computer," he told me stiffly, and he turned and walked away.

I got up and followed him. I watched as he disconnected, rewired, and reconnected for the download. I had never seen anyone do such a thing. Dad had once told me that only the police could deprogram a house computer. Once again, I wondered what Uncle Cristoff did for a living.

There was no evidence of the break-in. Somehow, it had all been erased.

"At least we've learned they were pros," my uncle said. "No local thug would know how to deactivate a house system."

"How do you know how, then?" I asked, probing curiously. Uncle Cristoff laughed but didn't answer. He scooted his chair around so he was sitting backward and began to eat the pizza I'd "made" while he was working with the house computer.

After we finished eating, I was ready to ask more questions, but he beat me to it. "Tell me about the spacesuit you wear. Is that a fad or something?"

When I explained how scholarships were earned by successful projects, he roared. "You still want to work for Cronoks Lab now?"

"Of course not. But I have to complete the project, or it goes down on my record as a deficient, and then no other company will offer for me."

Uncle Cristoff sighed and said, "Whatever. Let's go," but he continued to laugh and mumble, "Deficient," as I cleaned up.

We were just heading for the door when someone knocked.

"Lay low," my uncle ordered.

I had no idea what he meant by that, but it stopped me from answering the door. Cautiously, Uncle Cristoff whispered, "Open three centimeters," and then allowed the door to slide a finger space so he could see who was there.

Since he was blocking the door with his body, I couldn't see who was behind the door, but I did recognize the voice.

"Frall!" I screamed and almost ran over my uncle as I wedged myself in front of him so I could open the door the rest of the way.

"He's my friend from school," I explained. "What are you doing here, Frall? This is my Uncle Cristoff, by the way."

Frall took a double take. "A twin brother?" he asked as the two shook hands and then backed off to inspect each other.

"Why aren't you still in school?" I asked.

"I heard about your parents, Clista. I'm so sorry. Listen, uh, Mr. Pragan, isn't it?"

My uncle nodded. "Nice to meet you. I'm sorry, but we were just leaving."

"Wait. I have to talk to Clista. It's important," Frall told him. He held my uncle's gaze without wavering. Once again, I saw how Frall wasn't in the least unnerved by adults, even by an uncle who I considered extremely intimidating.

"Please, just give us a minute," I begged my uncle.

"Five minutes," he said, walking off to my parents' room.

Frall wasted no time. "Clista, I've been a jerk. I'm sorry," he said, taking my hand in his and moving in close.

I wasn't sure whether the "I'm sorry" part was about my parents or the fact that he was a jerk, but I was happy to see him. The reason

107

didn't really matter. "Thank you," I sighed, teary-eyed again at the reminder of my parents' death.

"The *Old Ones* came to me, Clista, just like you said they would. I tried to ignore them, but they won't let me. I'm supposed to go with you to the Stormian Caverns. That's where you're headed right now, isn't it? They've ordered me to accompany you."

"Time's up," my uncle said, walking back into the entry room.

I pulled my hand out of Frall's as if he was suddenly contagious, but my uncle had seen. He raised one eyebrow and gave me a "look." Then, his eyes narrowed, and he glared at Frall. "As I said, we're leaving now."

"Frall wants to go with us. Please?"

"I have to," Frall said. "The *Old Ones* have commanded it. You do understand that, being Clista's uncle, right?"

"I didn't explain about that part, Frall." I turned to face Uncle Cristoff. His eyes were glaring at me fiercely. I suppose he thought I'd lied to him again, but I hadn't; it's just that I left out the part about Frall.

"I'm sorry, Uncle Cristoff. I couldn't tell you about Frall because . . ." I started, but he cut me off.

"Never mind. I'll take you both so you can explain as I fly us out there. All right, kid," he said to Frall. "Come along, but you keep your hands to yourself, and you do what I say. Got that?"

Frall bristled at the orders. His eyes were flaring daggers, but he was smart enough not to allow his tongue to endanger the permission he'd gotten. He nodded silently.

As meek as five-year-old starter students, we followed Uncle Cristoff out the door and into his rented flyer.

Chapter Eleven

I'd never been to the Stormian Caverns where my parents' dig was. They'd always been too busy to take me with them, and I hadn't been invited to come on my own. School scooters were restricted. We were only allowed to fly back and forth between home and the Academy. If we tried a longer flight, the flyer shut down and called for aid. I looked forward to the time when I could choose where I wanted to go.

(How was it that Frall had been able to fly to my house, I wondered. Was there a way to get special permission to visit friends? Of course, Frall was a year older than most of us. Maybe that gave him privileges.)

The Academy allowed absolutely no student dating. We were only permitted at-school friendships, something that departed seriously from the movies we'd watched about life on Earth, where teenagers were in a constant flux of dating cycles. We at the Academy were even fed hormone reduction as part of our lunch meal. Perhaps that prevented the unplanned pregnancies and turbulence of Earth's underage population.

But because of that, when we arrived at the Stormian Caverns, it was the first time for me to see what I'd heard so much about. Yet, unbelievably, it was also very familiar. I had roamed there in countless dreams.

I told my uncle that, and he cast one of his strange looks at me. It wasn't as if he didn't believe me, but I could see that he was measuring my words.

"And you?" he asked Frall, not bothering to glance at him.

Frall shook his head and then told us that his dreams had been about me and about my danger.

Uncle Cristoff issued a strange noise over that, but when we landed, he turned around to glare at Frall and said. "Okay, give. What danger?"

Frall shot a glance at me. Then he shook his head. "It's not clear, but in my dreams, Clista was inside the caverns, and there was a tremor — no, more than a tremor, a full quake. I saw the rocks plummeting down on top of her. They were going to bury her beneath them, and I held up something. I don't know what it was, but I held it up in the air, and the rocks froze. They were in midair like they were floating. I took Clista's hand, and we ran out into the light."

"Either you have a good imagination, or a hero fixation — or both. But I'm not letting Clista go into those caverns, so, believe me, there's no danger."

"But I have to. I have to return the *Tworst of Trent*," I cried out.

Uncle Cristoff didn't respond. I stayed silent, watching him, wondering if my trip to see the Caverns had been wasted. Then I relaxed. If the *Old Ones* wanted me to do as they commanded, they would have to give me some help.

There were guards all about. Most of them had the Cronoks Lab crest on their jackets. I had the same crest on my spacesuit. I thought that it might help to get us past their restrictions. I needn't have worried. Uncle Cristoff flashed some kind of blinking digital read-out device, and we were passed through without a word.

As we walked closer, I staggered. Both Frall and my uncle were quick to reach out and assist me, but I was fine. It was just the incredible surge I'd felt emanating from the caverns. The *Old Ones* were calling to me. I walked faster.

We reached the opening. I saw piles of rock all around. They had apparently been hauled from inside the caverns — from the cave-in. Which one of them had brought about the death of my father or mother? I swayed with the thought. "I don't want to do this," I said.

"You don't have to do anything, Clista. I'll take you back to the flyer. I can look around another day," my uncle said, his eyes friendlier than usual.

"No. I mean, I don't want to go in, but I have to. They won't allow me to go back. The necklace is burning my neck."

Uncle Cristoff shot a glance around. "Be careful what you say, Clista. There may be listening ears."

"What are you talking about?" Frall spoke angrily. "Are you trying to frighten her? Hasn't she been through enough?"

Nobody had thought to fill Frall in on what we suspected. Frall was already irritated with my uncle for the slights he'd given out. Sparks were flying between them. I started to speak, to explain, but my uncle's upheld hand silenced me.

"I warned you to be quiet," he said sharply to Frall. "Not a single question, or you go back to the flyer right this minute."

Frall was all set to erupt, but Uncle Cristoff, obviously used to having his orders followed, turned his back and walked away, ignoring Frall as if his presence were of no importance. Frall glared after him.

I sighed and stretched out my hand to touch his arm. It brought no answering smile. Frall just edged away from me, apparently as angry with me as with my uncle. I let out an even bigger sigh and followed after my uncle.

The closer we progressed towards the site, the stronger the pull became. I couldn't hold back anymore. The compulsion was on me. When my uncle halted, placing his hand on my arm to control me, I shut my eyes and trembled. Then I took a step forward and another and another.

"No, you don't," Uncle Cristoff said, pulling me back. But as his hand gripped me, I whimpered.

"Let her go," Frall cried out, swinging a fist. The older man dodged and whipped me about, placing me behind him. That was exactly what Frall wanted. His fist flung out, making contact, and I, not thinking anymore, just driven, ran forward into the bosom of the *Old Ones*.

I didn't pay any attention to where I was heading. I knew the *Old Ones* would steer me. Instead, I thought about my parents and how they'd come here every day, scratching and digging for fragments of the past.

"Why didn't you save my parents?" I cried out. "You could have. Why didn't you?"

My questions echoed, but the *Old Ones* were silent. Perhaps they were ashamed.

The tunnel I was passing through offered several different channels. I closed my eyes and let my feet choose which way to go. I continued walking for maybe twenty minutes with no hesitation, although I could see nothing since the cave was dark. I didn't stop until I reached a large, open chamber. It was dark still, but I felt the openness of it, the feeling of great space.

My fingers knew exactly where to search. I reached up to the wall, and my hand closed on an orb, like those in my parents' basement, except this one was constructed to be placed on one's head. I fastened it on. Light glowed softly then. I looked about.

It was obvious my parents had never been this far inside the cavern, for there were artifacts on altars, empty pedestals standing ready for their statues, and several delicate-looking pieces of art just lying on the ground. With the light, I was able to see the entire room, but I didn't stop. I continued forward. The path beneath my feet was rocky and uneven, but I didn't worry about stumbling. I knew that the *Old Ones* were watching out for me.

At last, I reached my destination. I stopped and felt inside my pocket for the *Tworst of Trent*. Then, I placed it in a small niche I saw inside the wall. I heard voices then, thanking me, like echoes in my mind. "I wish you had saved my parents," I said.

"We could not," came the response, "but we will save you. You and the other will be our light to the future. Leave us now. There is danger."

I backed away and began my return.

Chapter Twelve

It was several minutes after that when the rumbles started. I didn't hear them at first. But when I reached the open chamber again, I felt the ground shaking beneath me. That was where I met Frall, and we rushed into each other's arms. Ignoring the sounds of danger, we held each other, and our lips met. Our kiss was sweet, even more so than the first one. Something clicked from that kiss. It was as if we knew we were meant to be together. When we drew apart, we gazed into each other's eyes, and then we smiled.

"I have to get you out of here," Frall said. I nodded. The *Old Ones* had told me that. They'd also told me what items he must pick up. I pointed them out, grabbed up several things I was told to take, and we ran forward. By then, another shake was sending its ripples across the floor of the cavern. The ground was dancing. It unbalanced us enough that our feet slid, and we were separated by the turbulence. I screamed at our parting.

Boulders were sliding off the tops of walls, and smaller rocks tumbled and cascaded down at us. I looked up and saw them falling. Just like in the dreams I'd had, they were descending faster than we could run. Instinctively, I threw myself to the right, hoping they would miss me.

They didn't. They never fell. Frall had remembered. He'd stopped the avalanche, just as the *Old Ones* had ordered him to do. He ran toward me, helped me up, and with his hand in mine, we ran through the rest of the corridors, heading up toward the light.

On several turnings, more rocks fell. Each time, Frall saved us. I would never have made it out if he had not been there, using the *Old One's* tool. We ran into my uncle in the seventh corridor. It was not a passage we needed to travel to make our way outside, but the *Old Ones* had taken pity on my uncle. They saved his life.

Perhaps they'd heard my words before and felt guilty for allowing my parents to die. Maybe they'd been away at the time or unable to save them. It's always possible that they needed my uncle and did not need my parents. As we broke out into the sunlight, I had many questions that needed answers, but the *Old Ones* were silent, even in the mouth of their Power.

We could hear the landslide of rock going on behind us. It was as if the caverns were imploding. But we didn't pause — not even to stop at the section where the cave had been reinforced. Instead, the three of us ran back to the flyer, wordless, each filled with our own thoughts.

We climbed into the seats where we'd sat before. Then Uncle Cristoff took off. In seconds, we were up in the sky. Then he flipped on the automatic and unlatched his safety belt. He turned so he could see both of us and demanded, "Input kids. What was that all about?"

I was amazed at his calmness. Frall had knocked him a good one, apparently. The knot on his forehead was an angry red, bloated with blood.

"Are you okay?" I asked. "Is there a first aid kit in here?" I unsnapped my belt and leaned forward to peer into the small front pocket.

"Get that belt back on," my uncle shouted.

Something in his voice sent chills down my spine. I leaned back in my seat and buckled it.

"Don't yell at her," Frall said, but his voice seemed shaky and weak. I glanced back at him and realized the problem. Just as I had done before, Frall had expended all his energy. He badly needed rest and food.

I explained the situation. "Frall saved my life, Uncle Cristoff, just like he said he would. Please, don't be angry. We each did what we had to do."

My uncle was staring at me. A facial tick in his cheek vibrated at super speeds. He smoothed it out and sighed. "You're all there is, Clista. Our family's gone. It's just you and me now.

"Do you know the risks you took walking alone into a dark cavern? There could have been snakes inside, and there are holes you could have fallen into. Or you could have gotten lost forever. Don't you understand that?"

"Of course, but the *Old Ones* said I had to go in. They took care of me. They told Frall what to grab from the caverns. They told him how to stop the rocks. The avalanche would have fallen on me. I would be dead like my parents, crushed under the ceiling of the cave, if it hadn't been for Frall.

"The *Old Ones* saved your life, too. You were in the wrong passage, Uncle Cristoff. They told us how to find you, and then they showed us the way out of there.

"Don't you see we had to do as we were told? We had no choice."

"I suppose they told Frall to hit me?" my uncle said sarcastically.

I looked back at Frall. He was sleeping. "I don't know, but Frall needs food, Uncle. Please, can we stop somewhere? It causes an energy drain when you work with the Power."

Uncle Cristoff was shaking. Then he groaned. "I don't know why I believe any of this, Clista. Maybe I'm crazy. But something really is wrong with the kid. I can see that."

He turned around, unhooked autopilot, and flew us through to a small flyby restaurant. We buzzed in and instantly downloaded the menu. I rocked Frall back and forth, but he didn't move.

He was worse off than I'd suspected. I was suddenly panicked with worry.

"I can't wake him," I said. "He really should have eaten before he went into this deep sleep."

My uncle laughed. "I bet the smell of some good veggie burgers and turnip fries will open his eyes. Don't worry about it. We'll order for him and douse him with ice if he doesn't move."

Uncle Cristoff gave our order to the dashboard, adding a special round of carrot shakes for each of us. Then, glancing back at Frall, he punched in an additional burger just in case one wasn't enough. He placed his hand on the acceptance port of the flyer, which would, of course, bill him for all charges. I heard the short beep of acceptance.

A moment later, when the light on the dashboard turned purple, we flew down to pick up our food. The server robot, extending its arm until it was over our skylight, dropped the box with all our food and drinks. It landed in Frall's lap.

Uncle Cristoff was right. One inhale, and Frall sat up and dug in.

"Did you get me something?" he wanted to know as he rifled through the box with the most painfully wistful expression on his face.

"Divvy it up, Frall. Clista said you'd be starving, so I got you two burgers."

Meanwhile, my uncle soared back up into the sky. He was just accepting his sandwich from me when he whistled. "Looks like we've got company, kids. Hold on to the drinks. I'm gonna have to do some evasive flying."

He didn't seem too worried. His hand still grabbed the burger I'd been unwrapping for him, and he took a big bite. "Stars, this thing's good," he said. "All right, here they come. Looks like they're not playing friendly. You kids both buckled in?"

Frall had his mouth full of fries and burger, but I answered for both of us. I had just turned around after a quick look at Frall's tight belt when my uncle dipped and bucked. The drinks were all in the drink holders with good, tight lids on them, and each of us was holding onto our burger with a firm grasp. Only a bag of fries went flying. I grabbed it and shoved it back into the box.

"Hey, aren't those mine?" Frall squawked.

"Later," I said, holding onto the side of my seat. Uncle Cristoff darted under a human passageway, the kind that keeps you out of the rain but lets you walk from building to building twenty stories up.

"It's Cronoks Lab, isn't it?" I asked.

Uncle Cristoff slid us to the left, completely around the space terminal, then darted us in and out of the terminal flyhop.

"That was close," Frall said, his mouth so full of food we could barely understand him.

"Yep, it's Cronoks, all right. Apparently, they don't like the little adventure you and Frall had this afternoon. I think they're kind of mad, in fact. Did you kids do something inside I should know about?"

118

I shook my head. "I told you everything. We just returned the *Tworst of Trent*, but they wouldn't know that. They didn't even know we had it — well, not for sure."

Uncle Cristoff chuckled. "I think they've got their suspicions. I would guess you're their number one candidate, Clista, and by the way, those two flyers are following us; it's certain they've decided they want to have a little talk with you about it.

"Whoa, these guys are good. I can't shake them. You kids don't happen to have any of that *Old Ones'* Power stuff you could use about now, do you?"

I turned around to look at Frall. His eyes were drooping again. He hadn't finished the second burger. It was still sitting in his lap, clasped inside his fist. He let out a soft snore. He wasn't going to be any help.

"Well, I do have the necklace," I said, "and there are some other things they told me to take, but I don't know what they do yet."

Uncle Cristoff looped and dodged again, this time clear around Semen's Financial Building. The other two flyers clung like dogs whose teeth were clamped on an escaping cat's tail.

I reached inside my shirt and touched the medallion of my necklace. It warmed to my touch. "I need help," I said aloud. "Cronoks Lab is attacking us."

I shut my eyes and concentrated. The stone grew hotter. It began to hum a single note. My neck burned. The chain was searing me, but I couldn't release it. I couldn't do anything but obey, humming along with that single note.

Then I felt the *Old One's* touch in my mind. I knew they were speaking to me. I hummed louder, and I began to speak in a language I didn't know. "*Speghartibutah. Frejuh. Speghartibutah Slema. Speghartibutah Threip.*"

I opened my eyes and looked at the flyers. They had trapped us. A third ship had entered the fray. It was now blocking our way.

"The mumbo jumbo isn't doing a lot of good, kid. I hope that's just a first course," Uncle Cristoff told me as his eyes searched for an avenue of escape.

I didn't respond. I was locked into my target. "*Teff!*" I spit out with the full force of my voice.

"Stars, Clista. What was that about?"

"*Teff!*" I said again, and then I looked at the third ship and once more boomed out, "*Teff!*"

"Clista, you're not going to scare them by barking at..." Uncle Cristoff stopped and cried out, "I don't believe it!"

A large mantle of rainbow-colored lights was surrounding the ships. The strange cloud of light blinked on and off in a sequence as regular as a pulse. The colors swirled about, increasing their speeds until suddenly, they burst into a huge flash of intense, white light. Almost immediately, each of the flyers who'd been attacking us drifted slowly down to the ground.

"What did you do?" my uncle whispered, each word a struggle for him to speak. "Do you have *any* idea how you did that?" he asked, letting out an impressed whistle.

"I didn't do it. The *Old Ones* did."

My eyes were sagging as badly as Frall's had a moment ago. I couldn't keep them open. "Fly us somewhere," I told my uncle. "I have to sleep."

My poor uncle did the best he could. He had no idea where Frall lived. He didn't dare take us back to my parents' house. He flew us to Ms. Evans'. I can almost picture the expression on her face when she saw us — two drowsy teens and my uncle, all of us looking like we'd been playing in a dust storm out in the plains. I hope she didn't slam the door in my uncle's face. I wonder if he had to talk her into letting us come inside.

Chapter Thirteen

I have no idea what Ms. Evans' reaction was, but when I woke up, I was back in the same bedroom where I'd spent the days after my parents died. I found out later that Frall slept in Ms. Evans' room, and my uncle and the school psychologist sat at the kitchen table drinking fresh coffee and staring into each other's eyes.

Later, I stumbled in, desperately hungry. I'd never finished my burger. The turnip fries were probably still in the box, soggy and cold. I wondered what had happened to the carrot shake. I never had time to drink mine.

"Hi, Ms. Evans, "I told her as I entered. "I'm so sorry to ask you, but is it possible I could have something to eat? Please?"

She laughed, rose up, and pulled out the pancakes she'd had the food hydrator fix. My eyes drooled. "Ah," I said, slipping into a chair at the table. "That's exactly what I need."

"Me, too," said Frall with a yawn, coming up behind me. "I hope you're planning on sharing those, Clista." Then, glancing at her kitchen clock, Frall let out a word I won't repeat. "I've got to call my folks. They'll be worried. Is it okay if I use your phone?" he asked Ms. Evans.

"I already called them," she said. "But nobody was there, so I just left a message."

"You what?" My uncle bolted up. "What time was that?"

"Why, just a few minutes ago," she told him. "I didn't want them to worry. Is something wrong?"

"Did you tell them where we were?"

"Of course I did. I didn't want them to think we'd kidnapped Frall."

"Come on, kids, we've got to go. You better come with us, too, Franca. Those guys may not be patient about your answers."

Ms. Evans' eyes widened with alarm. Then she let out a tiny screech. "I shouldn't have done that, should I? I didn't think ... oh, dear. I'm so sorry."

"Don't be sorry. Just let's just go. They're probably on their way here right now."

My uncle was up and heading for the door. Ms. Evans had bolted up to follow him. I was grabbing up the pancakes.

"Hold it," Frall said, dropping back down in his chair, attempting, I think, to ignore my uncle's orders. "I don't know why you're so worried. My parents aren't going to tell Cronoks Lab anything. They don't know what's going on."

I sighed and shook my head. Too many pancakes to hold in my hands. I grabbed the whole plate full and started walking. That was enough for Frall. He followed after, grabbing the top pancake. He stuffed it in his mouth greedily. I couldn't blame him. I was doing the same thing.

Outside, Uncle Clista unhooked the flyer's charger, checked that everyone's belts were on, and rammed it up into the sky.

I thought he'd get us out of there and take off for who knows where, but instead, he looped around and parked us inside the branches of one of the neighbor's big trees. "We'll wait here and see what happens. I hope I'm wrong about this. Frall, are your parents usually gone this early in the morning?"

"Shoot, never. They don't get out of bed until eleven most weekends, and this is Sunday. Of course, since I didn't come home last night, I don't know."

"Right. Let's hope they're just out looking for you."

"You don't think that Cronoks would have…" I stopped, thinking about my parents, remembering my suspicions.

"Would what?" Frall asked, his third pancake lay limp in his hand, his eyes round with worry.

"Here they come," my uncle said, and three flyers — different ones than the day before, bigger and meaner-looking — dropped down low over Ms. Evans' dwelling.

"Come out with your hands up," a voice ordered through the ship's amplified speaker. "We know you're in there. We just want to talk to you."

Of course, nothing happened. The men in the ships waited and watched. We lingered, observing them from our hiding spot in the tree branches.

"If you don't come out peacefully, we have authorization from the police to do whatever is necessary."

"Is that possible?" I asked. "Could they be working *with* the police?"

"Oh, dear," said Ms. Evans. "I never should have called Frall's parents."

"You didn't know, Franca," my uncle told her, patting her arm. He looked back at me. "I don't know what this is all about, Clista, but

I guarantee they're not working with the police. That's the one thing I do know."

"And how do you know that?" Frall asked suspiciously.

"Well, for one thing, I *am* with the police. I'd rather you didn't spread that around, though. You see, I work in a special department where it's best not to flash a badge."

"Wow!" I said. "You mean like a secret agent?"

"YOU HAVE TO THE COUNT OF TEN TO SHOW YOURSELVES," said a booming voice.

"Or what?" Frall asked. "What will they do?"

I'm sure my uncle had some ideas, but he didn't bother to answer. He just double-checked that the ship's cloaking device was on. "They might have a sound monitor. We're covered by the cloaker so long as we talk no louder than conversational decimals, but remember to keep your voices low."

I guess the Cronoks Lab's ships weren't really counting. About thirty seconds later, a net fell completely around the house. At seven, they turned on the sonics. If we'd still been in the house, we'd have come running out, screaming and crying because our ears were being blasted by high-pitched noise.

"I hope that doesn't harm my violets," Ms. Evans said, trying to smile with tears in her eyes.

The sonics continued for several minutes. Then, one of the ships lowered to the ground, and a group of men, all wearing the Cronoks Labs' uniform overalls, jumped out.

My uncle reached over and turned on his cellular. "This is agent 6847235 out of Steron. I need to report a break-in going on at Pluto Haven 44567. Send a squad over here, and better add a couple of police copters. These guys have big flyers. They may be packin' some high tonics."

"Wow!" said Frall. "You're the real thing!"

Uncle Cristoff stared at Frall a moment and then flipped the cellular back on. "This is agent 6847235 out of Steron. I just called in that break-in a moment ago. Would you send another flyer to …What's your address, Frall?"

Frall's eyes got bigger. He gulped and said, "I live over in the Asteroid Estates, Ceres 88954."

"Right. Send a flyer to Ceres 88954. Possible situation. Please check."

Meanwhile, men from Cronocks Lab were breaking through Ms. Evans' front door. They had some kind of machine that vibrated the door until the screws fell out, and the door just popped open.

"You nasties!" Ms. Evans cried out. "I just paid for that door. It was supposed to be reinforced for added strength."

My uncle put his arm around her and pulled her close. "They'll buy you a new one if they've done any damage, Franka. Cronoks Lab has plenty of money. We'll sue the pants off them."

"Uncle Cristoff, Why didn't you call for backup yesterday?" I asked. "Why did you…?"

He turned and eyed me. "Fair question. Look, Clista. You don't know me, and I don't know you. Not yet, anyway. I figured there might be a real, good reason for those guys to be chasing you yesterday. You told me as much. I wasn't about to let them have you, but I wasn't sure about the situation, either. But after what you showed me . . ." He stopped and glanced down at Ms. Evans. "Well, let's just say I got some new input. I saw things in a whole new light."

I suddenly felt sick. "All that stuff I told you about the *Tworst of Trent*... I didn't know you were a cop, then. I never should have told you. What are you going to do?"

My uncle wiped his forehead with the back of his hand. It was like he thought he could erase the stress by doing so. I was feeling it, too, but I knew such things didn't come off that easily.

He sighed. Then he turned to look at me again. "I don't know, Clista. I kind of wish you hadn't been so honest about it, but I did have to know. If you'd held it back, I'd have suspected you were hiding something. I guess telling the truth has its consequences, doesn't it? But let's not worry about that right now. I think we've got enough problems."

"What happens when they don't find us in Ms. Evans' house? You think they might start lookin' around here?" Frall asked, having finished off the last of the pancakes.

"Well, we're safely hidden, so we'll just sit tight for a while. We can't take off anyway. They'd see us then. Anyway, the squad flyers are on their way. Hey, you hear that?"

At the moment Uncle Cristoff said it, we all heard the high-pitched whine of approaching sirens.

"Way to go," Frall chimed in.

"Stupid! Why the heck did they turn those on?" my uncle said as he shook his head.

The Cronoks Lab men apparently heard the sirens, too. They came running out of Ms. Evans' house just as the police flyers came into the yard.

"Freeze," The order came from a siren-less vehicle that had slipped into their midst before the others arrived.

One of the white-coated lab men ignored the police order and kept going. He was halfway to his ship when a police ray zapped him and froze him into a human statue.

"That was dumb,' Frall said. "Boy, is he going to regret it tomorrow. I've heard that the police zapper gives a headache worse than any hangover."

"What would you know about a hangover?" my uncle demanded, eyeing Frall as if he could see right into him.

Frall's flushed. "Nothing, Sir. It's just what they said in the lecture at school."

"The police come in and talk to the kids about a lot of things," Ms. Evans said gently. "It's a good way to promote understanding and good choices."

My uncle smiled at her. The way he was looking at her told me that he'd forgotten we were even in the vehicle. I let out a big sigh of irritation. It was no time for the two of them to be getting love sappy.

Frall, noticing my expression, jabbed me with his elbow. "Hey, I think it's cool that your uncle likes Ms. Evans."

I rolled my eyes. It wasn't that I objected, exactly. Stars, it wasn't even my business what the two of them did, but …

Something the police flyers shot at the three Cronoks Lab flyers brought them down. The flyers landed in the street. On the ground, the ships were even more impressive looking. Their obsidian black outer layer glowed in the morning sunshine.

The police squad flyers were taking no chance with them. Nets dropped and coated the Cronoks flyers with a sticky spider web substance that would prevent lift up. The only way the Cronoks pilots could take off then was to be sprayed down with water, my uncle told us.

The doors opened in one of the flyers, and men in Cronocks lab uniforms stumbled out, hands over their heads. Then, the other flyers begin discharging their crew.

"Hey, that guy was at our school," Frall said. "He was one of the guys who gave the talks about the artifact. Remember when he went from room to room?"

I remembered all right. He was the man who'd tried to keep me at school when Mr. Grenan disappeared. I remembered him well.

I turned to my uncle and explained about Mr. Choffee. Ms. Evans had been there, too.

Seeing the guy, she grimaced and made a face. "Pushy man. He kept insinuating that Clista had something to do with Mr. Grenan's departure — as if Clista could suddenly make a man vanish into the air. It was pathetic.

"Poor Mr. Caroom, the sweetest principal we've ever had, finally had to eject the scientist from his office. That man just didn't understand the meaning of 'no'."

"And now I see he's part of *this* harassment. He's no gentleman. That's for sure!"

My uncle slid lower in his seat. "It wasn't just harassment, honey. They took your door off, remember? It's burglary."

Being enclosed in Uncle Cristoff's small flyer was making me claustrophobic. "Couldn't we get out of here now? I need to go to the bathroom."

Uncle Cristoff gave me the eye, assessing need. "Let me see what they found over in the Asteroid Estates."

He flipped on the cellular and mumbled off his police jargon: "Agent 6847235 out of Steron. Report on the response to Ceres 88954. What is the status?"

The dispatcher replied: "Stand by Agent 6847235. No party was found at that address. Signs of B&E. Investigation in progress."

"Copy. Thanks. "

"What does that mean?" Frall bellowed, scooting forward until he hung halfway over my uncle's shoulder."

"It means they've got your parents, and we've got a problem."

"But my folks don't know anything. Why would they take them? My mother writes children's books, for star's sake – books for toddlers. I doubt if she's ever heard of the *Old Ones*. And my dad, well, he's in finance. He sets up deals for space exploration, connecting investors with clients."

I really liked Frall, but I was finding it difficult to sit still. I *really* needed to go to the bathroom.

"Uncle Cristoff, please…" I said.

He started up the motors and lifted us up out of the tree. A shower of leaves filled his forward window. He hovered for a moment so the blowers could whisk them off, and then he shot us up into the sky.

The radio flared on, the dispatcher wanting information. "Uncle Cristoff answered, "Code four, in route to Ceres 88954. Out."

"Why couldn't we just land at Ms. Evans' house or go home to our house," I asked, crossing my legs.

"We'll go back there later. Right now, I want to avoid interaction with both the local police and Cronoks Labs, and your parents' house is still hot, Clista. I think we'd better stay away from there for a while."

I hoped that Frall's house wasn't too far.

Frall turned to wink at me. As if he could read my thoughts, he said. "Don't worry. We'll be there in a minute."

I smiled through gritted teeth, and he continued, "I'm glad we're going there, actually. I want to see what's going on, and I need to shower and change clothes. You could probably wear my mother's clothes if you want to borrow something, or you can wear a T-shirt of mine, although it might be a little big."

"I'd love to change," I told him, feeling dusty from our cave walk.

And Frall was right. It was less than five minutes later when we landed and were headed through the doorway. His front door had been removed, too, so we didn't even have to wait for computer identification approval. We just walked right in.

Following Frall's pointed finger, I ran into the bathroom and relieved myself. Then, I washed my face and tried to get some reality back. I mean, things just kept getting weirder and weirder. I couldn't believe I was standing in Frall's house. I didn't want to think about what had happened to his parents. It reminded me too much of mine.

When I came out of the bathroom, I discovered the whereabouts of the master bedroom, two different offices, and then a door, which I presumed must be his. I knocked softly. No answer. I put my ear to the door and heard the sound of running water. Frall was evidently in the shower. I remembered how he'd promised I could take a shower, too, and get some clean clothes. The thought of both was delicious.

I found my uncle and Ms. Evans in the living room. My uncle was on the phone. She was flipping channels for some news.

"Who's he calling?" I asked Ms. Evans.

"I have no idea. Are you okay, Clista? Today must have been very stressful for you after all that has happened."

I laughed. She didn't know the half of it. I wished I could pour it all out, but I couldn't. Look at the danger I'd put myself into by telling my uncle about Mr. Grenan. I closed my mouth tightly and sank down into the softness of the sofa.

"Stars and comets," my uncle said, turning around to face us. "Cronoks Lab already has a battalion of attorneys over there at the police department. It looks like those goons will be out on bail in less than 24 hours."

"But they're murderers and . . ." I began.

"They're only suspects in a B & E, Clista. There isn't anything else they can be held on. We have no proof of anything else yet. It's looking suspicious, but I still saw no evidence that your parents' death was anything but an accident."

"Yeah, and Cronoks Lab just coincidentally broke into our house and stole all the artifacts on the very same day?"

"Clista, are you still thinking that company is responsible for the tragedy of your . . .?" Ms. Evans said. "You mustn't believe that, my dear. Accidents happen. Your parents worked under dangerous conditions. Cave-ins occur all the time."

"I suppose parents disappear out of their homes, too," Frall said, walking in to join us. "Clista, I set out some pants and a shirt — if you want to change. I put out some of my mom's under things, too, if you want them…"

He was blushing. I ran over to him and kissed him on the cheek. "You're the sweetest," I said. "Thank you. I've had it with being saddled with the Cronoks Lab spacesuit. I have another week to go, but I just can't bear to wear it anymore."

"There are fresh towels on my bed, and, of course, you can order whatever shampoo or rinses you like. The bathroom's hooked up for it."

What could I say? He was the zenith of guys! I gave him a big smile, called out goodbye to everyone, and ran off to luxuriate in pleasantly hot water.

Everything was just as he'd said. I shampooed, cream rinsed, and dried, and then I eagerly slipped into the clothes Frall had brought me. However, when I picked up the shirt, I saw that he'd given me two choices. I could wear one of his mother's — a flowered T-shirt — or one of Frall's long-sleeved tees with blue comets and stars. No hesitation. I slipped the space shirt on and rolled up its sleeves.

Using Frall's comb, I smoothed down my hair and slipped on his mother's blue tennis shoes. I felt stupendous.

However, when I left the bedroom and went looking for everyone, I couldn't find them. They weren't in the living room or the kitchen. I called their names, but no one answered. It took me several panicky moments to find them outside in the backyard, barbecuing veggie steaks. Mostly, it was Frall and Ms. Evans who were doing the cooking, though. My uncle was back on the phone.

Frall scanned my outfit and gave me a thumbs-up. It was nice to be back in real clothing. I thanked him for sharing.

"Is it ready yet?" Uncle Cristoff asked, hanging up the phone. "We've got to get out of here."

"No, " I cried out. "We can't keep running. Why can't we stay here?"

My uncle came over to me, lifted up my chin, and said, "They've just been released, Clista. It isn't safe here. It's not safe anywhere they think you might be. We need to find someplace fresh, someplace they wouldn't think to look."

"And then what?" I questioned. "When does this all end? Or does it? Besides, we need to look for Frall's parents. Did you talk to the police about that?'

Everyone was looking at my uncle. Cristoff searched our eyes. Then he sighed. "First, we eat the steaks and whatever else we find. Second we leave and check into a hotel. Third we work with the police and some special friends I have. They will help us solve this case, and it will end then, but until that happens, we're just going to have to be patient. I can't make miracles happen. All I can do is make sure they put tails on the suspects and do some investigating."

My poor uncle. He looked ten years older than the day he'd arrived. I could see fresh gray hairs, bags under his eyes, and a few wrinkles he hadn't had before. Plus, his clothes, so immaculate the day he'd arrived, were crumpled and seedy looking.

"You want a shower, too?" I asked.

"Absolutely," he said, giving me a quick smile. Save me a steak. You wouldn't happen to have some clean clothes I could borrow, would you, Frall? I doubt if yours would fit, but maybe your dad's?"

The two of them walked back into the house, leaving Ms. Evan and me flipping the steaks. "Do you want me to see what else is in the refrigerator?" I asked.

A nod and a smothered sniffle was her reply. Ms. Evans was crying.

"What's wrong?" Dumb question with everything that had happened, but it was the instinctive one.

"I'll be fine in a minute," she said. "It's just nerves. Go on in the house and see what you can find, Clista. Check the cupboards, too. Some cookies might help all of us."

I gave her a quick hug and a peck on the cheek and went back inside to encounter oatmeal raisin and chocolate chip cookies, two bags of chips, sodas, and a large bag of carrot sticks. I was loaded down with them when Frall turned the corner. "Hey, raiding the larder, huh," he laughed, but I saw he wasn't upset I'd made myself at home in his kitchen. He took the sodas and carrots and carried them out into the backyard.

My uncle returned, looking a lot different. The clothes of Frall's father didn't fit Uncle Cristoff. I don't mean that they were too big or too little. They were just wrong, somehow. The white t-shirt still allowed his bulging arms and his six-pack to show, but the pants were completely unsuitable. They were like trying to put a clown outfit on a tiger. You still knew that the lithe animal was underneath, but the clothes interfered and looked silly.

However, Ms. Evans seemed impressed. "Feel better now?" she asked. Her eyes were glowing in a way I'd never seen on her pretty face.

We sat down and ate, managing pretty much to clean up everything on the barbecue grill, inside the potato chip bags, and, believe it or not, all the carrot sticks. The bags of cookies remained untouched.

I carried our dishes into the kitchen and was just putting them into the dishwasher when I glanced at the warning light of the computer system. It showed someone at the front door.

I dropped the plate in my hand and ran out of the kitchen. I wasn't fast enough. The guy cleared through the front door's safeties, popped open the door, and grabbed me.

"Uncle Cristoff," I screamed once before the man's hand covered my mouth.

"Settle down, little lady. It's your uncle I've come to see. Just don't scream, huh?"

His arms had me in a hold I couldn't break free from. I nodded limply.

"If I let you go, you going to scream again?" he asked, bending his face so close I was staring into his one-eyed, ugly pirate's face.

The scream was right at the back of my throat. I figured it was too late to hold it back, but I nodded. The moment the hand withdrew from my mouth, I let it out.

Uncle Cristoff was the first one in the room. "Let her go, Smog," my uncle called out, laughing.

That confused me. The pirate's hands dropped, but I stood frozen. I didn't know whether to run to my uncle or not. Then I saw Frall, his face fierce with anger, his fists all tight. I ran to him. His arms surrounded me, and he hugged me to him.

"Who is he?" Frall whispered into my ear when he should have been kissing me.

I pulled away. "I don't know."

Uncle Cristoff had slung his arm around the pirate's shoulders and was clasping him like they were good friends. How could he be friends with someone so frightening-looking?

"Darn," said my uncle. "We just finished the steaks. We can put another one on if you've got time to wait. The only thing is I'm worried we've overstayed our safety. They released the suspects at 14:06, and it's now 14:36. The cops have a tail on 'em, of course, so we've probably got some leeway, but I don't trust it. What do you think?"

Smog's eyes surveyed our small group. Ms. Evans was just entering the room. His eyes stopped at her.

"Who's the school teacher — and the boy? I've already met your extremely loud niece," he said, rubbing his ear.

Uncle Cristoff laughed again and walked over to Ms. Evans. He led her toward his friend. "This is my future wife if she'll have me when all this is over," my uncle said.

"What?" I yelled.

Ms. Evans blushed and smiled beamingly up at my uncle. "Yes," she said. "Yes."

Smog congratulated them. Then he looked over at Frall and me. "If that's her son, then you two have real complications."

I stepped away from Frall. "He's not Ms. Evans' son," I said, sounding bitterer than I meant to.

"That's my niece's boyfriend. This is his house."

"Ah, nice house, but the security system was lax. I was inside in under thirty seconds."

"Who is this person?" I asked finally because nobody else seemed the smallest bit curious.

"Smog, this is my niece, Clista. Clista, this is Smog, my partner and good friend."

Smog didn't sit down and eat. He agreed with my uncle that we needed to be gone.

"Get yourself some clothes, Frall," he ordered. "Plan on being gone at least a week."

"Oh, dear," said Ms. Evans. "I guess I should have done that, too. I never thought…"

"You and Clista, go make a bundle of clothes from what you can find around here. Hope that's okay, Frall?"

Frall looked uneasy, but he shrugged and nodded. Then he turned to go upstairs and pack.

Without being told, my uncle followed us into the master bedroom. He took each of the pillowcases off the bed and threw one at each of us. Then he took a third and did the same. We filled up our bundles, not even checking to see if things fit. Smog had given us only five minutes.

We each used the bathroom a final time and then piled into the flyer.

"Where's yours, Mr. Smog," I asked.

He chuckled, almost choking on the cookies he was stuffing into his mouth, one after the other. "Smog is bad enough, kid. Don't add the mister."

We took off, my uncle piloting. Smog sat in the front, Ms. Evans, Frall, and me in the back. I asked again. "Where's your flyer?"

Smog swallowed his mouthful and rinsed them down with a swig of cola. "Sent it home, kid. Same place we're going."

"Where's that?" Frall asked, looking worried again about his folks.

He had good reason. If they came back to the house while we were gone, they'd find a mess in the backyard, drawers dumped in their master bedroom, and unwashed dishes in their sink. Of course, that was IF they came back …

"Nothing fancy, like your house, kid."

"My name's FRALL."

"Right. Duly noted. You'll find my pad is rather primitive — but it's safe. No one knows about it, and I don't give people the addresses 'cause, I figure — if no one knows about something, it's a lot less dangerous."

Chapter Fourteen

So we flew and flew some more. I fell asleep against Ms. Evans. I think Frall did, too. I only woke up when the sound of the flyer changed. The quiet hum went down a decibel. I was pretty sure that meant my uncle was preparing to land. Except it wasn't my uncle who was flying then. He was snoring, leaning against the side of the door.

"How did you two change places?" I whispered since everyone else was asleep.

Smog chuckled softly. "Old trick, my dear. Your uncle and I got lots of them up our sleeves."

"Why are you called Smog?"

Once again, he snorted a laugh. "Smog is smoke and fog. The boys named me that 'cause I was good at hiding."

"You put up a smoke screen to veil yourself, right?" Frall asked, leaning forward and joining our whispers.

"You kids got your safeties on?" Smog asked, shooting us a suspicious glance.

"Yeah," Frall answered, pulling at mine to check. "We've just slid forward a bit. It accommodates for that, you know."

"I see." Smog looked over at my uncle, checking to see if he was still sleeping. "We'll be landing soon. Another five. Don't expect much, though. Treat it like a camping trip."

"It's nice of you to allow us to stay at your house. Thank you," I said.

Smog glanced back at me. "Did you smile at Grenan like that, too — just before you …"?

"That's enough," my uncle snapped, sitting up with eyes so sharp and knowing it was as if he'd been awake the whole time. "I told you things were not surface level. I'm not sure she was responsible."

"What did you do to Grenan?" Frall asked, looking from my uncle to me and back again.

"She didn't do anything," Ms. Evans said, yawning and stretching in the cramped space. "I was there, you know."

"Yeah, well, it's something we need to talk about, partner. A murderer is a murderer. No matter who she is."

I sat back against the seat. Grenan's face was suddenly in front of me. I wondered if he'd had children, a wife, parents …"

"Shoot, now you've got her crying again," Frall yelled out angrily. "She's no more a murderer than you're a.... a…" His eyes searched the flyer for inspiration, and they fell on Ms. Evans. "No more than YOU are a psychologist," he spit out.

Meanwhile, Ms. Evans had taken me into her arms and was patting my head. If she'd just left me alone, I would have been okay, but all the sympathy pouring from her made me cry even harder.

"It's okay, Clista. Smog just doesn't understand. Obviously, he's gotten his information wrong, and there's only one person who could have given it to him. Shame on you, Cristoff."

"Ouch," said Frall, apparently seeing the look passing between my uncle and Ms. Evans.

"All right, here we are," Smog said, spiraling downward.

"Oh, noooooooooooooo," cried Ms. Evans.

"I'm gonna be sick," sighed Frall.

"Are we going to crash?" I yelled out.

"It's all right. Just hold on. It's quick!" Uncle Cristoff assured us.

Smog said nothing, and the flyer's decibel level plummeted to almost nothing.

"We're crashing," I said softly.

We plummeted and dived. I shut my eyes. I prayed, not that we wouldn't crash. I knew that was inevitable but that our deaths would be quick and painless.

The flyer was spinning like a tornado. I couldn't hear the motor. I think we were in a stall. An alarm blared.

The buzz told us what we already knew. I didn't bother to look.

I reached over and captured Frall's hand. Ms. Evans had my other one. I was twisted that way, but it didn't matter. When we finally made an impact, it would be the end.

The seconds clicked. I could hear them. Or maybe it was my heartbeat. My mouth dried. I couldn't swallow. Did it matter?

"Smog," my uncle barked.

"All right. All right. It was good for them. It takes away their sass."

The motor caught. We felt the jar of it.

"Our Father who art in heaven,... Ms. Evans began. I mouthed the words, remembering them, needing them.

Frall's hand gripped mine painfully. "Frall," I said. "Please."

He didn't understand. "Look at me, Clista," he ordered. It was crazy, but I complied.

"If we make it, will you go out with me?" he asked, his eyes begging.

I laughed. Then I squeezed his hand, even though he was holding mine so tightly it hurt. "Yes," I said. "Yes."

The Academy didn't allow dating, but I was beyond caring at that moment. A flood of warmth spread through me. Frall wanted a date. I smiled.

We thought we were dying. I know it sounds stupid to be asking for dates, but it took our mind off the present. It made us smile. Ms. Evans squeezed my other hand. She was smiling, too.

"Good for you. He's a nice boy," she encouraged.

The flyer was jerking around, fighting Smog for control. He was talking to it. "Come on, baby. Give in to Daddy. Smooth out now. You know the way. Let's slide into home."

Apparently, it worked. The flyer quit bucking.

We could see the landing site then. We were coming at it too fast. Trees rushed by. We lowered. My ears popped. My stomach did loop-de-loops. More trees. A branch hit us in passing. It panged the window.

"Tight squeeze. Hold on, everyone."

Then we dropped. Elevator style. My stomach was in my mouth, my feet in my stomach.

Frall vomited, luckily into a bag he'd been holding. The smell made me ill.

My uncle opened the windows. The air was cold. Our exhale turned into dragon breath. But we made it.

I leaned forward and threw my arms around Smog's neck. "Thank you, thank you," I said.

"Get her off me," he griped, but I was back in my seat before my uncle could even move.

Smog parked us and shut down the engines. Then he hand-printed the doors open and let us out.

I jumped out first, and again, I threw myself at him. I don't know why. I didn't mean to.

"Do you do this often?" he asked, but he hugged me back. "Scared you, didn't I?" he laughed.

"Yes," I said, my teeth chattering, tears flowing down my cheeks again.

My uncle and Ms. Evans were hugging, too. Poor Frall, no one wanted to hug him. He was looking wobbly, and his skin had turned a pale green. He walked away from the flyer and sat down under a huge pine tree.

"Poor Frall," I said.

Smog laughed. "Yeah, there's something about being a killer that gives you an iron-clad stomach."

"I didn't kill him!" I screamed. "Stop saying that."

"Lay off her," Uncle Cristoff growled, giving Smog a warning look.

I walked over to Frall. "Feeling better?"

"What was that about?" he asked, referring to my temper flare-up with Smog.

"I don't want to talk about it," I snapped, turning away.

"Yeah, but you talked with Smog about it, huh?"

I wheeled about to glare at Frall. "I never talked to him about it. The only one who knows anything about that day is my uncle, and I'm sorry I ever told him!"

"You needed to tell me," Uncle Cristoff said, coming up behind me.

I shifted so I could look at him. I was ready to explode, but his expression caught me. His face was all twisted up with sympathy and concern. I lowered my head. I couldn't look at him.

"You had to talk about it, Clista. If you hadn't, it would have festered inside you. It would have made you sick. Do you understand that?"

I couldn't speak. It hurt too much. My sniffles started again. I wiped my nose on the back of my hand.

"Here," my uncle said, handing me a clean, white hankie. "You're lucky I still have that one."

I used it on my eyes and then on my nose. "What am I going to do, Uncle Cristoff? I can't undo it. The cavern collapsed. The *Tworst of Trent* is inside there. Besides, the *Old Ones . . .*"

"Hush. I know. I've been thinking about it, too. I think we need to talk with them. But not right now. Let's move into Smog's cabin and see how bad it is. Okay?"

I nodded, and Frall stood up. "Where should I put this, Sir?" Frall asked with embarrassment, holding up the bag with his vomit.

"Give it to Smog. Oh, and Frall, the first time he ever landed me here, I did the exact same thing. One gets used to even the worst of pilots."

"Did I hear that correctly?" Smog blared out, laughing. "You want to try getting us in this tight squeeze next time? It also keeps anyone unwanted from just dropping in, doesn't it?"

We walked forward to what Smog had called his "primitive living quarters." It was anything but. The outside was log-hewn, rough as a camper's cabin, but the inside, wow! For one thing, the inside was entirely finished off in wood and beautifully lacquered so that it shone. Even the floor, scattered here and there with textured burnt amber and cranberry-colored throw rugs, was polished cedar.

The bottom level held a giant fireplace, one that took up most of the sidewall. The furniture was all hand-carved and padded with colors that matched the rugs. There were hanging tapestries on the walls with scenes from nature. Each one included groupings of stars and strange suns.

"This is beautiful," I cried out. "I love it."

Smog beamed but pretended not to. He said gruffly, "It's a work in progress."

He showed us the kitchen with a table large enough to entertain six. It also was made of real wood. I touched it with wonder.

"Where did you buy everything?" I asked. "It fits so perfectly."

Smog laughed. "Buy? I made everything, kid. Each and every piece of furniture you see here. Only the appliances came from stores."

"Do you have a garbage can?" Frall asked, still carting around his bag.

"Go back outside. There's a dump out there. I compost everything, so your offerings will help a tree to grow strong and healthy."

"Ew!" I said, and then wished I'd kept my mouth shut as Frall's face turned red.

Smog lifted up a heavy metal pot. He filled it with water and then lit the stove. "There, that will start us off with some tea. I could use a pot right now. Anyone else like tea?"

"I'd love some," Ms. Evans said. She was leaning on my uncle, looking tired and overly stressed. She looked like she needed a nap more than tea.

"How many bedrooms do you have? We haven't seen those yet," I said.

Frall was just re-entering. He froze in the doorway at the mention of bedrooms. "I could sleep outside if it's a problem," he said. "Or on the floor?"

"I have four bedrooms. I don't care how you split them up, but one of them's mine."

Smog then led the way to show off the top floor. His stairs had a really cool banister.

"No, you will not," Smog told Frall and me when we hadn't even said a word about it. "I know just what you're thinking, but the angle's wrong for sliding. Anyone who tried it would fall from about ten feet AND would get my boot in the butt after they landed. Got that, kids?"

Frall and I nodded, but I don't think Smog noticed. He was heading up the stairs.

Uncle Cristoff caught up with me. "You and Ms. Evans will share one bedroom. Frall and I will share another."

"But that doesn't make sense," I said. "There are four bedrooms. Why should Ms. Evans have to share?"

"Don't fight me all the time, Clista. Save some of it for when you're bored," my uncle said, as his legs did double-time, carrying him upward to rejoin Smog.

"Duh, Clista. Don't you get it? They don't trust us," Frall told me.

"That's dumb. Neither of us would…"

Frall was looking at me strangely. I bit my tongue. Sometimes, there was such a thin line between things you could say and things you shouldn't. I mean, I really liked Frall. He was cool, but that didn't mean that I wanted our friendship to deepen into something else. We had too much to accomplish before either of us would be ready for that.

Then I remembered our kisses in the cavern. They'd been pretty intense. I turned red and suddenly walked the steps a bit faster. I felt Frall's eyes on my back as I did so. What was he thinking? Was he remembering how it had been between us inside the cave?

Ms. Evans was agreeable to sharing a room with me. I thought she'd object, but she just smiled and said, "What fun. We can talk late in the night about girl stuff."

I couldn't say anything then. I didn't want to hurt her feelings. We had twin beds. I asked her which one she wanted. She shrugged and let me choose. I chose the one closer to the window. I wanted to see the stars. I bet they'd be beautiful in the forest, far away from the city lights.

There wasn't much else in the room. I guess Smog had had little reason to do interior decorating. The beds had pillows on each of them, sheets, and a couple of blankets — no bedspreads, nothing fancy. There was a nightstand in between the beds. I opened it, curious. It was empty.

A single chair sat in the corner, nothing else. There wasn't even a closet. I wondered where Smog expected his guests to put their clothes. Of course, we had next to none, so it really didn't matter to us. I threw my backpack on the bed. Ms. Evans placed her pillowcase full of clothing down on hers, too. That was that.

Then we walked into the hall to see where the others had gone. My uncle and Frall were arguing about the bunk bed. Neither of them wanted to be on top.

"Cool," I said. "I'll take it."

Ms. Evans said she didn't care, so we swapped rooms. Good thing we hadn't done any unpacking.

I climbed up on the top bunk. The bed was up against the window. I had a perfect view outside. Funny how there are moments of perfection even amid so many things gone wrong.

Of course, we had to barge in on Smog. He was nice about it, showing off his room. He gave us a tour. His was not only the most finished of the bedrooms, BUT he had a telescope.

"That is so star search cool!" I told him, and Frall seconded it.

Smog let us look through it, but we really couldn't see much since it was still light outside. Smog promised to let us take a peek before going off to bed. That was something to look forward to.

Once at school, we'd gone up to the observatory. We only got to stay until ten o'clock, but the sight was something I'll never forget. When you see the rings of Ploutomia, and then one of its moons comes into focus — Wow! It's hard to imagine some people get paid to study the stars. I wonder what that would be like.

We finally wandered back downstairs. Somehow, we all gravitated to the kitchen, and we stared at Smog like hungry puppies.

"All right," he said, laughing. "I'll fix something. Smeghett or Plushpup?"

Frall and I looked at each other. Then we glanced at my uncle and Ms. Evans. They both had the same blank expression on their face. It was obvious that none of us had any idea what Smog was talking about. He laughed again, pulled up his sleeves, and started washing his hands.

"No free service," he said. "Everyone pitch in."

Smog had NO food hydrator. He had no food zapper. He had no modernistics at all. We had to do everything by hand. He gave Frall potatoes to peel. I had carrots. Uncle Cristoff had to scout the yard for firewood. Ms. Evans had to set the table and fix some kind of fruit compote, which was something else I'd never heard of. Smog started opening food packets.

Everything turned out okay, but it was a strange bunch of ingredients. No one complained, and everyone was hungry enough to eat it, but I sure wished we'd brought some techno stuff from home. This cooking stuff would get old fast.

Chapter Fifteen

After our meal, we went hiking. That was the highlight. We saw several small rodents, a zimpoo, a mistock, and a molor. Frall said he saw a tuck, the largest member of the cat family on Rwawan, but no one else saw it, and we all thought he'd imagined it.

We headed up to the top of the mountain, scaling it, which I thought was pretty scary. I was shaking by the time Smog finally pulled me the last step up.

"This is so high," I said, spinning about so I could see all around us. Smog and Uncle Cristoff laughed.

"This is nothing. It isn't even a climb, Clista."

It was for me. I sat down and let my shaky legs unwobble a bit. That's when Smog and my uncle decided it was time to bring everything out in the open.

"I want you to tell the whole story, Clista," my uncle ordered.

I shook my head. "You don't understand. It's not something I want to talk about."

"But you have to, Clista. We have to unravel this, and you two kids are at the heart of it. Each of you, including you, Franca, knows a little piece. You're not telling the others what you know. You're hoarding it inside, which means there's too much secretiveness. Smog and I are experienced detectives. It's time we put all the pieces together and see what it looks like."

While Uncle Cristoff talked, I'd stood up. I guess I was backing away. I didn't even notice until Ms. Evans stopped me.

"You don't have to talk about it, Clista — not if you're not ready."

"Franca," my uncle said, giving her a look that more or less meant *stay out of it*.

But Ms. Evans was stauncher than I'd thought. She turned to my uncle, put her hands on her hips, and said, "You may be an efficient police officer, but I'm a skilled psychiatrist, and I won't have Clista pressured. She's been through too much."

My uncle gave an enormous sigh. I could see that he didn't like her invasion into what he considered was *his* problem, but he had welcomed her into the Makeshift conference. He couldn't suddenly uninvite her.

"Hold it, you two. What if it's good for Clista to be talking about it?" Smog asked. "What if Frall needs this too? Do you have any idea how deep these kids are in this, Franca? We call it murder, you know."

"There is no proof that Cronoks Lab caused the death of Clista's parents," Ms. Evans cried out before she realized what she'd said. "Oh, I'm so sorry, Clista. I shouldn't have said that, should I?" she told me, paling.

"No, she's a tough girl. She'll pull through," Smog said, "except you misunderstood my meaning. I wasn't talking about *that* murder. You want to explain it, Clista?"

Did I want to open a can of stinging gnats? No way. Ms. Evans was a counselor, but she wouldn't understand what I'd done. She didn't know anything about the *Old Ones*. She wouldn't believe me.

I looked at Frall, then at my uncle. "I don't know what to do," I said. "I can't. No one can understand what it's like — no one would even believe me…"

"I believe you. Now, at least. They'll have to believe when they hear what I've seen. Frall believes it, too. He knows," my uncle said, taking my hand and leading me back to the others.

"Franca and Smog will have to accept what we've seen — what we saw you do. But Smog is right, Clista. You can't expect others to risk everything – maybe even their lives, without knowing the big picture truth. We have to lay it all out and compare notes. Hopefully, it will make more sense then than it does now."

"But it doesn't make any sense to me either. I don't understand any of this. And, Smog already said…"

My stupid tears had started up again. I hated them. They made me feel weak.

Frall moved closer. He touched my arm. "I want to help," he said. "Whatever it is that Smog is talking about, I'll understand. It was that guy at school, wasn't it? You did something to him. Did you kill him? Is that what Smog means?"

"Of course, she didn't," Ms. Evans interrupted. "What are you saying? I was there. There was no blood in that room. No signs of violence. How could you think that?"

My uncle was watching me. He'd already said his piece. He was waiting to see if I'd do as he'd asked.

"You're all going to hate me. I know you will, but it's true. I did it. Mr. Grenan, I mean. I think he's dead."

"Wait a minute. What's this, I think business?" Smog asked. "Either the guy is dead because you killed him, or he isn't. Which is it?"

I was sobbing. It was all rushing back at me. I thought I'd locked it away. I'd promised myself never to think about it again.

"The *Old Ones* told me to do it. They showed me how. I did what they said."

"Could we start at the beginning? Who are the *Old Ones*?" Smog asked.

"The *Old Ones* were the ones who came before us. They were here and on all the moons and the planets we've landed on. There were always signs that they'd been in all those places first. They left artifacts and pictures. Text even. We don't know that much about them. My parents were researching them. That's what the grant was for. Dad found things in the cavern. They were from the *Old Ones*."

"All right, so we're talking about dead guys here? Dead as in *centuries*?"

"Thousands of years. We don't know if their civilization is gone from all existence or whether they just moved somewhere else. But they're not exactly dead."

"Wait a minute. Thousands of years ago … and they're not dead. Did you bump your head on something?"

"She's right. They're not dead. We've both felt them. They talk to us," Frall said, throwing his arm around my shoulder and giving me his support.

"So you've both knocked your heads? Is there such a thing as a shared hallucination, Ms. Evans?"

She hushed Smog. "Go on, Clista. Tell us more. This is fascinating. I knew your parents were researchers and scientists, but I never knew what they were working on. Tell us."

I inhaled and held it for a moment. I used the hankie Uncle Cristoff had given me. Then I continued. "My parents found evidence of the *Old Ones* inside the cave, and they …" I looked over at Uncle Cristoff. Did I dare keep talking? Was it okay?

He nodded for me to go on. I sighed and continued. "My parents brought some of the pieces back to our house. They began to analyze the writings they'd found, probing them, trying to understand what they said, but no one could read the words of the *Old Ones*. No one knows how.

"Then, one night, Mother let me go down to the basement where they kept it all. She showed me what they were working on. I'd never seen artifacts before — except once when I went to the museum. Yet those were behind glass. These were lying on the tables. I touched something, and it tingled."

Smog was making a face. I saw his disbelief. I didn't know how I could explain it any further.

"It did that with me, too," Frall said. "I came over to visit Clista. Her dad invited me down to the basement to look at the artifacts. I wanted to study them, you see. I wanted to work at the site with her parents.

"Clista's father let me touch something, and it was super weird. It called to me. Then the other pieces beckoned. Not with a voice, exactly, but with a ringing in my head, an insistence. It guided me toward…"

"The *Old Ones* communicate with both of us. I think we're connectors," I said.

"Connectors?" Smog repeated. "All right. Could we get back to the story, Clista? Frall, let's wait for yours. I'd like to hear Clista first and *then* your version. That will help. We should separate you and hear the sides one at a time, but that isn't going to work here. Not if we're trying to piece together everyone's knowledge."

"Well, there was one piece that especially drew me to it," I told him, keeping my eyes down and staring at my lap. "It was a necklace. I don't mean that I wanted it. It wasn't that pretty or anything. I mean, it called me. I touched it, but that's all. Then I went upstairs, and I went to bed.

"That night, I dreamed about the necklace. I dreamed over and over that I'd put it on. It was a horrible dream. The necklace burned me. It burned into my skin and melded itself into me, and I couldn't get it off. In my dream, I even took a knife to it and tried to cut it away. I was bleeding from the wounds I was making in my neck, and yet the necklace couldn't be pried off."

"This was just a dream, right?" Smog said. "You didn't really do this or anything, did you?"

"No. *Then,* it was only a dream, but the next night, it happened. The necklace was around my neck when I woke up."

"Wait a minute. You dreamed it was there, and then you woke up, and it was there? I bet you were still dreaming."

"No, she wasn't. I've seen it," Frall burst in. "She has it on. It doesn't come off, no matter what you do to it."

"Right now?" Smog was looking at both of us as if we were touched by Asteroid Sickness.

"You can see it if you want. It's always on me, permanently on me," I told him.

I no longer had the spacesuit on. It was very easy to unbutton my collar and show him. Ms. Evans and my uncle peered down at it, too, but Smog tested it with his fingers. He withdrew immediately and began shaking his hand.

"What the . . . ?" he cried out. Then he reached into his pocket and brought out a knife. He poked and prodded with that for a moment.

"I don't believe it," he said. "What kind of trick is this?"

"There's no trick," I said. "It just doesn't come off. It's one of the *Old One's* artifacts, and from the day they put it on me, it has remained around my neck. I wish I could take it off. My folks tried. Believe me."

"I don't believe in the *Old Ones*," Smog said, twirling me around so he could inspect the necklace in the back. "I've always found that the seemingly impossible always has an answer."

"Yeah, that's what I used to think," my uncle laughed. "Funny how it took my teenage niece to change my thinking. Lately, I've had a good dose of attitude adjustment. When I think about how Clista used the necklace to deprogram the Cronoks Lab' flyers..."

"Are you saying she can use this thing to do magic?" Smog asked.

"Not magic," I explained. "I can't really do anything myself. It's not like I wish for something to happen, and it does. I think the necklace just provides a connection that helps me to communicate with the *Old Ones*."

"Like a conduit," Ms. Evans said, peering down at the necklace. "May I touch it?" she asked.

"Sure," I said, my tears were forgotten. Frall was leaning over as if seeing the necklace for the first time, and then there was Ms. Evans and Smog staring at me. I was beginning to feel like I was the freak in a freak show.

Smog pulled back his knife, and Ms. Evans reached out. "Oh, it's warm. It looks like metal. I just assumed that it would be cold."

"It's cold," Smog told her, touching it again. "It's like dry ice. It burns."

"How could that be?" Ms. Evans questioned, staring up at him in wonder.

I had felt the change in the necklace, too. It heated for her touch. "You're a conduit, too," I cried out. "It likes you."

My uncle and Smog laughed, but Ms. Evans didn't. She stared into my eyes. Then she reached out and touched the necklace again. "Yes, I feel the *Old Ones*. They want me to get something from…"

"What!" yelled Smog. "I thought you were a normal, intelligent person. What is this? Are you encouraging the kids?"

"Lay off, Smog," my uncle said. "Let's see where this goes."

"No," Smog said, glaring at us. "Has everyone forgotten the reason for this little hike? There has been a murder. Can we get back to that? Forget the loony bin stuff.

"What about this guy, Mr. Grenan, Clista. What did you do to him? How did you kill him?"

A monkey-bird was chattering from up in the pine that leaned over our resting spot. Its impatience at our temporary visit was a querulous burst of noise.

"Get out of here," my uncle yelled at it.

But monkey-birds do not scare easily. It persisted, growing louder and louder, even hopping down to a lower branch.

I started to laugh. "Let him tell the story. He obviously knows all about it."

Frall, standing beside me, almost protectingly while everyone was inspecting the necklace, threw his arm around me again. "You don't have to talk about this, Clista. I understand that whatever you did, it was the *Old Ones*, not you. I know you better than everyone else. I know you'd never hurt anyone. I'm sure of that."

He was wrong. I'd killed someone, and I was making jokes just to get out of telling about it. Feeling his support helped me, though. I looked around the circle of eyes. Yes, it was time. I wanted to tell Smog, to get it over with, to confess. Maybe he and my uncle could help me, but whether they could or not, I was tired of carrying the guilt, tired of keeping it a secret.

I picked up a broken branch, one newly fallen from the tree. Its pine needles were still green and soft with newness. I snapped off a section and peered down at the pointy edge. The layers of stringy-like fiber opened to my inspection.

Layers — there were layers in everything. Layers of guilt, layers of blame. Would Smog condemn me when he heard the whole of it? Yes. No matter what excuses and reasons I came up with, I was guilty. I had no right to do what I did. And I couldn't blame it on the *Old One*. They hadn't forced me, had they? But had they influenced me? Had they made me kill?

I closed my eyes and tried to remember. What had I been thinking? Had I believed that I could take away someone's life and that it was the right thing to do?

Layers. I'd unravel them. I'd dig down until I reached the core. That would tell me who I was, and then? What if I lost everyone's faith in me? That was possible. Would Frall still say he understood? Would he still keep his arm around me? Would Ms. Evans still believe

I was a good person? Or would their eyes turn cold? Would they all desert me like I deserved?

I nodded. The chattering monkey-bird, tired of his protests, took off, soaring into the sky. I watched him, wishing I could join him.

But I couldn't. I cleared my throat, swallowed hard, and began to talk. I told everyone how the Cronoks Lab scientist had cornered me, how he'd refused to give up the *Tworst of Twent* even though I'd explained about its evilness . . .

"Wait a minute. The *Tworst of Twent* was evil? I thought that was one of the *Old Ones'* artifacts?" Smog questioned.

"The *Tworst of Twent* is an expeller," I said. "It's as old as the *Old Ones*, but they didn't create it. They keep it hidden away so it can't cause harm. Unfortunately, it can't be destroyed."

Smog's dark-blue eyes continued to look at me with distrust. "Can you explain that?" he asked, wiping a dirty hand through the tousle of his blondish hair.

"An expeller is one that channels negativity, I think," I said, attempting to clarify what I really didn't understand. "Mr. Grenan was melding with it, had melded with it. He was becoming more evil, allowing the *Tworst of Twent* to become stronger. Do you understand?"

Smog sighed. "No, but go on. There was this thing that was bad, and you told Grenan to put it down, and he didn't. Was it endangering you, this *Twist of Twent*?"

"*Tworst of Twent*. Yes, it endangered me and our entire world. It leaked evil."

"No, Clista. I don't mean that. I mean, did Mr. Grenan threaten you in some way personally. Was he causing you pain or about to cause you pain?"

I glanced at my uncle, but his face gave me nothing. His eyes just watched and recorded. I looked up at Smog again and answered him. "Yes. My neck was burning, and the *Tworst of Twent* was making me ill."

"All right. Cristoff, you hear that? We can claim she did it in self-defense. I don't know how that'll stand up in court, though, if the victim didn't have a weapon. But go on, Clista. What happened then?"

"The *Old Ones* channeled their Power through me, and I wrapped Mr. Grenan in a web of it."

"You did what? A web of what? You mean rope?"

I looked over at my uncle again and then at Ms. Evans. They were both listening, her face as expressionless as my uncle's.

"No, I didn't use rope. I used the Power, the energy that flowed through my fingers."

"You're not trying to tell me — you choked him?" Smog asked.

"No. Of course not. I never went close to him. I certainly didn't touch him! He had the *Tworst of Twent*. It was burning me, even from a distance. No, when I said I wrapped him in a web of it, I mean the Power. I put my fingers together and drew in the Power of the *Old Ones*. That Power, like long strands of a spider's web, dangled from my fingers. Then, without moving, I sent the strands forward, and they fell around Mr. Grenan."

"Clista, are you telling me the truth? You didn't have any weapon except this magic stuff that you made from your mind?" Smog asked.

I shook my head. Then I scanned the faces across from me. My uncle already knew the story. He was looking at me with knowing eyes, his face composed and set. Ms. Evans was leaning against him, inside the v-shaped space of his legs. My uncle's arms were surrounding her. She was listening, but there was a contentedness in her expression as if my story were not all she was thinking about.

Frall, who sat beside me, with his arm still around me, I couldn't see. I felt his closeness, the warmth of his body. I pictured his face, his coffee-brown eyes absorbed in seeing the picture I was showing. So far, it hadn't turned him away from me. Not yet.

The scent of the pines brought me calm. The tranquility of the place, without the monkey-bird, slowed my breathing, making it easier to say the words.

"No, I had no weapons, Smog. My father was there with me, but I asked him to let me deal with Mr. Grenan. He remained in his seat while the Power grew in my fingers and while it covered the scientist.

"I repeated to Mr. Grenan that if he would set down the *Tworst of Trent*, he could go free. I begged him to release himself from its evil, but it had already taken him. His face writhed in hate. I think the *Tworst of Trent* does not like the Power of the *Old Ones*. I believe they are enemies, yet they attract each other. That is odd. I do not understand it."

"You and me both. I don't understand any of this. Is this what Clista told you, Cristoff?"

"As far as she's gone. There's more. Keep going, Clista. Tell him the rest," my uncle ordered softly.

Ms. Evans' eyes were on me, also urging me. I stumbled on. "Well, the strands of Power wrapped themselves around and around Mr. Grenan, coating him as if it were a string. He clutched the *Tworst of Trent* against his body, but he didn't move. He was bound to that spot.

"Then, when he was thoroughly cocooned inside, looking like a white, stringy balloon, he began to spin. I think the Power was setting him, drying the fibers of Power. After that, the other scientist knocked, asking for Mr. Grenan. I placed my hands on the drying ball, and through the Power, the ball began to shrink.

It grew smaller and smaller until it was so tiny I could pick it up. I placed that ball in the pocket of my spacesuit. Then, when the other scientist, Mr. Choffee, came into the room, he couldn't see Mr. Grenan. He couldn't see anything but the room with my father and me."

Smog didn't say anything. He stood up and walked away, leaving us sitting there.

"Where's he going?" Ms. Evans asked, but my uncle just shrugged and shook his head.

"You did a good job of telling that, Clista," Frall said. "I remember seeing you that day. You were as pale as a ghost. You looked ill. Now I understand what happened. I'm glad you trusted me with it."

"It's awful, Frall. I don't know why I didn't see it at the time. I guess I didn't think about what I was doing. I didn't realize that I was probably killing him. I didn't mean to kill someone. Can you believe me?"

"Clista, I do understand, and I know something else. The *Old Ones* have no evil in them. They don't kill. Mr. Grenan's not dead."

I pulled away so I could look into Frall's eyes. "How do you know that? Are you sure?"

Frall reached out with both hands. Then he reached forward and touched his lips to mine. "I'm sure, Clista, but we can summon them to us and ask, you know."

"Summon them? Wouldn't that make them angry? I've only summoned them once to save us from the flyers."

Frall's hands cupped my head. He was staring into my eyes. I breathed in the scent of him. It felt so right to be close to him, whispering, touching. We were meant for each other.

With that thought, my hands removed his, and I backed away. Was this the *Old Ones'* influence? Was this their imprinting? Or was it wistful thoughts? I focused on breathing in and out, slowly and surely.

Frall just sat there with the biggest grin on his face. "That just hit you?" he laughed. "It conked me over the head days ago. It seems that they've made some choices for us. Do you mind too much?"

"What? What do you mean?"

"Clista, what did you do with the cocoon you put in your pocket? Where is it now? May I see it?" Smog was back, dealing out questions as if he'd bundled them up and carried them to me.

"We took it to the cavern — Uncle Cristoff, Frall, and I."

"You left it there? Did you see this thing she was talking about, Cristoff?"

"Yeah. It didn't look like much — maybe a ball of white thread. But I was reading Clista's eyes, and when she told me the story both times, she wasn't lying. Whatever you think, she believes it."

Frall was watching me, too, still tuned into the feelings we'd been talking about. I was split between the two worlds. I needed concentration for both of them, yet I had no answers for either of them.

"Clista," both Smog and Frall said at the same time. I stood up and walked over to the pine tree to touch its rough-textured bark. I needed to feel something with solidity.

"You'll get pine sap on your hands," Ms. Evans called out.

Pine sap. That was the least of my problems.

"Leave her alone," Frall said to Smog. "Can't you see what you're doing to her? She can't control the Power. They made her do what she did. Now she's all …"

"All what? Twisted inside? Is that what it is, Frall? Am I mad?" I asked, turning to face him, to face all of them.

"No, that's not what I meant. Confused, maybe. Rebellious. I was. But I don't mind now, Clista. I don't mind at all that they've chosen for me, because I like their choice. It feels right."

"What are you talking about? What choice?" Smog asked. He was darting quick looks back and forth between us, his face creased with puzzlement.

I opened my mouth to explain, but I didn't. It wasn't Smog's business anyway, and besides, I wasn't sure how I felt about it. I'd really liked Frall before all this business with the *Old Ones*. I still liked him, but I wasn't comfortable with the way the *Old Ones* were leaning on me, pushing me in directions that maybe I didn't want to go, or at least — not yet.

"The *Old Ones* have chosen me as Clista's mate," Frall said. "Clista isn't comfortable with that."

Of course, she's not comfortable with that. I'm not, either. She's too young," my uncle said, butting in.

I turned. "Listen. Do you hear that?"

"Yes. I think it's a flyer," Ms. Evans said.

The buzz of the approaching craft was a low throb in the south. Smog motioned us to take cover under the trees. We ducked into the heaviest foliage and stood watching the sky.

Uncle Cristoff was the first to whisper, "It's a police flyer. What do you think, Smog? Do we stay hidden or show ourselves?"

Smog studied the flyer. It was flying near to the ground, searching. It located the cabin and circled.

"He's found the cabin. Darn. How in the world did he locate us?"

"They had to have used a tracer," my uncle said. "They must have planned this, but why? Is there something else we should know, kids? Any other crimes?"

Frall and I both shook our heads.

"If the tracer's on the flyer, they won't be able to find us. If it's on us, we'll know in a minute," Smog said.

"But if you guys are police, won't they know we're with you? Why would they search for us?" Frall asked.

"That's right," said Ms. Evans. "I don't understand what's going on. I thought we were running from Cronoks Lab. Now we're running from the police? I don't like that."

"You misunderstand. We're NOT running from the police. If it's *really* the agency, everything's fine," my uncle said, watching Smog as he crept closer to the edge of the foliage cover. "What do you think, Smog?"

"The police don't put tracers on people, not unless they have a warrant. There's been no warrant issued for any of us — not that I know, at least," Smog answered. "Tell you what. I'm going to go smoke 'em out. I'll sing if it's legit."

"But what if it's not? Smog, please don't go. Not if you think it's Cronoks Lab. Don't trust them," I said, panicking.

"Keep your niece close by, Cristoff. I still have questions for her. Be watchful. Adios," he said, slipping off deeper into the forest."

"He's going the wrong way," Frall said. "I thought he was going to check the flyer out?"

"Sh," my uncle hissed, watching the vehicle scanning over us. "Trust him."

We quieted then, leaning back against the giant tree trunk and staring upward.

"If they are the police, how will Smog know?" Ms. Evans whispered after a moment.

"Police code," my uncle answered, barely audibly.

Several minutes passed. The monkey-bird came back and began to wage his verbal assault. Frall threw a twig at it, but it didn't fly high enough to scare him off.

"Leave the bird alone," my uncle said.

"But he's giving away our position," Frall argued, picking up another twig to throw at the scolding bird.

"If those guys up there have an infrared scanner, that bird and all his wild friends may save our life. Wildlife throws the thing off. We need that bird until we know more about our skyward friends."

Frall dropped the branch and took my hand. "Okay," he shrugged. "Have it your way.

"Are you mad at me now?" Frall whispered in my ear. "I hope you understand that I was just trying to tell you how agreeable I was to the relationship the *Old Ones* have pushed on us."

The police or Cronoks Lab were overhead, scrutinizing sections of forest. Smog was crawling further into the bushes so he could pop out and question the flyer. We were hiding under a two hundred foot-tall pine, itchy from pine needles, and Frall wanted to discuss our relationship?

I swallowed and opened my mouth to say, "Not now..." when Smog suddenly flung himself out of the forest on the other side of the clearing and, waving his hands, started calling out, "Hey, this is private property. What do you guys want?"

"Good job, my friend," Cristoff mumbled softly. "Be quiet and listen, folks," he told us. "We may be running for our lives in a minute."

"I'm not running from the police," Ms. Evans said firmly.

I think my uncle was about to dispute that when the flyer dipped back Smog's way and fired down on him.

"That settles it. It's not the police," my uncle said. "Come on, run..."

Frall was up, and on his feet at the same time I was. We darted towards the darkness of the thick, heavy growth of the inner forest. Unfortunately, the dangled vines, the ferns, and the thick padding of the forest floor made running difficult.

"Use this," my uncle said, tossing a machete at Frall. Frall caught it cautiously. Then he swung it around, saying. "Stand back, Clista."

I didn't wait. I saw another pathway and darted forward, heading around the overgrowth.

"That a girl," said my uncle when he caught up with me. "You have good eyes. I don't suppose the *Old Ones* can do anything about covering the trail we're making, can they?"

"That's Frall's area," I told him.

Frall gave me a quick look. I think he was a little upset that he hadn't had the opportunity to play machete Man of the Forest, but he smiled at me.

"Sure. No problem," he said. He stuck his hand in his pocket and pulled out one of the *Old Ones'* artifacts. It was a new one that I hadn't seen. How had he known to bring it? Were the *Old Ones* still guiding us?

Frall held his hand out flat with the rock-shaped artifact in the center. Then, he began to speak in the Old Language. "*Trepok trezet, Trepok trezot, Trepok trezit, Trepok trezut…*"

The rock glowed. I walked closer and touched the artifact. It was hot. Keeping my left hand there, I moved my right hand to touch my necklace. Then, I joined Frall. "*Trepok, trezet, Trepok trezot, Trepok trezit, Trepok trezut,*" I chanted along with him.

"What are you doing?" Ms. Evans asked, her hand reaching out as if she wanted to join us.

"No, you don't. Two of them are enough," my uncle said.

We didn't need her help. A wind swept out of the artifact in Frall's hand and the necklace around my neck, forming a current that traveled around and around in a circular v-shaped cone.

"What in the stars is that?" my uncle whistled under his breath.

Neither Frall nor I had time to answer. We were concentrating, focusing on the trail we'd walked.

"*Trepok, trezet, Trepok trezot, Trepok trezit, Trepok trezut,*" Frall chanted, with me echoing and then joining in.

The twister lifted up and blew itself forward and down to the ground. Then it grew larger, man-sized, twirling faster and faster, lifting up dirt, pine needles, and twigs and carrying them off down the trail.

"I don't believe what I just saw," Smog said, stepping out from behind a large redwood. "You kids do the strangest things. Were you really responsible for that?"

"You're okay," I said, almost losing my focus until Frall called me back to task.

"*Trepok, trezet,*" I said, and Frall's eyes stared into mine.

"Clean the path and clear our passage," Frall intoned.

"Hide our passage. Keep our presence secret."

The winds of the torret, the cone-shaped wind we'd sent forward, were still as loud as thunder. I noticed that the others were covering their ears, but the sound didn't bother Frall or me. We fed on it, sharing our chant and our soul-piercing eye contact.

Smog and my uncle sat down beside us. I could feel Ms. Evans' movement beside them, but the force of the torret and the strength of the communion between Frall and myself was what centered my mind. I looked inside Frall, and I saw.

I suppose all that continued for fifteen minutes or so — that's what my uncle later told me — but for that period when Frall's eyes and mine were joining inside the force of the power, there was a pathway we soared together. It was overwhelming, consuming, and heady.

"*Trepok, trezet, tezert, kopert,*" Frall chanted, and I copied. Then, together, we repeated the words over and over.

Finally, at last, the sound died. The winds that had lifted our hair backed off. I fell against Frall, and he against me. It was as if we dissolved inward into each other.

"I understand," I said. "You were right."

"It doesn't do any good to fight it, does it?"

I was still shaking my head when my uncle lifted me away from Frall. "That's enough of that, Clista. You two are too young to be pairing up."

It was obvious he didn't understand, but I was suddenly too tired to argue. I shrugged and sat down where he indicated, on the other side of Ms. Evans. "Uncle Cristoff, Frall, and I really need something to eat," I said. "Do we have any food with us?"

Luckily, Ms. Evans was our rescuer. She had a candy bar in her purse, which she split in half and gave to each of us. Frall and I were grateful.

"What did you find out?" my uncle was asking Smog as soon as the candy was parceled out to Frall and me.

"Not much," Smog told him, scanning the area above our heads. "They shot at me too soon. However, I guess it was pretty evident that they "fingered" the flyer and not us. They've been scanning, not coming at us directly."

"Did you see if they landed?" my uncle continued.

"No way," Smog said, wiping his face with a dirty rag. "Their ship is too large to land here. They won't be joining us, not with that flyer. However, now that they know where we are, it won't be too difficult to send for reinforcements. We can't go back to the cabin. We'll have to move on.

"But I still don't understand all this. What are these fellows after? Surely not the kids. This has gotten too involved for them to be chasing around after a kid who's killed one of their scientists," Smog said, eyeing me strangely.

"I think they want the necklace," I said. "I don't know how they could know about it, but that has to be it."

"But of course, they know about it, Clista. Didn't you say they took your parents' books," Frall asked.

I hit my forehead with the back of my hand. "How could I be so stupid? Of course. My parents must have mentioned the necklace. They're scientists. Of course, they recorded it. I bet they gave the whole history, maybe even telling how the necklace came to me and that it had power."

"Do you mean Cronoks Lab stole some books from your parents? When did that happen, Clista? Why would they do that?" Ms. Evans asked, her eyes still tearing from the stirred up dust.

My uncle sat down beside her. "I know we've kept a lot from you. You saw what Clista and Frall did. You heard about the *Old Ones* and their power. And apparently, you're woven up in this as tightly as the rest of us, maybe even more so. Why did you start to touch the rock?"

I stopped chewing to listen. I wanted to know that, too. Was Ms. Evans one of us? Was she meant to be a conduit, as she'd called us?"

"Why, I don't know. Did I reach out? I don't remember." She was wrinkling up her nose in puzzlement. We could all see that she was confused and a bit disoriented. That I could identify with. I felt the same way. Why was all this happening?

"There's a sacred spot in the mountains. It's a cave. No one will go near it. I think we need to go there. How do you feel about that, kids?" Smog asked.

"You mean it belongs to the *Old Ones*?" Frall asked.

"Yes," Ms. Evans said. "Yes, that's where we should go. I feel it now. I didn't a moment ago. But now it calls."

Smog shook his head. "This just gets stranger and stranger. What next?"

Frall stood up. He walked over to where my uncle was standing and said, "Clista and I must be together. You must not try to separate us."

I opened my mouth to argue, but there was something in Frall's eyes. I stared into them, allowing us to forge that mysterious bond we'd had a moment before. Then I saw what the *Old Ones* were sending me to see: Frall and I were walking together, hand in hand. The others were behind us. My uncle stopped us, and he took my hand, pulling me away from Frall. The necklace burned. My head hurt. My blood ran cold and I suddenly couldn't breathe.

"No," I shouted out, and my uncle dropped my hand and moved away. Once more, Frall was at my side. He took my hand, and we walked on. The Old Ones were watching us. They were in the sky and in the trees. They were all around us. One of them, an old man with a long, crooked nose, white-white hair, and eyes that burned into me, nodded his head at me. I lowered mine respectfully and then looked up again. I saw him smile.

"Clista, what is it?" my uncle was asking me, tugging at my arm, demanding my attention.

"You can't separate us. Frall is right. The *Old Ones* demand that we walk together."

"Separating you? No one's separating you two," Smog said, trying to understand the direction of the conversation.

I stood up.

"Sit down," Uncle Cristoff ordered, but I ignored him.

"We have to go now. We have to leave this spot. They're coming."

I walked toward Frall and placed my hand in his. We walked in the direction we needed to go. He knew as well as I. The *Old Ones* were calling.

"Now, just a minute…" my uncle argued, but he didn't continue to speak. I think that was because Ms. Evans was following us. I could hear her lighter step.

"All right," my uncle growled. "I give up. But I'd sure like it if the *Old Ones* would have a conversation with me. I'm getting tired of playing catch-up."

Smog must have decided to accompany us, too, because I heard him slap Uncle Cristoff on the back as they walked.

Then Frall tugged at me, and I sped up. Thus, we journeyed forward into the thickest part of the forest, heading further away from home and everything we'd ever known.

Chapter Sixteen

"How are we going to stop this?" I asked him. "I feel like we keep getting in deeper and deeper. And your parents? What about them? Do you think the *Old Ones* will help us?"

Frall kept walking, his eyes scanning ahead of us. "I don't know, Clista. They help sometimes and not others. I don't know if we can demand things from them, but I think they owe us, don't you? Especially with my parents. If Cronoks Lab has hurt them, well, there's going to be some fireworks. I won't take it."

"They've got to be okay, Frall. Why would Cronoks Lab hurt them? They don't know anything. I bet the Lab is just holding them to try to get us."

Frall stopped and looked at me, searching my face. "You think so? Stars, I hope so. Mom is kind of innocent, and Dad, well, he sure doesn't know how to… Do you really think they'd trade us for them? I would, you know. I'd give up if I thought it would save my folks."

"But we can't trust Cronoks Labs to keep their side of the bargain."

Frall nodded. He kept going but turned to watch the adults behind us. "Your uncle's driving me nuts, you know."

I nodded. "But he's kind of cool, sometimes."

"Yeah, Smog, too."

Frall held back a limb and let me step through before he let it swing. The adults were lagging. We could hear Ms. Evans panting from the speed of our pace. Several times Smog had called out for us to slow down, but we hadn't. We continued on, speeding up as the *Old Ones'* calling grew stronger.

"I need to ask for Mr. Grenan back, Frall. Do you think they'll do it? I can't go on like this."

"I know," he said. "I read it in your mind when we were forming the torret."

"You don't think the guy's dead, do you? Do you think I killed him?"

"You didn't kill him, no matter what happened to him, Clista. It was the *Old Ones*, and I don't think they kill. I once read a text about them that said that they never…What is that?"

The way forward was blocked by a deep gully. It looked like a river spanning about twenty feet across, but there was no water in it. The banks were steep and soft, sliding down into the ditch when we tested the edge.

"Stars! Where did that come from?" Smog said, stepping closer. "Back up, kids. That looks dangerous."

"We have to go on," Frall said. "We can't retreat, and there's no way around it."

Smog examined his face, but he didn't question how Frall knew that. Smog was starting to recognize the look that contact with the *Old Ones* brought to our faces.

"Then we'll just have to climb down," Smog said just in time for Ms. Evans and my uncle to slip through the forest growth and catch up.

"Climb down what?" Ms. Evans asked before she saw the chasm in front of us. "Oh, my. I'm not much of a climber."

"There's no way we can climb down that. It must be twenty feet to the bottom and an equal upward climb on the other side," my uncle said.

"Do you see any choices?" Smog asked. "The kids say there's no way around it."

"And I suppose the *Old Ones* told them that?" my uncle asked, his left eyebrow raised in doubt.

"We have to go forward. That's what the *Old Ones* tell us," I backed Frall.

"Did they assure us it would be safe?" Uncle Cristoff questioned.

I had no answer to that. The *Old Ones* were sparse with information.

The vines hanging from the trees all around us made adequate rope. Smog showed us how to strip the leaves and tie them securely. Ms. Evans tried to help, but her hands had begun to shake. It was obvious that she was our weak link. I worried that she wouldn't make it.

"Smog, have you noticed Ms. Evans' fear?" I asked, whispering when he and I were off to the side. "Do you think we ought to leave her behind?"

"First off, I don't think your uncle would agree to that, and secondly, if Cronoks Lab is really following us, that might not be the safest thing to do. Thirdly, would she stay? I thought she was under the same inducement you kids were."

I shook my head, unsure. "I don't know. The *Old Ones* haven't mentioned her. I haven't seen her in the visions they've sent, either. Do you think my uncle is that attached to her?"

Smog began to laugh. "Does a man propose if he's not rather fond of a woman?"

"Well, she's going to be difficult. I bet she's never even hiked anywhere before. She's a psychologist, you know. She stays inside all the time. I wonder if my uncle thought about that when he suggested she come with us. All you have to do is look at her, and you can see that," I said as I turned away.

"Is that right?" Smog laughed. I felt his eyes on me as I scuffed off.

I cut a couple of vines with Smog's knife and began tearing off the leaves. As I did, I sat by myself, thinking about the things I'd said to Smog. Had I been fair? Had I been honest? How did I know Ms. Evans wouldn't be able to keep up with us? I sighed and stripped faster.

I finished my rope and gathered the ones the others had done. The ropes had to be dried before we could use them, but Smog had a policeman's device that not only dried the vines but also cured and strengthened the fiber. He did a couple of them and then took off, heading into the forest by himself, saying only that he'd return in a while. While we waited, Frall kept urging us to go forward. He was too restless to sit. He spent the time pacing and complaining about stopping.

However, when Smog did come back, he brought a shirt full of fresh fruit he'd found. It was obvious; he was a pretty good guy to have around.

We started our descent right after eating the sticky fruits. First was Smog, then me, then Frall, then Ms. Evans, and last was my uncle. It was a good line-up. I trusted the males on each side of me. I hoped Ms. Evans wouldn't cause the problems I envisioned.

Smog started down, his feet wedged into the soft and crumbly soil. He had told us to search with our eyes for rocks to give us toeholds. I noticed he was doing exactly that. In a minute, I followed, my feet searching for his toeholds. I was doing fine when I felt the tug of Frall's start downward. I looked up and then looked down to see how far Smog was. That was my undoing. I froze.

"Clista, keep going, girl," Smog called to me.

Do you have any idea what that's like? One moment, you're fine, and then your limbs just won't support you. They won't move. You have the image of the great height you are hanging to, and you see yourself falling and falling. There are rocks down below. You know it will hurt. Painfully. Your hands are sweaty — a river of sweat, yet you can't move them. They're frozen, too. Frozen and cramping because you're clutching so hard.

"I can't," I told them, clinging to an exposed root as if it were my last lifeline.

I shut my eyes, but that didn't help. The images were still there. "I can't move."

"You can't stop. Frall's coming down. He'll be reaching you in another minute. Keep going, Clista."

That was easy for him to say; he was almost to the ground. I took another look and clung harder.

"Clista, what's the matter?" my uncle cried out. "Don't look down; just keep moving your feet, searching for the toe holds."

He was simply repeating what he'd already told me before. My mind was chanting the "don't look down" words over and over, but I had looked — twice — and now I couldn't move.

"It's all right, Clista," Frall called out, about two body lengths above my head. "No one expects you to climb down by yourself. You're a *girl*. Girls can't climb well. Everyone knows that. *I'll* be down to help you in a minute."

I stared up at him. I couldn't see his face. I could only see his boots coming closer. His words infuriated me. Thousands of years of programming, and it still came back to that. Men thought of us as incapable.

Only a girl? Fueled by my anger, I stretched my foot further and further down, searching for the next toehold. I found it. I was still clinging to my root, but I could feel Frall coming quickly. He'd reach me in another minute. Then he'd hold me in his arms and help me down – like a baby — like a weakling *girl*. I had to move. I had to let go of the root.

"I'm almost there, Clista," he called out. "I'll take care of you."

I let go and dropped down to the next toehold. "I'm fine, Frall," I yelled back. "Females are as fully capable of climbing as everything else."

I didn't look down from then on. I just kept hugging the wall and searching for toeholds and finger grips. So when Smog's hands swung me off the cliff and down into the gully, it shocked me so much that I screamed.

"Good girl," he said. "You scared me there for a minute. Then you started up again. What did Frall say that got you going?"

"Nothing. I just got my second wind," I lied.

Frall was just reaching the ground about then. He let go and walked closer. "Come here, Clista. You do know that I was kidding you, don't you?"

I knew no such thing, and I glared at him. Then I saw the twinkle in his eye. "You just said that to make me keep going, didn't you?" I asked, feeling an incredible relief as well as embarrassment that I'd been so easy to manipulate.

He nodded and took another step closer. "Of course, silly. I know there isn't anything you couldn't do if you set your mind to it."

What could I do then but forgive him? We both took a step and ended up in one of those mutually agreeable embraces. Unfortunately, Ms. Evans and my uncle were descending rapidly. She with not a single frozen moment. I broke away with a final, quick peck on Frall's cheek.

"Just wait," I said. "There will be payback time for that remark,"

Frall laughed. Then he caught my hand. "I look forward to it, Clista."

The moment my uncle landed, he was glaring at Frall. "Keep away from her," he ordered. "I don't like the way you're eyeing my niece."

Frall's eyes, which had only been smiling at me a moment before, suddenly blazed with anger. "Sir, I think you're overreacting. Maybe you're doing transference, which, as I understand, means shifting your own private thoughts for Ms. Evans to…"

"Shut up," my uncle thundered and stepped menacingly toward Frall.

Smog intervened, leading my uncle to the side. I did the same with Frall.

"We have to get along," I told him. "No matter how much he rides you. We have to not fight."

"He's pushing me, Clista. I don't know if I can keep holding back. He has no right to say the things he keeps saying to me. I know we're too young, but we have no choice. Sometimes, events change the order of everything. For us, it has. You know that, Clista. You feel it."

I nodded, but I wasn't exactly agreeing with him. I knew what the *Old Ones* wanted, but I also knew that they couldn't push me into something I wasn't ready for.

But I didn't try to explain that to Frall. We moved out, following the gully, heading where we were compelled to go.

"Clista, you do know that I wouldn't hurt you, right?" Frall asked a few minutes later.

"Hurt me? Of course. Stop worrying about it. My uncle's new to this guardianship business. I don't think he understands what his role is. He'll calm down when all this is over. Relax. Adults get all touchy about things when they're under stress — irrationally, I mean."

"No kidding. He rides me like I had the horns of a devil."

I laughed. Frall was being rather melodramatic, but we were walking at a good speed. The prickly feeling that I'd felt in my neck when we stopped settled back down to a dull ache.

Chapter Seventeen

We trudged on, always heading for the mountains, never able to see them but feeling the call of them. We knew their direction with the same certainty as if we had a compass rose or a Directional. My mouth grew parched. My stomach growled, but still, we walked, our feet pounding a steady rhythm on the soft forest floor.

Occasionally, monkeybirds scolded us, flitting from tree to tree to watch as we traveled through their territory. Once we saw a coogle. It snarled, jumped up into a tree limb, and sat there watching our passage, its sharp, pointed teeth grinning as we continued on.

At one point, the gully became too difficult to walk in. Then, we had to reverse our prior descent. That was an uneventful climb. When we reached the top, we took a break. Even Frall sat down then, I at his side, despite the glowering looks of my uncle.

Then, too quickly for me, we were up walking again, threading our way through the tall mystrend trees and heading for what? Going where?

About twenty minutes later, the forest began to change from ferns to tangled vines that hung down from the trees, draping everything like green-leaved streamers. Sometimes, the vines spread from tree limb to tree limb high above, forming hanging bridges for small animals. Other times, the vines traveled along the ground, filling in treeless space with thick shrub like growth. I saved Frall from more than one fall when his foot got caught in tangles of it, and he disconnected me when I became knotted in its tight, rope-like growth.

"How much farther do you think it is?" I asked at one point, wanting to know if the *Old Ones* were more communicative with Frall than with me. He just shook his head, shrugged, and kept going.

We came to water. We were both unsure whether to drink it. I touched the necklace and pictured drinking it, asking if it were safe, but there was only silence. The necklace did not heat up, nor was there an answer in my mind.

I could barely swallow. I knelt and put my hand in the water, stirring it longingly. "We should at least boil it," Frall told me.

The others behind us had been making their way through the vines very noisily. We had heard Smog cussing several times — each time he tripped, we later found out. Ms. Evans' higher pitched voice especially carried well. She'd been telling my uncle all about the school and the students who came to her for counseling. I stopped a moment to listen. My uncle's voice was too low and soft to be heard. I wondered if he was asking her questions that involved me.

I was thinking about that when my uncle suddenly sprang out of the bush. Of course, I screamed.

"What are you trying to do — scare us to death?" I panted, my heart pounding.

But Frall apparently hadn't gotten a good look at who was leaping out from behind the vines. He lurched at the body, grabbing for the knees.

"Stop it, Frall. It's my uncle," I called out, but the two of them were wrestling on the ground, turning over and over like writhing hands. "Smog!" I called, frantic that one of them would be injured.

Smog came charging through the foliage, ready to fight, dragging Ms. Evans like she'd been too slow. "What's going on?" he bellowed. "What happened?"

"Uncle Cristoff frightened us, and Frall attacked him. I don't know why they're fighting now. Stop them, please."

Luckily, he didn't have to. My uncle sprang up, dragging Frall into an upright position. "Knock it off, kid," he ordered, securing Frall with a chest-hugging diagonal arm hold.

Then he released Frall, throwing him to the side. My friend sagged and collapsed on the ground, heaving for breath.

"Sorry about that," my uncle said, grinning like a schoolboy. "I didn't know of any other way to stop you kids. You've been stampeding forward like a herd of grecks. I had to slow you down so we could all have a rest stop."

"Ever heard of talking to us?" Frall asked, spitting out a mouthful of dirt.

"Here, have a drink," my uncle told him, handing him the canteen.

The two of them were still glowering at each other, but it was a sure thing that my uncle had stopped us. I walked closer, putting out my hand for the water.

"Did you notice the stream? Do you think it's fresh water? I'd love to wash up in it, and maybe we could even fill up the canteen if you think it's good water," I said.

Smog walked closer to check it out. "Well, it is moving water. I suppose I could test it. How much water do we have left?" he asked my uncle.

Uncle Cristoff took the canteen from Frall and shook it. My hand waved up and down. I was dying of thirst. Couldn't he see that?

"Hey," I said. "My turn."

My uncle saw my expression and let out a laugh. Then he tossed me the canteen. "Not much," he said, "at least, not until we test the water. If the water's good, you can drink all you want."

Smog bent down, collected a sample, and used a water strip that issued an almost immediate chemical analysis. The water was potable. I drank most of the canteen. Water is the most delicious drink in the world when you're really, really thirsty.

All of us collected wood, cleared an area for a fire, and set about boiling the water so we could replenish our water container. That wasn't easy since we had no pot to boil it in. Smog had to find a suitable log, carve out the inside, and scoop the water into it. As that boiled, the sediment from the log's interior settled into the liquid. It didn't look inviting to drink. Guess whose job it ended up being to scoop out the bugs and tree dirt with a twig?

Actually, that was better than what my uncle and Frall had to do. They went hunting for food with a homemade spear that Frall made and my uncle's jet blaster. While they were gone, Smog went fishing, an equally unpleasant task. Only Ms. Evans was free from chores, but she set about to make sunhats for us, something I doubted any of us wanted.

I had never envisioned going native, but all of the students were given instruction in survival skills. It was a required course since there were many poisonous planets and even a few dangerous animals on Rwawan. Both Frall and I had taken the class the year before, but like all the other kids, we never thought we'd use any of the training. As I helped Ms. Evans with her hats, I tried to recall some of the class's more helpful hints.

My hands had gone into automatic by the time I started on the second hat. The vines were easy to weave in and out of the branches that formed each hat skeleton. The finished product might not be fashionable, but Ms. Evans had done a good job of bending the limbs so they not only framed the head, but stayed on easily.

I put down the hat I was working on and did another scoop out with my debugging stick. Then, I picked up the hat and continued my construction.

"Do you think the Academy is looking for us?" I asked.

Ms. Evans blinked as if she'd been thinking of other things. Then her eyes cleared, and she focused on me. "I hope so, Clista. I'm sure the police are. I don't know what the school will think. When you didn't come back, and then Frall disappeared, well, let's just say that someone will be putting all the pieces together and asking questions."

"I had a big test yesterday. I never studied for it."

"You can take it when you return, Clista. I'm sure your instructor will understand about your not being at school when he hears that you were being chased around the countryside by people with guns. That is an extremely valid excuse, and I'll be happy to write you a letter of proof."

"Will they be mad at you because you didn't show up?"

"I'm afraid so. I'm not sure they'll be as understanding in my case. It's possible I'll have to find a new position when we finally return."

"I'll write you a letter of proof for it. Okay?"

Ms. Evans laughed and started on another hat.

"Is that the fifth one? Are we done?" I asked.

Her eyes counted the pile, and she nodded. "I suppose we could make an extra, but there's no sense in carrying something we don't need. I'll just take some extra vines in case the forest opens up more and doesn't have any. Then, if a hat starts falling apart, I can make repairs."

"But how do you know that we'll be walking where there's no cover? We've been under the trees all day."

"It was something Smog said. Between the forest and the mountain where we're headed, there's a stretch of chaparral. I figure there's no sense us all getting sunburned noses."

I smiled and scooped out more bugs from the heating water. The evening air was getting chilly. I was very content to be sitting right next to the fire. I threw another log on it, tended to that, and settled back beside her to continue my weaving.

"Do you think Uncle Cristoff, Frall, and Smog will really catch something to eat? I'm so hungry."

"I think we're very lucky, Clista. I have perfect confidence in them. I can't think of anyone I'd rather be stuck here with," she said, laughing.

"That's just because you really like my uncle, don't you."

She blushed and looked down. "You have a point there, Clista. Do you mind too much?"

I studied her before I answered. It wasn't that I minded exactly. It was just that it seemed like everything had happened too fast — the cave-in, the necklace, communion with the *Old Ones*. Then I met an uncle I'd never met before. He became my guardian, and before I could adjust to that, he was wooing my school counselor. It was a lot to swallow in one gulp. I tried to explain it, but Ms. Evans seemed to understand perfectly.

"We won't be rushing into anything, Clista. Once this is over, anything between your uncle and me may just fade away. There are many romances built around stressful conditions. They're usually hollow. Don't worry about it."

"Hollow?" my uncle said, plopping down something he'd killed that I had no intention of looking at.

"I need to borrow you for a minute, Franca. Will you come with me?"

She didn't argue. She put down her hat, stood up, and looked Frall and me over. "Smog isn't around, you know," she warned my uncle.

"That's okay. Frall and I had a nice talk. Just exactly what you and I need right now."

My uncle's face was all dark and closed off. He looked angry. If I'd been Ms. Evans, I think I'd have said "no," but she went off with him, acting like he didn't scare her in the least.

"The water hasn't boiled yet," I said, scooping out another bug.

"Aren't you going to ask what your uncle and I talked about?" Frall asked, plopping himself down beside me.

"Was it bad? Did he lecture you again?"

"Actually, no. He wanted to know what my intentions were. He's really old-fashioned, you know."

I stirred the water with the stick, wondering if Frall would go on. The smell of the carcass was sickeningly strong. I put my stick down and moved back over to the hat I was working on. "All right," I said. "You're waiting for me to ask, aren't you? What did you say?"

"I told him 'yes.'"

I looked up at him. "Yes, what?"

"You're not ready for marriage, Clista. I know that, but I am. No matter how long it takes, I'll wait for you."

I laughed. "You're nuts, Frall. Marriage? You'd let the *Old Ones* push you into something like that? We're not even through our studies yet. We're way too young."

"Sometimes people know, Clista. I know."

The fire cracked. I jumped. Frall grinned at me.

"But I don't know, Frall, and I don't like being pushed. I mean, I like you and everything," I said softly, unsure how to explain what I was feeling without hurting him.

"I know," he said. "I told you. No pressure. I just thought you'd like to hear what I told your uncle. He's okay with it now."

"So you guys won't be fighting anymore?"

Frall grinned even wider. "I can't promise that," he laughed. "He's really protective of you, which is weird since he didn't even know you before your parents…"

I was glad that Frall didn't finish the sentence. I sighed and put down the hat. It was finished. All of them were done, ready for the long trek across a chaparral somewhere between here and the mountains.

"Thanks for telling me, Frall. And thanks for not expecting me to answer you right now about what our future looks like."

Frall laughed again. "You'll come around. The *Old Ones* have told me that. No pressure, though," he said, laughing again.

Frall had started skinning the dead animal. I couldn't bear to watch. I stood up and walked over to the dead tree we kept raiding for firewood. I started gathering up some more wood.

I was dumping it onto the pile when Smog came up carrying a string of fish.

"You had success," I said. "I don't believe it. What did you use for bait?"

Smog laughed, his eyes scanning the area. "Jerky," he said. "It works every time."

He raised a questioning eyebrow and asked, "Where are the others?"

"When my uncle came back with the dead thing, he took off with Ms. Evans. They had some talking to do," I said, rolling my eyes.

"I see. Smog set one of his fish on a log and began to carve it up. I turned away, ready to get more wood.

"Don't go far. I saw something considerably bigger than a monkeybird," he said.

"Like what?" Frall asked, looking up from his animal dissection.

"Have you kids ever heard of a gogo bear?"

"No way," Frall said. "Here? I thought they weren't found this far south."

"Tell that to the gogo bear," Smog laughed.

I scooted back closer. "What's that? How big is it?"

Smog looked up at me. He'd just caught off the head of the second fish. Its single eye stared up at me, all red-streaked with blood.

"Let's just say that if you need to go to the bathroom, you better take someone to watch your backside. Gogo bears are bigger than a flyby and more dangerous than your Cronoks Lab goons. You certainly don't want to run into one."

"What's that?" my uncle asked, startling us.

"I spotted a gogo bear. From now on, no one goes anywhere alone. One of those bears would scoop up a human in the blink of an eye, and I doubt that anything short of a singeing by a fire stick would stop them. We need to be extra careful tonight and tomorrow when we continue."

Ms. Evans sat down next to me. Whatever my uncle had told her must have gone down well. The lady was beaming from ear to ear.

"Everything okay?" I asked her needlessly.

She smiled. "Your uncle is a mighty persuasive man. You don't *really* mind if I like him rather a lot, do you?"

I laughed. What else was there for me to do? Even I, a teenager, could tell that she'd fallen in love with him. I hoped he didn't hurt her. I really knew nothing about him. Why had he never married? Why had he and my father never talked?

"Of course, I don't mind," I whispered back to her. "I'm happy for you."

She stirred the fire. It really didn't need it, but I tossed another log on, getting a yell from Smog. "Hey, knock it off, Clista. We need the fire to die down a little to cook dinner," he censured me.

"I thought you wanted a big fire to keep away the gogo bears," I retorted.

"She's right, you know," my uncle said, looking slightly worried. "Can you pick up some more kindling for it, Clista? Not far, of course, staying in sight."

I walked back over to the dead tree and selected some small pieces. I was thinking about what Ms. Evans had said and about Frall's words. I never heard the bear's approach. But when I stood up, I saw him standing there, sniffing at the raw meat. He roared at my presence. Of course, I screamed. I think we were pretty well matched. No one needed to rush to my defense. The bear fled, not even looking back over his shoulder.

Frall dropped the carcass he was working on and dashed over to me. "You okay?" he asked, sweeping me up in his arms.

I was shaking. The animal had looked even larger than Smog described. "He was standing there, right next to me," I sobbed into Frall's shirt. "He might have…"

My uncle and Smog were patting me, too. "It's all right now, Clista," my uncle said. "You did just right. I can't believe that he got so close to us."

"It must have been the meat," Smog said. "Gogos never come near a fire."

"This one did," I said, showing them with my arms spread apart how close he'd come. "He was standing right where you were! I even felt his breath on me. His teeth were longer than my hand."

"Bring her back to the fire," my uncle ordered Frall.

Admittedly, I was shivering, but I wasn't cold. Frall scooped me up and carried me, although I protested that I could walk. All I got for that was a forehead kiss. Then he set me down beside Ms. Evans. She put her arm around me and hugged me, too.

"No more firewood collecting for you," she said.

Normally, I would have argued with that. I hated being babied, but gogo bears have small, beady red eyes. The thought of the one who'd been standing there made me shiver again.

Smog dumped a pile of kindling by the fire. "She scared that one off. Good job, Clista."

"Not funny," I told him, but I smiled.

Sitting next to Ms. Evans, whispering about school and about how brave Frall had been to come to save me when he'd thought the beast was attacking, I calmed down, but I didn't get up to help again. That stupid bear had taken away my courage. I hated the thing.

The men cooked the meat and carried on as if nothing scary had happened. When the fish was done, we each had more than enough for dinner. The buckdore that Frall and my uncle had killed was cooked more slowly. It would be our meal for the following day. The smell of it permeated the small meadow we were in. I looked around, expecting to see the gogo bear coming back, but it didn't. I guess my scream was more potent than I'd known.

It was embarrassing to have my uncle tailing us when Ms. Evans and I used the bushes for our toilet, but we were both done quickly. Neither one of us wanted to see a giant rug with teeth popping up behind us. The thought of other animals, ones we hadn't even seen or heard of, made us even more cautious.

There were no ghost stories that night. I slept between my uncle and Ms. Evans. Frall and Smog were nestled at our feet. I thought it would be impossible to sleep. There were too many noises everywhere — the fire cracking, the stream babbling, twigs cracking as some beast moved nearby, and a monkeybird that kept scolding us from a tree. Unfortunately, he'd joined us just as we were bedding down. All those sounds were accompanied by the snores of Smog, who crashed almost immediately. But I was warm, and I felt safe. I closed my eyes — just for a moment and didn't wake up until morning.

Chapter Eighteen

In the morning, by the time the sun was peeking into the forest, my confidence had flowed back in. I accompanied Ms. Evans for our morning necessaries and then went back to the stream for a quick wash-up. We ate no breakfast but started out fording across the small stream barefoot. I was wishing for a cup of coffee when Ms. Evans mentioned it.

We'd both started to say the same thing at the same time, so we burst out laughing and everyone wanted to share the joke. Unfortunately, there wasn't one. The looks the others gave us told us that everyone was missing their favorite brew. But it was Smog who complained the loudest about the rotten bed.

That brought our laughter again. Since he'd been the first one to fall asleep and the loudest snorer, he got little sympathy. When he tried to defend himself, saying he didn't snore, we could hardly walk straight. It's strange what's humorous when you're dealing with too much stress.

When we made it to the other side of the stream, we put on our shoes and trekked on. The sun was already warm by that time. Smog told us we'd be having a hot day. We were glad when the forest thickened again, and we were able to walk under its canopy of leaves and vines.

Frall and I were leading once again, but the others stayed close. Remembering the gogo bear, I didn't want to leave them behind. I made sure that Frall didn't rev up his motor to speed us out of sight again. Glancing at my face, he kidded me, but not harshly. He knew how badly I'd been scared.

As we walked along, Smog passed out strips of the buckdore we'd cooked the day before. Its flesh once pounded and molded, didn't look like the bloody, dead carcass of the day before. Even so, I didn't want the meat, but my hunger pains changed my mind. I nibbled on it the same as Frall, glad that we had food.

The forest was dark under its heavy matt of leaves. We could no longer look up and see the sky. I breathed it in and smiled. I loved trees, the smell of pine, and the softness of the ground beneath my feet. A stray needle pricked my calf. I reached down and pried it out of my sock.

"What's the matter? You tired already?" Frall asked, smiling down at me.

I held the needle up, not saying anything, and jogged forward. It would have been more successful had Frall not swung his arm around me and swung me behind him.

Of course, it didn't stop there. It turned into a game, darting, dashing, and trying to be the first in line. The only thing is that it wasn't fair anymore. Frall had suddenly grown another inch or so, and his body had hardened and strengthened. I think he realized it about the same time I did. His eyes softened with the knowledge, and he eased off and let me go first.

"You seem different lately," I told him, not meeting his eyes but instead keeping my attention on the trail, or rather the lack of it.

"No doubt," he said. "There have been a lot of adjustments. Neither of us is the same, Clista, and we'll never change back again. We have to move forward, just like with the trail. We feel it calling us. Life is like that, isn't it?"

"I didn't want more change. I liked the way things were — or, at least, the way they used to be. I loved school. Now, maybe we'd never get to go back.

"Do you really think that's true, Frall? Will things never smooth out? Won't it ever be normal again?"

I stopped, having come to one of those spots where the vines were too thick to go forward. I glanced about, searching for an easier route. Frall brought out the knife my uncle had given him and whacked at it.

"Here, duck under. It gets better up ahead," he said.

We could hear Smog and the others coming up behind us. We shot forward, bending low. Inside, there was a completely sealed-in room, ivy hanging all about us. Frall pulled down a couple of strands to cover our entrance.

"What are you doing?" I giggled quietly.

"Sh!" Frall said before he gathered me in his arms. His lips were on mine before I realized what he was doing. We were suddenly shut off from everything inside our small, secret garden room. I should have slammed on the brakes, but I didn't. I savored the moment. Frall's kiss was a journey I didn't want to miss.

He didn't hold me long. His eyes stared down into mine. "You feel it, too," he said. "I knew it wasn't just me. And it isn't just the *Old Ones* pushing us together, is it?"

Frall's eyes were swallowing me. I felt the earth tremble, the sky move, and bells tingle in my ears.

"I don't know. Could we try it again?" I asked.

Once more, Frall bent his head, pulled me close, and our lips met and merged. The symphony played with a choir of a thousand angels.

When we broke apart, it was because we heard my uncle calling. We were both smiling.

"We're here," Frall called, and he turned me about. Without a word, we began cutting away an exit, heading always to the mountains. We'd just broken through and were slipping under our hewn outlet when my uncle came plunging into our hidden garden.

His eyes viewed us strangely, but he had no reason for suspicion. "Over here," he yelled for the others, and they came pushing their way inside our secret world. But Frall and I were plunging forward already. We didn't look back. Our secret had climbed inside us.

All that day, we walked, mostly hand in hand. Frall and I had passed beyond the questions of the day before. We both knew a bit about our future. Sometimes, that's comforting.

When we stopped in the late afternoon, it was by another small stream. It also tested out as good, safe drinking water, so we built a fire, heated up the water, and the men went off to hunt and fish. Ms. Evans and I stretched out by the fire, exhausted. We were too tired even to talk. We nodded off and only woke when Smog returned with fresh fish.

I felt guilty for my laziness and insisted on preparing what he'd caught. It wasn't as bad as I'd remembered. As long as I didn't think about the fish being once alive, I was able to concentrate on cleaning it.

This time, Smog had us put the heads and inside parts of the fish into our boiling water along with some greens that he'd found beside the stream. Amazingly, the smell of it cooking was delicious.

Frall and my uncle returned much later. Frall had a black eye. He said it was from the backward swing of a branch, but it looked more like a fist to me. I glared at my uncle. That night, when he gave the sleeping orders, I shook my head and went to sit by Frall.

There was an ugly silence following my uncle's sternly barked command to come lie down. I ignored the order, the silence, and his glower. Then when Frall lay down, I lay beside him, sandwiched in between Ms. Evans and Frall.

Smog, bless him, laughed. Then he brought up the rear, placing himself behind Frall. "No funny stuff, young man," he told Frall. "I sleep light."

The night was short. No monkeybirds screeched down at us. No gogo bears growled or attacked the fresh meat we were smoking on the low-burning fire. There was only the wonderful, perfect silence of forest trees and the melodious rhythm of the steady stream of water gurgling along its pebbled path.

Of course, I had, also the feel of Frall's arm around me, and his warm breath on my neck. The night was magical, full of placid dreams that flowed as sweetly as the stream of water in a peaceful happiness, which was something I hadn't felt for a long time.

The next morning, when I woke, Frall's eyes were on me. He smiled and kissed my cheek. "Thank you," he said. "I wanted you to do that, but I never thought you would."

I rose and washed my face in the creek. Smog had started a pot of bark and water. We drank it from a wooden cup we passed around. It wasn't coffee, and it was bitter-tasting, but we all felt better somehow. Perhaps morning needs the symbolism of the shared warmth of a blackish liquid.

Frall and I claimed our jerky from the meat he and my uncle had killed the day before and immediately set off, the inexplicable pulling we both felt making us nervous and irritable until we'd begun our day's journey.

My uncle tried to join us with words carefully controlled and stiffly cordial. Neither Frall nor I responded, and he finally dropped behind, apparently deciding to let time soothe my anger. But Frall's black eye looked worse that morning, and I had no patience for my uncle's domineering guardianship. Silence was the best I could do.

There was an easy, relaxed swing in our stride that morning. It was as if the previous day had ironed out our indecision, or I guess, at least mine, since Frall had already passed that border sometime before. It was stress relieving to be through all that, to know my mind and to feel right about it.

I started whistling, and Frall smiled. "I could feel your contentment before you expressed it. Isn't that strange?" he asked.

He was holding my hand as we walked along. I fingered the ring he wore, the *Old Ones'* ring, the one he'd found in the cave. I closed my eyes and tuned into his thoughts. He was right. I could feel his mind — not what he was thinking exactly, but what he was feeling, the emotion on the surface. I withdrew quickly, blushing.

He laughed. "I guess I'll have to tone that down. I don't want you reading *everything* I feel."

I looked away, although I felt his eyes still on me. He was studying me, worrying that I'd misunderstood.

"I do understand," I said. "I just can't think about that, not like you do."

He didn't laugh. He nodded. "I know," he said. "I agree, except I can't help having thoughts like that. They flit about. You'll just have to ignore them."

We were walking steadily, dodging vines and heavy limbs. Frall often held them back for me, reaching up further into the branches than I could. I liked that he did that for me. I liked the way he cared. I even liked his thoughts, the ones I shouldn't be reading.

I started whistling again. It was a strange song, one I'd heard somewhere, but I couldn't place it. It had no words that I could recall, just a haunting melody.

"I know that tune," Frall said. "It's from the *Old Ones*, isn't it? It's inside me, too."

I tripped over a fallen root. Frall kept me from falling, his arm coiled protectingly around my shoulder. "The *Old Ones*? I don't think so. It's probably from school or off the broadband or something."

"No, Clista. Listen to it harder. Don't you hear the difference? That's not one of our tunes. I bet no one else could even follow the melody. Let's try later, shall we? We'll see what your uncle thinks of it."

"Why did you fight with him?" I asked, leaping from one subject to another.

Frall stopped, unbuckled the water jug that Smog had passed to him, and took a drink before handing it to me.

"You can guess that. He's not crazy about having me in the family."

I handed back the jug, and Frall hooked it back onto his belt. "Want to take a break?" he asked.

I nodded and plopped down on a soft patch of moss-like greenery. "But I thought the day before he was okay with it."

"I don't want to talk about your uncle, Clista. He has nothing to do with us. You know that, don't you?"

I shook my head, not following where he was headed. "He's my guardian, Frall. How can you say that?"

"You don't know yet? The *Old Ones* haven't sent you any dreams?" he asked, staring into my eyes, searching for knowledge that wasn't there.

"Don't talk in riddles. Just tell me. What have you dreamed?"

Frall avoided my eyes. He looked up at the branches of a tree across the way. "Maybe I'm wrong," he said. "Maybe they're only dreams."

"Frall, tell me, please. You've always dreamed of the future when the *Old Ones* were part of it. Tell me."

He sighed, still not meeting my eyes. "Maybe we should move on. They'll be catching up any minute, and that's always a negative, especially with Cristoff."

"I refuse to budge from here until you tell me, Frall. You told it to my uncle, didn't you? That's why you guys fought."

"Refuse? You refuse to move, do you?" he said, laughing. "Do you know how easy it would be to lift you up and continue?"

He was teasing. I knew he wouldn't do that, yet I was also aware of how much his body had changed these days in the forest. His muscles bulged beneath the shirtsleeves. His chest had widened and broadened.

Ignoring that, I reached out and touched his arm. "Maybe the *Old Ones* want me to know, and you're supposed to tell me about it."

Frall looked down at me and sighed again. Then he glanced off into the bushes. "It's crazy. I can't believe it myself, but if the dreams are right..."

He knew the others were coming. I could tell from his manner. Then I heard them, too. Ms. Evans was trading recipes with Smog. Her voice was laughing and happy. But it wasn't Ms. Evans who arrived first. It was my uncle who pushed himself through the maze of vines and limbs. "Taking a breather?" he asked. "Good idea."

He walked closer and reached down into his pockets, pulling out a handful of nuts. "Here," he said. "We found these on the way. We all ate our fill and saved you some."

So saying, he poured some into each of our cupped hands.

"What are they?" Frall wanted to know.

I didn't care. I cracked one open with my teeth. The shell was thin. I tossed it down and chewed the nutmeat. It tasted sweet and crunchy. "Hey, these are great! Thanks, Uncle Cristoff," I said, smiling up at him.

He smiled back. "How about you and Ms. Evans take one of those little walks while I talk a bit with Frall," he half-asked, half-ordered.

"Why? So you can hit him again?" I demanded.

"Clista," Frall reproached me. "I don't need you to protect me."

Of course, that made me madder. I stood up and trudged off, stomping a bit, I'm afraid. I heard them following me.

Ms. Evans looked really happy to see me. "Clista," she called out. "I've been dying for your company. Smog is nice, but he's not the bathroom partner of my preference. Will you walk with me?"

Her eyes were on my uncle. I knew what she was up to, but I nodded in agreement. We strode off, Smog two steps behind us.

"Thanks for the nuts you collected for us, Ms. Evans and Smog," I said. "That was nice of you."

"Please, we're not in school now. Call me Franca."

I nodded and walked on. The forest suddenly seemed to have grown much quieter. I turned around to ask Smog about it, but he hushed me with his finger. "Be silent, ladies. I think we have company," he whispered.

Then we heard it. A jasmire —the largest cat of the Rwawan forest.

Franca and I turned frightened eyes on Smog, listening for his directions. "Hug the tree," he whispered, "and make no sound."

We did so, but our eyes continued to survey the space around us. Smog cracked a limb off two trees. The sound made both of us jump, but we didn't scream. Our mouths were too tightly closed.

Smog tiptoed toward us, his knife sharpening the top of each manmade spear. "Here," he said. "Pray you don't need them. I'm going to make a couple of others, just in case."

He returned to the lowered tree branch, but the jasmire was suddenly there. Its sabered mouth snarled in anger. Its eyes glared as it scanned the three of us. Then, it shifted and concentrated on me.

Its mouth opened, and it roared a challenge.

"Put up your spear, Clista. Be ready," Smog whispered.

I raised it, but I was still staring into the eyes of the jasmire. "Claydeah," I said. "Claydeah."

The jasmire took a step closer, growling and lowering its head, although its eyes didn't break with mine.

"Claydeah," I said louder. Then I shouted, "Claydeah!".

The jasmire's tail lowered down between its two back legs. It yelped, and then it leaped into the air in a spin that took it within a breath of Smog. But it wasn't attacking anymore. It was running. It sped back into the forest, whining like a frightened child.

"Whoa," Smog exclaimed. "What in the world did you just say to that critter?"

I shrugged. "It's what the *Old Ones* told me to say, but I really have to go to the bathroom now, Smog. Can you please turn around?"

He nodded, but he didn't speak. He just kept shaking his head and staring off in the direction the jasmire had fled.

When Franca and I returned, Frall and my uncle had apparently finished their talk. We all sat down to eat some jerky while Smog told them the story about the jasmire. I didn't want to hear about it anymore, but he persisted, going over and over it like it was an incredible miracle.

"So the cat didn't attack," I finally snapped at him. "Maybe it wasn't hungry. Maybe we just lucked out."

"There was no luck to it," Smog said. "I believe in your power, Clista. I believe now wholeheartedly."

It wasn't long before we continued on. I pumped Frall for information, but he refused to discuss what had occurred between my uncle and him, and he also wouldn't tell me the things he'd been steadily dreaming. Frustration comes in many packages, the biggest of which is unanswered questions.

Later, when we stopped for the night, there was no discussion about the order of sleeping. I sank down next to Frall, Franca at my other side. If my uncle glared, it was too dark to see. There were no stars, at least not under our canopy of vines. Frall's arm almost immediately slipped about me, and he slid me close. I felt his lips on my neck, and I smiled. Then, I slipped contentedly into sleep.

Chapter Nineteen

In the morning, Frall was already up when I woke. So was everyone else. I rose, yawning. "Why didn't you get me up?" I asked, but no one answered. Franca, busy with the fake coffee and turning the cooking meat, only waved and smiled.

"Frall was up early and went fishing," Franca told me as I yawned my way over to her. "We have a good breakfast for a change. Smog left to see if he could find more nuts. He said he knew where to look, and your uncle and Frall just went down to the water to refill our canteens."

Franca poured and passed me a cup of the bark coffee. I sipped, expecting the same bitter taste as before, but the brew tasted sweeter.

"This is good," I commented. "What did you do to it?"

She laughed. "That was Smog's invention. He dumped in a handful of nuts. It really does improve the flavor, doesn't it?"

I passed the cup back to Franca, and we sipped companionably for a moment. Then we took our trip into the bushes, one guarding while the other one did what was needed.

We washed up back at the camp as if we were dwelling in civilized conditions, laughing as we used the pink blossoms Smog had brought us with the assurance that they were like soap. Both of us tested the flowers on our faces. They not only had a pleasant smell but also left our skin soft and tingling pleasantly.

Then, it was time to turn the meat. The smells were delicious. Franca scooted a cooked fish onto a broad-shaped leaf. In a minute, it was cool enough to tear pieces off. We nibbled carefully so we didn't choke on the tiny bones.

Frall and my uncle returned a while later carrying dead trophies of several small creatures they'd caught down by the water. "No time to cook them now," my uncle said. "Isn't Smog back yet?"

We waited and waited, even putting out the fire so we could leave the moment he arrived, but he didn't return. Frall and I were just heading out, no longer able to still our restless need when Smog finally showed ups, naked waist up, and carrying a bundle of something inside his shirt. I was curious about the find and wanted to hear what had kept him, but Frall was so impatient, he jerked me forward.

"Hold it," Smog cried out, chasing after us. "I hit the jackpot, kids."

Frall ignored him and kept going, swinging me forward. But Smog stopped Frall and shared his loot, a bundle of thin-skinned nuts. What a treat! Unfortunately, Frall and I had no place to put them. My clothes had no pockets, and Frall's jeans already held his precious knife and some fishing twine Smog had given him.

No problem. Ms. Evans had washed everyone's socks that day. Ours were dangling from Frall's belt loops. He handed one over impatiently, and Smog filled it up. A bag of nuts was added then to Frall's belted waist.

We set off at a half-run, which I knew I couldn't sustain. I complained about it, but Frall razzed me, calling me "lazy" asking if I couldn't keep up because I was a *girl*. I knew he was only teasing. I didn't get mad this time, but the truth is that I didn't feel well.

My leg muscles weren't throbbing as they had been for days, but my back hurt, and I felt achy all over. I didn't want to admit that. Frall was in a strange mood, overly bossy, and already annoyed at the lateness of our start. I tried to ignore the way I felt. I kept going, plodding on, doing my best to keep up with him.

We were hand in hand as usual, the others following at a distance. It was the way that Frall demanded it. He'd told my uncle that he couldn't focus clearly, with all of them distracting him. I felt the pull of the *Old Ones* the same as Frall did, but he was the one who always seemed to take the lead, to push us forward. On that day, I cared even less about who led and who followed.

We walked several hours like that, Frall slowing down after it was clear the others were a good distance behind. Several times he complained, though, about my lagging. I'd speed up a bit, but I couldn't equal his speed, not that day.

The air was warmly shaded, not uncomfortable, but I felt sticky and hot and even worse as we continued on. About an hour later, I finally recognized the problem when my cramps started. It was a familiar ache and one that I had absolutely no provisions for.

"I need to talk with Franca," I told Frall, stopping and looking behind us.

"Just go in the bushes, Clista. I won't watch, I promise," he urged.

My face grew red. I didn't know how to tell him my problem. "You don't understand," I said. "I need to talk to her *now*. I need her."

I guess it had already started. Frall's eyes got big, seeing the front of my pants. "You're bleeding," he said suddenly. "Darn, I'm sorry, Clista. I've been a bear today. I didn't know why you were being so slow. Could you use leaves?"

He was looking at me strangely, not embarrassed like I was, but as if he was intrigued by it.

I suddenly couldn't stand his presence. I moved away from him and sat down, shaking my head. "I don't know what to do, but I don't want to talk about it. Please, just get Franca, and don't tell anyone. Just get her."

"I won't leave you alone, Clista. You know that. It would be even more dangerous in your condition. Wild animals will smell the blood. The others will be coming through the vines in a minute."

It was all so stupid. Frall hadn't done anything, but I started to cry. I was having horrible cramps, much worse than usual, and I felt unbelievably miserable. Bleeding all over my clothes was just the last straw.

Frall walked over to me and touched my shoulder, wanting to console me, but I jerked away. "Leave me alone," I cried, swatting at his hand. He stepped back and began to pace like a restless jasmire.

Smog was the first to come through the vines. He must have heard my tears. "What's wrong?" he demanded.

"I'm not allowed to say but go get Franca. Clista needs her."

In a minute, she came running, and as soon as she understood the problem, she sent the men away. I hated being a wimp, but I was so glad she was there. Franca even had an aspirin in her backpack and more clean socks to use for my needs. With wet vine leaves and some water, I cleaned myself off, although there was little I could do about my sticky, stained pants.

It wasn't time for a rest period, but we took one anyway. I sat, drank some water, ate some jerky, and finally, unenthusiastically agreed to go forward.

But it wasn't easy. Frall kept trying to touch me, and I couldn't bear to have his contact. Even when he was only just there beside me, he irritated me. I preferred walking beside Franca — that seemed to relieve some of my crankiness.

However, it soon became evident that Frall had been correct. When he and I didn't walk together by ourselves, the group ended up going in circles. After discovering that fact, we sat down to rest, disappointed with our failure. Smog set off to explore. He found us a small stream, and we backtracked to it. Then we quit for the day. I was relieved, although I could tell that Frall was bugged, but my cramps were back, and Franca had no more aspirin.

Luckily, it's true that all things pass — even the bad ones. The next day was better than the first. My cramps were gone, and I got used to dealing with the problem. At each stop, I washed out the socks I was using and hung them up to dry. Hanging over the fire, they dried quickly, but during the day, when we didn't stop to build a fire, Frall would carry the damp socks on his belt.

That bothered me, but not as much as the way the socks chafed my legs. No matter how much I used the flower blossom soap on them, the socks dried rough and stiff. But having rough socks was better than not having anything to stop the flow down my legs.

It also meant that Frall and I had become a team again. He shrugged off my tears and bad temper from the day before and more or less ignored the temporary breach in our friendship. Again, his hand held mine, and he teased me with sweet smiles and looks that, sometimes, made me feel dizzy.

A few days later, when my period was over, we came out of the heaviest part of the forest. The trees became sparser. Blooming plants replaced the ferns, and the vines no longer tried to trip us or halt our progress forward. The scenery was beautiful. We heard the monkeybirds again and several other small creatures chattered down at us from the treetops. I placed flowers in my hair and savored the peat moss smell all around us, laughing because I felt good again.

Many times, as we walked through the area of less dense forest, we saw jasmires. They seemed to like watching us, although none of them ever came close again. Their eyes were nightlights through the darkness, and their hunting snarls, the music of our nights. We didn't see any more of the gogo bears, but my uncle, several times, found their tracks. So, always, as we walked through the forest, we were alert and wary.

On day eleven, if we'd kept track correctly, we came out of the woods. For the first time, we saw the flat, sand-colored chaparral that Smog had told us about. We stepped out onto its soft, dry, sandy dirt, and in hours, the muscles in our legs were cramping. Smog stopped us and showed us how to rub each other's calves to relieve the pain.

I didn't mind doing that for Frall, but when his fingers took away the ache in my legs, his eyes on me were overly hot. It embarrassed me and made me blush. I wished someone else could massage my pain.

The hats Franca and I had earlier fashioned were, for the first time, appreciated. The men stopped making fun of them and yanked them further down over their sunburned noses. Otherwise, we had little relief from the burning sun, except underneath the chaparral's lightly populated trees. We hugged them and rested beneath their shade. On the second day, the intense heat forced us to change our usual pattern. From then on, we had to walk in the dark and sleep during the day.

We worried about finding water, for the chaparral stretched out as far as the eye could see, but the closer we came to the mountains, the more streams and rivulets we found. It quickly became apparent that water was not a problem. The biggest difficulty proved to be Frall's increasingly rotten temperament.

Throughout the forest, he'd been his usual self — mainly courteous and friendly, but in the chaparral, he began to snap at everyone. I became cautious of talking with him because his tongue had turned so sharp and cynical. I no longer wanted to be by his side, knowing he'd probably say something that would bring me to tears.

Several times, my uncle drew him aside and lectured him about his attitude, but that did no good. I kept thinking that maybe Frall had changed because he wasn't sleeping well. I still lay next to him during the sleeping times, and I heard him tossing and turning. Often, he'd rise up angrily and storm away, ignoring the others' concerns about his safety.

However, when he came back a while later, he'd often fondle my hair or give me a half-smile and a pat. Then, most often, his arm would hold me close, and I'd hear the quick beat of his heart. It often played the symphony for my dreams.

Crossing the wide expanses of the chaparral seemed to last forever, although it actually took fewer days than our forest jaunt. But we were vastly relieved when we reached the base of the mountains. Their coolness washed over us and brought back our smiles. Even Frall seemed more himself by the time we reached their shadows.

The mountains had been our beacon, and both Frall and I were confused. We'd spent so many days traveling there and listening to the mysterious call. Now, all those days seemed wasted, for there were no *Old Ones* waiting for us. For the first time, Frall and I didn't know what to do. No inner voices guided us. They were silent.

That night, Frall slept with his back to me, and it was I who couldn't sleep. I rose up in the pitch of dark and stumbled away from my sleeping friends and family. I sat apart on a boulder, watching the flickering of the campfire. I was tired, worn out from our travels, yet too antsy to lie down and shut my eyes. I couldn't sleep. Instead, I listened.

I suppose I'd been sitting there at least an hour before I heard it. *Waken your mate and come to us,* the voice inside my mind called. I shook my head, thinking I'd only dreamed it. Could a person fall asleep sitting up?

But Frall rose up and came to me. "You heard them, didn't you?"

"I thought it was a dream," I said as I stood.

"They call. We must go, Clista. Come."

I argued with him. How could we walk away without telling the others? And Frall had been so strange lately. I didn't feel our bond as tightly. I pulled away from his arms and stood apart, stepping back as if to be by myself.

"I understand. I'm sorry," Frall said, slipping up behind me, his arms once again encircling me. "Remember when you had your period and wouldn't let me close to you?"

"Don't talk about. . ."

"Sh. Listen to me, Clista. There are times when we can't communicate our needs. We're still young. This is new, but it will get easier. I love you. I want you. I need you. Do you understand that? Can't you trust me? Can't you forgive me?"

I sighed, unstiffening a bit. He felt it and turned me around. His lips pressed against mine. They called as surely as the *Old Ones*. They called me back to Frall. We pressed against each other tightly. My mind plunged into his. I knew then. The *Old Ones* told me. My heart commanded me to trust.

213

When Frall eased the kiss so he could whisper in my ear, I nodded. "Okay. I trust you, Frall. I know you're right. We have to go."

The others were still sleeping. I thought that was very strange. My uncle and Smog both slept like cats, one ear listening for sound. I questioned Frall. He laughed.

"We could probably yell, and they wouldn't wake. They sleep under the *Old Ones'* spell. They will not awaken until we return."

"But what if…"

"There will be no danger to them. This place is sacred. They will be fine until we come back. You know that, Clista. You're not listening to the *Old Ones*, are you?"

I buried my head on Frall's shoulder. "I'm afraid. That's silly after all this time, isn't it?"

Frall tightened his arm hold. "No. They ask a lot of us, Clista. You and I haven't had time to talk for at least a week. I should have told you."

"That they want us to marry?"

I couldn't see him. The night was dark, with no stars or moons. Yet, I felt his nod, and I knew there was more.

"They want us to live with them, Clista. To study and learn. I'm willing. Are you?"

I stopped, but Frall pulled me forward. "We have to keep going, Clista. I want you to say 'yes.' I need you to say 'yes.' Please. Will you?"

"But I don't understand. Go where?"

Frall sighed. "They'll explain. I don't know why they send me the dreams and tell you nothing. They want us to go together. You know that. They've told you that much. Where they'll take us, I don't know, but we'll be safe. They won't allow us to be harmed. I trust them, Clista."

I tripped over a rock, and Frall saved me from the fall. It was just like in the forest. I melded closer to him, feeling the bond we'd shared so often.

"My uncle . . ."

"I'll be with you, Clista. Isn't that enough?"

I was thinking about that as we entered the side of the mountain where some bushes had covered a small cave. We crawled inside and then stood up and walked further into the depths. I could hear the *Old Ones* then more clearly. They were murmuring to me, calling me, asking me to come to them.

"They killed my parents," I said, stopping suddenly.

Frall caught me just as I was about to turn around and run back out. "You know that's not true. They didn't do that. Cronoks Lab killed your folks and mine."

"We don't know that. Your parents might be…"

"They're gone, Clista. The *Old Ones* told me in the chaparral. Cronoks Lab shot them when they tried to escape."

I threw myself into Frall's arms and sobbed for his pain. "Why didn't you tell me? Why did you carry that wrapped up inside you? Why?"

"I wasn't ready, Clista. Not to share it. You didn't even know them. How could you mourn their death?"

I felt the tears on his face and knew that he, too, was crying. We held each other and wept, grieving together as we should have before.

"This is good," a grave voice said from behind us.

Frall and I separated and turned to stare. A Goliath man stood before us, one clothed entirely in yellow from his shoes to his shirt. His face was covered with a long, gray beard; his eyes were as blue as sapphire blooms.

"Who are you?" I asked, but I knew.

He smiled and nodded. "I am Thornic. Welcome, Clista and Frall. We are pleased you have come. We have been waiting a long time."

He gestured for us to walk beside him, and so we did, Frall and I walking hand in hand. He noticed that and nodded his head. "This makes us very happy that you have found each other. We worried through the flatland. You seemed so separate."

"How did you know?" Frall snapped, his irritation evident.

"Ah, yes. The young practice frequent, sharp spurts of rebellion. How relaxing you must find them. We have not engaged in such for many millenniums. We shall savor your sparks of anger, enjoying their energy and the fervor in which you harbor them so closely to your souls."

I don't think his words comforted Frall. If anything, it probably kindled his annoyance, but he took several deep breaths, squeezed my hand, and calmed down.

"We left my uncle and the others sleeping. You'll take care they're not hurt?" I asked.

Thornic smiled down at me. "Gentle Clista, I promise they will be safe. We will not allow more of your friends and loved ones to be harmed."

Once more, Frall squeezed my hand, and I signaled back. Thornic took no notice. He continued on, stepping firmly into the deeper darkness of the cave.

"Ah, don't you have a light?" Frall asked.

Thornic stopped, clapped his hands, and the whole cavern lit up. "Sorry," he said. "I forget sometimes."

The walls were sparkling. Frall whispered that it was probably gold. Thornic overheard and stopped. "Yes, you can find gold, copper and several jewels in the cavern's rock. Would you like some?"

Of course, we both nodded. He pricked at the wall with his fingers. A ruby fell, and then a rock of gold. He handed the gem to me and the rock to Frall. "Satisfied?" he asked, "or would you care for more?"

"Are they real?" I questioned. "Why would you give them to us?"

Thornic laughed. "You may have all the ore and jewels you want, children. We only wish you happiness."

"Bring back my parents then," I said, "and Frall's."

Thornic stared into my eyes. "Life cannot be created by us. When a soul departs, it is gone. Only the inanimate can we gift you with. I am sorry for your grief, children, but we cannot fulfill that wish."

"But you didn't kill them, did you?"

"Kill them?" he repeated, taking a step back from me in shock. "We do not take life ever. Life is sacred."

"Clista didn't mean that. Please don't be offended," Frall assured the *Old One*.

Thornic studied me. "She needed an answer. I see that. It was the *Tworst of Trent*, Clista, that took your parents and Frall's."

"How can that be possible? I buried it in the Stormian Caverns. How could you say it was responsible for Frall's loss?"

Thornic sighed. "I should have waited for this discussion. I see that now. You are both tired and yet I keep you standing here in conversation.

"Ah, well. The *Tworst of Trent* vibrated evil. It caused the ruin of Cronoks Lab. They are polluted now. I believe that is how you would say it."

I had been rude, and I felt sorry. I reached out and touched Thornic's garment to ask his forgiveness, but my hand passed through him. I gasped and stepped away.

"Do not be frightened," he said. "I am not here. I am still on OUR planet, a place far from Rwawan, but I wanted you to know me as a being like yourselves."

"You're not real?" I asked, struggling for breath.

"I am as real as you, but I am not where you stand."

"You're a holograph, right?" Frall asked.

"You made us walk for weeks just to see a holograph? You could have come to us," I said angrily.

"No, Clista, your journey was necessary. You were not ready when you stood inside the Stormian Caverns. This place is another site where I could come before you. There are only four such locations on your planet, and one has now been destroyed."

"But that's what I needed to ask you. Please, could you let Mr. Grenan go? I didn't mean to trap him inside. It was wrong to do that. Can you let him go even though he's in the other place? I mean, he's not dead, is he? Please?"

"Come. I have kept you here too long. We must continue to the throne room. You will be more comfortable there."

He began walking faster then. We could barely keep up with him. I think his speed was intended to keep Frall and me from asking more questions.

When we entered the room he'd spoken of, there was no doubt why he'd called it the throne room. Two huge stone chairs towered over a chamber bigger than a sports field.

"Sit down," Thornic ordered.

I looked about me, not wanting to sit on a throne, but Frall dropped my hand, climbed up the stairs, and went to sit on one of the huge stone seats. "He wants us to," Frall said, looking back at me. But I didn't move. It didn't feel right to sit on it. Yet, the room was large, and I was frankly ill at ease. I followed Frall and stood beside him hesitantly.

Frall laughed. "You're not going to sit?' he asked.

When I shook my head, Frall reached over and laughingly pulled me down in his lap. "Okay," he said, "then I'll share my throne with you."

Thornic was still standing there watching us. He smiled at our exchange. "Would you like me to sit, or does it make you uneasy if I stand?" he asked. "Since, as you have discovered, I am merely a holograph, it really does not matter to me, but I wish you to be comfortable."

I shifted, hoping I wasn't too heavy on Frall's legs. I certainly didn't care what Thornic did.

"Sit still," Frall chuckled at me, pulling me closer with arms that encircled me. "And you're not in the least heavy," he added picking up my thought.

I felt silly perched on Frall's lap, but I took a moment to scan the room we'd entered. First off, the ceiling was at least fifteen meters above us, so far up, I had to tilt my head to study it. The walls, on every side of us, looked to be made of stone with some kind of white mortar in between. There were no decorations in the room: no paintings, tapestries, or murals, and the room seemed odorless with no breeze or air circulation, yet its temperature felt just right.

"You can stand or sit. It doesn't matter to us," Frall was telling Thornic, "but could you answer Clista's question, please. She's been fretting over Mr. Grenan for some time."

Thornic sighed. "I am aware of her concern. However, although he is not dead, the man cannot safely be freed. He is permeated in evil."

"We are working on a solution to that problem, Clista. We do not like it that we have erred so greatly in respect to you. We shall restore the man as soon as possible, not because he is worthy, but because it brings you grief. Such a burden should not be felt on your delicate shoulders. Believe me, it is *our* responsibility."

I wiped a tear from my eye. I was trying very hard not to cry again, but I was so very relieved to hear that I hadn't killed Mr. Grenan. "Thank you," I said as I swabbed at my eyes.

Thornic nodded. "I have not been a good host. What would you like to eat and drink? I can supply whatever you would most prefer."

Frall laughed. "A cold root beer and a hot fudge sundae."

"Oh, that would taste so good," I said.

Thornic smiled. We didn't see him gesture, and he didn't call out, but almost instantly, an automated man came toward us with exactly what we'd both ordered. I stood up in preparation.

"A table would be nice, would it not?" Thornic said, and immediately, one was there in front of us with two seats and yellow place settings.

"Sit down," Thornic said. "We shall talk in a moment. But first, you two must enjoy yourself. You have experienced great hardship for a number of days."

I guess that was the time to question why he'd forced us to endure it, but the ice cream was waiting, and the fudge was hot. Frall and I spooned it up and ate and drank until we were stuffed. Then we sat back and sighed with contentment.

"Where did he go?" I asked, just noticing that Thornic had disappeared.

"He left for a reason, Clista. He uh…"

Frall was looking very strange. He'd paled, and his face looked feverish.

"What's wrong?" I asked.

Frall didn't answer. He stood up and walked toward me. "You know how the *Old Ones* talk to me sometimes, Clista?"

I nodded. "Thornic told me to get on with something I haven't really done right. Not because I didn't want to, but because I don't think you're ready. Except they don't want me to put it off anymore. They want me to…"

"What? What is it?"

Frall stepped closer. He took my hand. I thought he was going to pull me up, but he didn't. Instead, he went down on one knee and said, "Please, Clista. Please, will you marry me?"

Frall's dark hair was shining in the room's light. It was almost a romantic scene from a novel set in a castle, but . . .

"Oh, stop it," I cried out, bolting up. "You know we're too young for that."

Frall hadn't let go of my hand. "Sit down, Clista. I'm trying to do this properly. Please."

I sat back down on the chair at the small table where we'd eaten our ice cream, but I was still shaking my head. "No."

"They want us to go with them, Clista. I told you that. They want us to marry first. Please say 'yes.' You know how I feel about you. I love you. I want to do this. They're not forcing me."

"But I don't want to. I'm not ready." I knew my words were a slap in his face, after he'd offered me his charming knee bent proposal, but I wasn't about to do something I didn't want to do. How long had I known Frall? As my mother used to say, "A mere drop in the bucket of time."

Frall sighed, nodded his head, and stood up. "I tried," he said, shrugging. "I told you she wasn't ready." I knew he was talking to Thoric, even though the Old One seemed to have disappeared.

"Too bad, too bad, but she cannot be forced," came a voice from all corners of the chamber. I hunted for the holographic image Thoric had earlier shown us, but I still couldn't see him.

And then, suddenly he was back, with a flicker of light that grew more solid in appearance as I stared. "You do not find Frall pleasing?" Thoric asked.

I sighed. "Of course I do. I love him, but I'm only eighteen. That's way too young for. . ."

"I see. In this time period, people marry later in life perhaps, but there were other periods where females married at age fourteen," Thornic said, eyeing us peculiarly. "But the here is now. I see that. But this does complicate things."

"What things?" I asked, gazing at Thornic, then Frall.

"We will need your uncle as a chaperone, I suppose," Thornic said.

"Could you please explain what you're talking about a bit more? I'm feeling really lost here. Frall says you want us to go with you to your planet? Why?"

"You have been chosen as our queen. The necklace rests on your neck. Frall wears the crest on his finger. We must prepare you both. You are our mated couple."

"Prepare us for what. What do you mean, queen? I'm just a kid. None of this makes any sense."

Thornic nodded. "There is much you will learn when you are on Flagan Pren. We will explain it all to you then. You will adapt and acquire the knowledge that you keep asking for. Be patient, child.

"But first, I must call to the others. Must they all come with you?" Thornic asked.

"The others? You mean Smog, Franca, and my uncle?" I questioned.

Thornic nodded again.

"You can't make your uncle go without Franca, Clista. They love each other," Frall urged.

"Why would I make anyone go?"

"Because you've refused me," Frall said, looking crushed.

I went to him and circled his waist with my arms. "I didn't refuse you, Frall. I really do love you. It's just…"

"I know. I told them you weren't ready. Maybe that's my fault because of the way I acted in the chaparral. I closed you out then, but we can't change that now, can we?"

"It had nothing to do with that, Frall. I understand now. You'd just learned about your parents. You had every right to be . . ." I was trying to finish diplomatically, but he beat me to it.

"A grump?"

"It is done," Thoric said, breaking into the discussion Frall and I were having.

"I have awakened the others. They come now," Thornic continued. "I must go to them and help them through the cave." So saying, Thornic winked out.

"Oh, boy, do I ever know someone who's going to be super angry, Clista," Frall warned.

"My uncle? He's going to be furious. I think we should hide."

"I think you should marry me. Then you wouldn't have to hide, Clista. You and I could go off to Flagan Pren, and we wouldn't need to deal with your uncle. We'd have each other."

I backed away. "You're pressuring me, Frall. Don't. Maybe the *Old Ones* are making you do this. Did you ever think about that? Maybe you don't *really* want to get married, and they're…"

Frall huffed as if I'd hurt his feelings, even more so than when I'd refused his proposal. "Don't say that, Clista. You can tell me you don't want to. You can tell me 'no' a hundred times. But don't tell me what *I'm* feeling. I know the truth of that. You'd know it, too, if you looked inside me and read my thoughts."

"But what if your thoughts are because of them?"

"Darn it, Clista. You're making me mad now."

I guess I would have had a response to that, too, but Frall kept me from giving it. He seized me in an embrace, one that took my breath away. He lifted me up and held me there over his head. Then he captured my lips.

When he had thoroughly kissed me, he set me back down and said, "Any questions now?"

It was very hard to be firm under those conditions. I was about to cave in. "Yes" was at the tip of my tongue, but something still prickled. Maybe it was my mother's face, the thought of what my father would say — or my uncle. It was just that I knew marriage was wrong — wrong at that moment, wrong for me. I loved Frall. I wanted his kisses. Sure, it would be easy to give in to him, but I also knew that I wasn't ready for that kind of commitment.

He read the answer in my face and turned away, disappointment in his eyes. "I love you, Clista," he said, not looking at me. "I'll wait for you. I'll wait as long as it takes."

With those words lying there in the air between us, it was even harder to keep saying 'no.' My heart hurt. I felt Frall's pain and mine in a kind of echo that reverberated back and forth between us.

"I'm sorry," I said. "I'm so sorry."

He turned back to me and pulled me up against him. We were hugging each other like that when my uncle and the others came in. It wasn't a passionate embrace but a comforting one. It just said that we cared for each other.

Chapter Twenty

Of course, my uncle didn't understand that. He started yelling right off and strode directly to us, ready to tear us apart.

Thornic moved to block him. "You will not scold the queen with that voice. She is above reproach, although we find it disappointing that she has refused him."

My uncle's face turned a dark red. "Disappointing?" He coughed, choking on the word. "Listen, you; I don't know why you think my niece should be ready to marry at the drop of a hat. She has a lot more sense than that," my uncle thundered, stepping to the side so he could reach me.

"Enough," Thornic said, holding up his hand. "Be still," he commanded, and my uncle's eyes bulged from his efforts to continue. "It is necessary for you to accompany her to Flagan Pren. I do not wish for your presence, but under the circumstances, it would be better if you would join us. Will you voyage with your niece?"

My uncle was apparently frozen to the spot, but it didn't keep him from giving his opinion. "No way," he yelled. "Clista's not going anywhere except back home — preferably to *my* house since hers seems rampant with danger. Now let me go."

Thornic was patient. He sighed, just like a human. Then, he restated the problem and tried again. "You do not understand, Cristoff Pragan. Your niece *must* come with us. She is to be trained. Her mate will journey with her, also. It is important for both of them to meet the *Old Ones* and to discover what capabilities they have been given. I ask for your presence merely to provide the queen with an acceptable guardian."

I was trying hard not to react to the scene. There was too much information being served right and left. I couldn't take it all in. I wasn't sure if I should demand that Thornic let my uncle go or just keep quiet. I was almost about to argue when, instead, I let out a great, heavy yawn.

My uncle glanced at me. "This is crazy. Can't you see she's exhausted? Let us go.

"It's the middle of the night. We're all tired. Do you have beds around here, Thornic? We need to sleep. We can talk about this madness of Clista being *a queen* and whether the kids should or shouldn't be traveling somewhere when it's daylight," my uncle said, giving into a yawn that all of us reciprocated.

Thornic bowed his head and said, "As you like. Follow me. I shall provide you with such needs."

Thornic gave Franca and me a room with twin beds. I suppose the others got adequate bedding. I didn't speak to Franca. I simply explored the bathroom, learning that there was a shower for the morning, tried out the luxurious indoor plumbing, washed my face, and then slid under the covers of the bed, laying my head on a real pillow. It was heaven. I wish I could have stayed awake to appreciate it more fully.

In the morning, when I woke, Franca was sitting up on her bed, staring at me. "Did you hear the things the *Old One* said last night?"

I swung out of bed, laughing. "It's all about the necklace," I said. "If you were wearing it, they'd name you queen. Do you want it?" I joked.

She didn't answer. Instead, she threw another question. "Are you going to this place they've named, then? Will they force you?"

I didn't know the answer to either question. It didn't look like I had a lot of choice, yet they hadn't made me marry Frall. I shrugged.

"Did you notice that there's a shower in the bathroom?" I asked her. "I get first dibs."

She nodded. "He brought us clothes," she said. "He's rather a nice old man, don't you think?"

I hadn't noticed the clothes. I went to inspect them. They were both dresses, one in blue and the other in a cherry-red. It was obvious which was meant to be mine. Thornic had written my name on the blue one.

The note also mentioned "other garments." I pulled out the drawer to see what else the Old One had brought us. Everything we needed was there, including slippers to match the dresses.

"Be right back," I told her, grabbing up the underclothes that were in my size. Franca stood up, rubbing her back. Then she started in on bending and stretching exercises in what was obviously some kind of exercise routine.

When you haven't had a shower in weeks, water is the biggest luxury you can imagine. I spent much longer than I'd planned soaping up, rinsing off, and washing my hair.

When I came out, Franca went in, smiling in anticipation. I called out that it was heavenly, but I'm not sure she heard me. She began singing the moment the water flowed.

I slipped the new gown over my head. It was perfect. I wasn't the kind of girl who wore dresses much, but the material was soft and velvet-like. It had sparkles in it that glowed as the room's light fell across it. As I walked, the material flowed with me. I felt beautiful. Such was the quality of the exquisite gown.

I towel-dried my hair some more and then let it fall. I knew it would dry quickly in the warmth of the room. There were two brushes in the drawer. I set to work detangling.

When Franca came out, she was also pleased with her gown. Unlike me, she said she adored dresses. "Wait until your uncle sees me in this," she sighed happily.

That reminded me of something Frall had said the day before. "If my uncle did decide to go with us, would you be willing to go, too?"

"To another planet?" Franca asked, staring at the blank wall. "I don't know. He'd have to ask me. He'd have to want me there. Yesterday, it sounded like he was still. . ."

Someone knocked just then. We looked at each other and shrugged. "Come in," Franca called out. It was Frall and my uncle. They came striding in, as did Smog, who'd been hanging back a bit.

"Wow!" Frall said, taking in my changed appearance. "Wow!"

My uncle's eyes moved over me. His were quietly approving but not as appreciative as when he saw Franca. Then his eyes lit up, and he grinned.

"Well, ladies, I don't know how far you can walk in those outfits, but I must say it's a pleasure to see you in them."

"I second that," Smog said, crowding into our circle.

Frall's eyes were saying much more than my uncle's words. I blushed and looked down. That was apparently his cue to move closer. He took my hand and led me to the side. My uncle glared at him, but Frall ignored his glowering looks.

"You're so very beautiful," Frall told me, kissing my lips with the briefest of pecks.

"I like the way you look, too," I whispered in his ear, impressed with how handsome he was in his new dark-blue uniform-like suit.

"Enough of that, you two," my uncle barked out. "Let's find the alien and get out of here. You ladies better bring your other clothes. As I said, you won't be able to do much walking in those."

"There is no need for that," Thornic said, barging in. He glanced at our camping clothes. They burst into flame, becoming ashes within seconds.

"You had no right to do that," my uncle roared.

"Please," I urged. "Don't yell, Uncle Cristoff. Thornic would produce others if we asked him to, wouldn't you?" I questioned, turning to regard him.

He nodded. "If you would like it so, Clista. Of course, but let us discuss that over breakfast, shall we?"

Franca sighed. "Breakfast? How delightful. I'm famished. Please, don't tell me we get cooked fish, though."

Thornic smiled. "You may have whatever you would like, Franca. Simply ask, and I will make it so.

"Pancakes," Frall and I called out at the same moment.

Thornic nodded. "And you others? What would you like?"

"Freedom," my uncle said. "Let us go. Release my niece and round up Cronoks Lab so we can get back to something that resembles normality."

Thornic shook his head. His eyes passed over the rest of us with the same look. "I'm afraid that is not possible. They have burned Clista's house," he said sadly.

"No!" I cried out. "Don't tell me that!"

Frall stopped me from sinking to the floor. It wasn't that I'd fainted. My legs had just failed to support me for a moment.

"It doesn't matter, Clista," Frall said. "We'll all start again. They destroyed our past but not our future."

"But my books, all my things, the pictures of my parents …"

"I am sorry, little queen," Thornic said. "Since your parent's death, we have protected you from harm, but we cannot shield the inanimate."

My uncle remained silent, watching me, his thoughts probably on Frall's closeness more than the discovery of our loss. I wiped my tears and stood up straighter. They'd destroyed my parents' house. But that didn't really matter, not really — except for the pictures. That was the part that hurt. Cronoks Lab had stolen even that.

We were all silent as we walked the rest of the way into the dining chamber. Frall seated me and then sat beside me, his chair as close as he could make it. He served me first, taking two pancakes off the platter in front of us and placing them down on my plate. I smiled at him for doing so, but I'm afraid my smile was rather weak and wobbly.

The others found plates of scrambled eggs and soy products, the kind that imitated bacon and sausage. There was toast, too, and, of course, lots of pancakes. Frall expressed delight when he discovered a pitcher of berry syrup, a personal favorite of his. I nibbled at my pancake without anything, still thinking about my loss.

Thornic stepped closer and whispered into my ear. "We can recreate a picture of your parents from your memory," he said. "Would that help?"

"You could? Does it hurt? Oh, I don't care. Do it, please," I told him.

"There will be no pain, my queen. I shall return."

He nodded to me and then faded out. I wondered how he did that, and then I remembered that he was just a holograph. Could a holograph truly do everything it promised?

I shouldn't have doubted. Thornic was back in minutes with a picture frame wrapped in silvery fabric. I untied the pink ribbon that bound it and pulled out a photo of my parents. "You did it! I don't understand how. But I love it! Thank you, Thornic. Thank you so much."

For a moment, I almost hugged him, but I remembered how that wouldn't work. Yet he was smiling at me so humanly. It was hard to remember that he wasn't really there.

"If you want to show your joy by embracing me, do so with Frall," Thornic laughed. I can feel it in that way," he spoke into my mind. So, of course, I pounced on Frall and kissed his cheek.

"What brought that on?" Frall asked, but he draped his arms around me and hugged me back.

"Clista," my uncle barked out.

I backed away and turned to show the picture to all the others. They stood up and crowded around, except for my uncle, who pretended he wasn't interested. Smog asked to see it, then took the picture to my uncle. "Look at it," Smog ordered. "That is your brother and the woman you once loved. How can you not want to see?"

My uncle's eyes dropped to the photo. He seized it in his hand, looked, and then thrust it back at Smog. His face turned ugly, his cheek twisted in grief. He looked ready to slug Smog.

"Do you think I don't know that?" he shouted. "Do you think I don't see her every time I look at Clista? Clista is her mother — the eyes, the hair. I look at her every day, and I see Clara."

"Then you must hate me," I whispered, only just beginning to understand.

My uncle lurched toward me. It startled me. I moved backward against Frall. His arms went around me protectively. But my uncle wasn't attempting to grab me as I'd thought. He fell at my feet.

"Hate you, Clista?" he said. "How could you think that? I adore you. When I look at you, I see Clara, but I also see myself. I know you're my niece, but I see my own flesh and blood in you. I see the daughter I never had and might have had. Do you understand? Can you forgive me?"

I felt the force of Smog's gaze on me. He was telling me to say something, but I was speechless. I bent down and hugged my uncle. It was all I could do. I couldn't accept him as a father, and his confession made me feel awkward and unsure about what to say.

He'd loved my mother? Was that why he and my father hadn't spoken? What had happened between them? How had it all come about?

My uncle stood up, drawing me up with him. "We won't talk about it again, Clista. Not unless you want to. Darn Smog and his openness."

"I'm glad you told me. I just don't know how to . . ."

"You don't have to say anything, Clista. I'm not asking you for that. But Franca and I could be your second family if you'd accept that. Would you be willing to try?"

I glanced at Thornic. He was studying the scene, or I suppose recording it somehow for the real Thornic, the one on Flagan Pren. "I don't know. I can't stay here if that's what you're asking. You see, I'm leaving Rwawan. Both Frall and I are going with Thornic."

My uncle backed away. "That's ridiculous. I won't let you. You're still underage. You have to do what I tell you."

I shook my head sadly. I had hoped it wouldn't come to that. I stepped back into Frall's arms.

Frall laughed. The hall echoed with it. "You have no choice, Cristoff. Don't you see that? Do you really think the *Old Ones* will allow you to oppose them?"

It was the wrong thing to say to my uncle. I'd noticed he didn't take lightly to such challenges, but Frall was correct. The *Old Ones* would not allow my uncle to interfere.

"They want all of us to go. It will be an adventure, too, and a lot safer than it is here with Cronoks Lab constantly hunting for us. Please say you'll go," I begged.

"How do we know we can trust you?" Smog asked Thornic. "Show us what you really look like." he dared the holograph.

That was something I'd never thought about. Didn't the *Old Ones* look like us? I glanced up at Frall, questioning.

"We would all like to see," Frall said, as he squeezed me a bit too tightly in his fear.

"Frall," I complained, but he didn't understand. He bent to kiss my neck, and in so doing, his arms loosened slightly.

Thornic nodded. "You are prepared, my queen?"

I nodded, not as bravely as I should have, but Smog was right. We needed to know what we were getting into.

It's strange that it should matter. Frall and I had been speaking with the *Old Ones* in our minds for so long. Yet, appearance is important. I trembled, waiting.

"I am the same inside," he said. "The outer shape makes no difference." So saying, he melded into someone taller and thinner. His face elongated. His nose became more regal and slightly pointed at the end. His lips thinned, and his skin color darkened. Yet his robes remained unchanged, and his face, although slightly odd and nonhuman looking, was not that much different.

I sighed with relief. Frall kissed me again. "It's all right," he said, sighing with relief. They're humanoid."

"So, this planet where you're taking us to has air and water and all that we need?" Smog asked.

"Yes," Thornic said, smiling at him. "We would never endanger the queen or her family and friends."

"All right. I'll go. Nothing here for me anyway with Cronoks Lab burning buildings right and left. Is my cabin still there?"

"Yes, but they have damaged it," Thornic told him sadly.

Smog lifted his hands. "Don't tell me the details. A man can only stand so much pain. I don't suppose you can pick me up a female before we leave, can you?"

"Smog!" Franca said, laughing, but her arm was holding onto my uncle.

"That is not possible, I regret," Thornic said, smiling at Smog's quip.

"So that leaves us," my uncle said. "It seems that I have little choice about the matter. You will take my niece whether I go or not, right?"

"That is correct," Thornic nodded in his usual, stiff manner.

"This has been quite a trek for you, Franca. Are you game to continue?"

"I will go wherever you go," she said quite romantically.

I sighed and leaned back against Frall. He used that as an excuse to kiss me again. My lips opened to his.

"Clista, stop that," my uncle barked out. Glaring at me, he said, "I guess I have no choice. Someone has to chaperone you two, and I think it's going to take all three of us to do it."

I smiled at him across the room. Then I nodded my head. "We're ready to go, then, Thornic. Do we have to walk far to get to the spaceship?"

Frall laughed, knowing the secret that Thornic had told him.

Thornic's eyes surveyed the group. "You all agree that you wish to journey to Flagan Pren then?" he asked, verifying their wishes.

Smog said, "You bet. Why not? How often do we get such an offer? It's a free vacation, right?"

Franca and my uncle glanced at each other. She was still clutching his arm. My uncle gave her a quick peck on the cheek, and they nodded to Thornic, my uncle looking a bit uncertain about it but Franca smiling broadly.

"Good," Thornic said. "Well done, my queen. We are ready for take-off."

Almost instantly, we heard the motors start up. The vibration jiggled the floor.

"What the..." Smog let out as his eyes widened, and his face turned pale.

"We're already on the ship? Hey, don't we need to buckle in or something," my uncle questioned. Not waiting to hear, he led Franca to her chair and gently pushed her down.

But Thornic was shaking his head. "There is no necessity for that. Our technology does not require such things. The thrusters have already fired. We have achieved lift-off, and are on our way this very moment. You will find the ride quite smooth.

"We will journey for a little more than a year. This evening, when you bed down, I will place you all in sleep mode, and you will awaken when we arrive at Flagan Pren.

"But in the meantime, perhaps you would like to enjoy your day. Feel free to explore. There is nothing that can harm you onboard. The ship has a full library."

I disconnected myself from Frall and took a step closer. "But shouldn't we spend the time studying and not sleeping? Don't we have a language to learn and customs to be trained in?"

Thornic bowed to me. "All that will be attended to. Learning tapes will acquaint you with our language while you rest in deep sleep. They will also give you whatever information is needed. Until then, I shall leave you to peruse the ship and amuse yourselves. Call me if you need anything."

He blinked out just like that. I whirled around to look at Frall. Nothing was going quite like I'd imagined it. "But what about…" I started to ask.

"When you are hungry, simply say what you would like, and it will appear on the table," Thornic said, blinking back in. "You were about to ask, my queen?"

"What if we need something else?" I asked.

"What if the ship has problems?" Smog butted in.

"Merely speak my name, and I shall return. Is there anything you desire now?"

"Yeah, a million dollars," Smog said.

Instantly, bills were floating in the air. I grabbed at one. "It's a thousand dollar bill!" I shouted. Franca collected several. Smog dived for them since they were scattered all over the floor.

My uncle just laughed. "And where do you plan to spend that?" he asked. "On Flagan Pren?"

We each handed the money to Smog and backed away, our smiles of glee gone, but he stuffed the bills in his pockets and said, "When we return, friends. When we return."

Chapter Twenty-One

Everyone split up then, and Frall and I went exploring. That didn't last long. There was nothing much to see. So we returned to the dining chamber and ate pizza, washed down with several combinations of sodas, all combined. The rest of the day, Frall and I played cards and talked about Flagan Pren, wondering what it would be like.

My uncle and Franca had disappeared right away. We had no idea where they'd gone. Perhaps they went investigating also, but I think they just wanted to be alone. Smog took off, too. We didn't see him until lunchtime when he came back to share our pizzas.

Everyone returned at dinner. In essence, we ordered a banquet as everyone kept calling out for something else they remembered liking. Afterward, so stuffed we couldn't move, we sat around talking long into the night. Nobody wanted to go to bed. That was something we didn't discuss. It was scary thinking about sleeping a whole year of your life.

But when the yawns came, we eventually hugged each other good night and stumbled tiredly off to bed, keeping to the same rooms we'd had the night before.

It felt strange going into our room that evening. For so long, I'd been sleeping outside under the stars. The night before, I'd been so tired that I'd hardly noticed being in bed, except for how comfortable it was. But that night, the bed seemed too luxuriously soft and lonely. I missed Frall, the way he'd held me in the forest just before I fell asleep and the way the others had all curled close around us.

But it was Frall my thoughts dwelt on mainly. I was remembering how he'd gone down on his knee, how he'd asked me to marry him, and how sad he'd looked when I said 'no." He was so sweet. I really did adore him. Was that love? Maybe I did love him, but how could I know that it was the kind of love that would last forever? How did anyone ever know?

When I married, I wanted a relationship like my parents had, one that went on and on. I wanted a husband who'd be at my side even when things went bad. I wanted someone who'd love me when I got old or fat — or grew warts, I suppose. That was the kind of marriage my parents enjoyed even to their dying day.

My father used to tell me that he'd rather be weeding the yard with my mother than going to a party with someone he didn't love. Would I feel that way with Frall?

Maybe if he hadn't turned away when I'd first told him about the *Old Ones*, would I feel different? Or if we'd known each other a lot longer, would I be sure then? What if he hadn't withdrawn and gotten snappy when we crossed the chaparral? Would that have made any difference?

A huge yawn hit me. Franca turned in her bed and looked. "Are you still awake?" she asked.

"I was just thinking," I said. "How do you know you love my uncle? Couldn't it just be everything that's happened? I mean, we've been under all this pressure and running from Cronoks Lab and stuff. How do you really know?"

Franca laughed, not meanly, but as if she were glad I'd asked her. "Ah, I know what you're thinking about — that handsome Frall."

I nodded, glad she was awake and willing to talk. "He asked me to marry him, you know, and I turned him down. Tell me, Franca, please. How do you really know when it's real, when it's the forever kind of real?"

There was a nightlight in the room. I could see Franca's eyes studying me. Was she being the school counselor now or the woman my uncle had offered up as a substitute mom? I liked her. I would be happy to have her as a friend, but no one could ever take my parents' place. That just couldn't be. I closed my eyes and waited for her response to my question.

"That's a hard one, Clista. It's hard for adults even to know the difference. But when you can't stand NOT being with someone, when you want to share every thought, every sight and sound, when happiness comes from just holding hands or sitting in the same room with them, when your heart speeds up whenever they come close or when you see them across the room, when joy fills you, just at the thought of being with them, I guess that's what it's all about. That's being in love."

I sighed. I liked her answer. It sounded like she'd already felt those emotions with my uncle. Her conviction was too solid, not to have run that through her mind.

"I feel some of that with Frall, maybe even all of it, but how do you know that it will last? How can you be sure of that?"

"You're never sure of *forever*, Clista. We can plan and dream of the future. We can schedule our life around that plan, but we're never really sure how it's going to unfold. You know that. Look at what's happened to all of us. Chaos. Beautiful chaos in terms of meeting and falling in love with Christoff, but it's a future that's certainly been unpredictable."

"Do you think I should marry Frall or wait?"

"I think you're awfully young for marriage, Clista. How many men have you gotten to know? You haven't even had a chance to date. That's not essential. There are many women who've loved their first boyfriend and married him, then lived happily.

"But it often helps if you have the opportunity to meet different men, to compare and contrast, so you can format what your standard for a good marriage partner should be. Sometimes, we just need time to figure out what we want from life before we can actually decide who we want in a life partner."

"So, the answer to your question is that I don't know. These are just my thoughts on the matter. You probably think I have all the answers, but I don't. I think you just have to listen to what your mind is telling you, as well as your heart. You have to give yourself time so that you know that the decision is right for you. Does that help?"

I nodded. "Thank you, Franca. I'm glad you and my uncle have found each other. I hope it works out for you. And I'm really glad you came along. Thank you for that, too."

I was yawning through my words, barely able to keep talking. My eyes were closing, and I knew I was drifting into sleep. I heard Franca call out "good night" softly, but I didn't answer. I was going to, but . . .

I didn't hear Thornic come in during the night. I don't know if he needed to switch us over into deep sleep. My dreams were filled with strange customs and places, and I remember speaking another language in my sleep.

When I woke, Frall was sitting on my bed. He kissed me into wakefulness. It was pleasant to wake up to Frall sitting there beside me. Thornic had initiated his waking cycle earlier than the others, so we would have time together. I think Thornic was still matchmaking.

Somewhere, buried in the tapes played throughout that year of sleep, there was input about Frall and me. I couldn't remember it exactly, but as I blinked and woke up, I understood a little more why it was desirable for us to marry.

I knew also that the *Old Ones* could have influenced my thoughts while I was asleep, but I don't think they did because although I was glad to see Frall, I was still unsure about whether we should get married or not. There'd been no decision made during my year of deep sleep.

But enough of that.

I left Rwawan and came to live on Flagan Pren. The journey that took me through those days of loss and pain as we ran from Cronoks Lab really hadn't taken that long. My parents and Frall's had only died a few weeks past. (Well, unless you considered the year we'd all spent in deep sleep? Was I now a year older?)

Thornic said my story has only just begun. Isn't that true for everyone? Every day is a new beginning, a progression of strange events, some stranger than others. Sometimes the strange is only a teacher growing a moustache, someone's odd comment, or learning something you didn't know, but my story seems weirder than most.

Like most people's, it's full of the mistakes I made, like being too blind to see how special my parents were EVERY DAY. I wish I could see them one more time and tell them thank you and that I loved them. And I gave my uncle a bad time at first. He didn't deserve that. But I have a second chance to make it up with him.

Those are only some of the mistakes I made. We all do that. Unfortunately, some of my mistakes were worse than most people's, like how I dealt with Mr. Grenan. And most people don't wake up to find themselves wearing a necklace or communing with a race of aliens that lived a thousand years ago. Was that a mistake, though? And was it something I could have changed?

But it's time to put the *should have, would have, could have's* behind me now. Frall, whose kisses are sweeter than even that hot fudge sundae we ate back on Rwawan, is beside me, bidding me a good morning. I bet he cleaned his teeth and brushed his hair before invading my room. I haven't done either of those things yet. Did I drool in my sleep?

I smiled at him, but then budged him off the bed, and told him that I needed to get dressed, and he nodded. I think he read my embarrassment, because the moment I stood up, he grabbed me and kissed me anyway.

"Your hair is beautiful," he said, "and your breath is fine. Oh, and I don't see any drool."

It wasn't going to be easy having a boyfriend who could read my mind. But, I refused to be pessimistic, because today we've landed on Flagan Pren, and it's going to be our new world. And as soon as I have showered and dressed, we're going to wake up the others, and then we'll get to start a new life.

Thornic says it's good to close one book when you start a new one. So after we meet the *Old Ones*, I'm sure I'll have new stories to write, but for now, today, this moment, my tale is done.

To continue this adventure with Clista, Frall, and the Old Ones on

Flagan Pren, read:

Dream Visions

Book Two of the Dream Series

www.ingramcontent.com/pod-product-compliance
Lightning Source LLC
Chambersburg PA
CBHW071300250626
47159CB00004B/1251